Demons

Who, or what, dunnit?

Barrie Condon

Demons © 2024 Barrie Condon

Barrie Condon asserts the moral right to be identified as the author of this work in accordance with the Copyright, Designs and Patents Act 1988

This is a work of fiction. Names, characters, places and incidents are either the result of the author's imagination or are used fictitiously.

All rights reserved. No part of this publication may be reproduced, stored in or introduced into a retrieval system or transmitted in any form or by any means (electronic, mechanical, photocopying, recording or otherwise) without the prior written permission of the author.

Isbn: 978-1-914399-61-9

This book is sold subject to the condition that it shall not be resold, lent, hired out or otherwise circulated without the express prior consent of the author.

Printed by Ingram Spark

Cover Design © 2024 Mercat Design. All Rights Reserved

The dream is the small hidden door in the deepest and most intimate sanctum of the soul, which opens to that primeval cosmic night that was soul long before there was conscious ego and will be soul far beyond what a conscious ego could ever reach.

Carl Jung

CHAPTER ONE

Life really does begin at forty. Up until then, you are just doing research.
Carl Jung

Behind the skeletal Gothic tower an array of smaller but very pointy spires made the university buildings look like a nail bed for a dodgy fakir. In the drizzling rain, a specialty of Glasgow, the tower looked Mordor-like, the product of centuries of backbreaking toil by malformed hobgoblins in pursuit of unremitting evil.

Ironically, these gloweringly medieval-looking buildings were a Victorian confection less than 150 years old. They'd been designed to mimic the equally bogus Houses of Parliament. I was looking at a fake based upon a fake.

For a supposed centre of international learning this sham Lord of the Rings vibe sent out all the wrong signals; orcs and quantum computers are never going to make comfortable bedfellows. After a drink or two I wasn't shy of pointing this out to my colleagues. In today's up-and-at-'em, erect-and-thrusting world of academia, illuminating comments like that are as welcome as a cobra in a crib.

Nevertheless, the University of Glasgow was a fine institution of higher learning and research.

If only I worked there.

No, my university lay just beyond in a warren of reclaimed tenement buildings and old sandstone villas. Many years its junior, the University of West Scotia lay just on the edge of Glasgow University, perhaps in the hope of catching academic excellence by proximity alone.

Where Glasgow was high and refined (at least in its own estimation) we were down and dirty. Where they went for substance, we went for gimmick.

And there was nowhere more redolent of the gimmick than the Department of Metaphysics and Psychology, known by the local news rags as *The Lair of the Soul Hunter*. This had infiltrated a whole row of tenements and that's where my pokey little office was to be found.

The usual ragtag bunch of Christian fundamentalists were standing around the short flight of steps leading up to the entrance. Today their pinched and self-righteous faces seemed almost relaxed. Even they were looking forward to the summer vacation. Elsie, a florid woman in her fifties whose regular fire and brimstone diatribes livened up our early mornings, had put down her *Burn in Hell, Blasphemers* placard against some railings and was having a fag. I gave her a disapproving look but she just shrugged.

"Schools nearly out, Dai," she said.

"I thought the Lord's work was never done."

"That's right, with sinners like you around."

From the truculent Elsie this was almost like a benediction. I felt even more depressed. Everyone was getting ready for the summer vacation except me.

"How dare you enter without permission!" Though the accent was genteel the voice was sharp and penetrating. We all turned as Ms Murdoch, the departmental secretary, dragged a young man out of the department and down the stairs. That he was wearing a suit meant he wasn't a student. Indeed, his whole buttoned-up vibe exuded offended Christianity.

"Hey, leave him alone!" Elsie said, stepping forward to protect one of her own. I guessed that the coming holiday had turned the young man's head and, bored with standing around brandishing a placard, he'd decided to storm the heart of evil.

Ms Murdoch turned to face her. I'd never seen anyone in the department dare to stand up to Ms Murdoch and was intrigued to see what would happen next.

She moved a little closer to Elsie, not Glasgow-pub-just-before-a-fight-close, but enough so they could probably smell each other's toothpaste. Ms Murdoch wasn't big, and her nicely tailored designer suit suggested an unfamiliarity with street fights, but there was always something hard and implacable about her. Elsie visibly flinched.

"Get your placards and your acolytes and get out of here, Elsie, before I call the police!"

"It's a free country, at least the last time I looked. We can protest wherever we like."

"Not on university property you can't. And you can't go around physically assaulting the young girl on reception."

"I was just waving my banner. I didn't see her," said the young man miserably. Whatever Christian spirit had vitalised him seemed to have fled, leaving behind a rather worried individual.

Ms Murdoch ignored him. "He'll have a record, Elsie. Whatever employer he has in future I'll make it my mission to make sure they know all about his criminal activities."

I'd noticed that with Ms Murdoch. No matter how gently I'd demurred with her on some trivial administrative matter, things had got dark really quickly.

Elsie was an annoyance but over the many months we'd all sort of grown used to her (it's always good, no matter how benighted you are yourself, to have at least one person you can feel superior to). Now she looked like someone who had brought a knife to a gunfight and I felt sorry for her.

So much so, I had no stomach to stay and watch the climbdown. As I edged forward towards the stairs, my movement must have caught Ms Murdoch's eyes for she turned to look at me.

I didn't like what I saw. Usually calm and expressionless, the little fracas must have cut through her sang-froid and I glimpsed both disdain and triumph.

It would seem she knew something I didn't and that thing was bad.

More than a little unnerved, I entered the department. The interior of the tenements had been redesigned by a madman and I made my way through its Escher-like convolutions until I got to my third-floor office. I shared this with a post-doc called Hutchison whose earnestness and enthusiasm was always wearing but today I feared it might make me kill him.

Sure enough, early though it was, he was already there.

He looked up and smiled. "Good morning, Doctor Younge."

Sometimes, when your mind teems with rude retorts, they somehow cancel each other out and you're left with nothing.

"Yeah, morning," I grumbled.

I clumped my battered old briefcase onto the top of my desk. Apart from some deodorant and mints (you never know when you might strike lucky) it was empty. In the small, closed world of the university, briefcases were definitely retro. Most academics favoured backpacks as they zipped home on their emaciated bicycles with wheels so thin that should they collapse, the razor-sharp seat would cause a nasty injury (wishful thinking—my weakness).

Hutch, as he liked to be known, sat back on his seat. "Last day of term. Can't wait! What are you getting up to over the long summer months, Doctor?"

I'd long since given up being rude to him; it just didn't work. The man didn't have skin, he had a carapace an armadillo would have found a trifle thick. He was a mature student and was well into his thirties. He was thickset with a bushy beard, a feature so behind the fashion curve it might actually be far ahead. Just like his heavy tweed jacket.

"Not sure I'll be doing anything over the summer."

"How so? Japan's your favourite, right? Last year you were out of here like shi…"

I waved him into silence. I didn't like the rare expletive that escaped his otherwise blameless lips. It was like a fine piece of lingerie soiled by an unmentionable stain. "I've been told not to book anything in July. High command from Rettner and Donlevy."

The insides of his big bushy eyebrows twitched down as his forehead creased in concern. "Why?"

"Don't know. Got a meeting at ten where there's going to be a big reveal. Whatever it is, it can't be good." I remembered the look Ms Murdoch had given me.

The eyebrows now arched up in surprise, their movements more revealing than a lie detector. "And they're both going to be there?" he squeaked.

Donlevy, the Soul Hunter himself and our departmental head, was OK on his own. He was a bastard but a rational one. You might not like what he did, but at least you could see where he was coming from. Dean Rettner, on the other hand, was sweating dynamite in haute couture.

I nodded, lest a vocal tremor give too much away.

"Best of luck, old chap," he said, like we were back in the fifties.

I brought up my emails by poking at my laptop which, for the record, I hate. The way you have to lay your palms almost flat but still have to push down with your fingers. Is there any better way to mangle your finger joints? Give me big heavy keyboards you can seriously poke. Proper keyboards are for people who can express themselves, who can let it all out; laptops are for repressed people with buttoned-up backsides.

Just saying (don't you hate that passive-aggressive expression?).

If you are one of the benighted who do like laptops then think about this. Try typing on a laptop aggressively. You just can't. As your hands are pretty flat, it forces you to sit back and upright like a Victorian spinster in a church as your fingertips peck daintily away at the keys. No matter how vicious and blood-curdling your sentiments, all that animus, rather than being sublimated by brutally poking away at a chunky keyboard, is internalised where it will fester until it emerges years later in some unconscionable sexual act. Or a blood vessel will burst or your heart will clench like a miser's fist and never relinquish its grip.

Let it all out—that's my advice. I'm a psychologist so I should know.

As a psychologist I couldn't fail to notice that picking desultorily away at my emails was pure displacement activity. The truth was that the only thing on my mind was the forthcoming meeting. Face-to-face with Rettner was always bad news. In my chequered career I had left behind too many hostages to fortune, too many tempting cracks in my facade to be opened up by someone as determined and ruthless as Rettner.

There was a window in the office and down below I could hear students saying their goodbyes before returning to Chengdu and all points East, leaving the few token home-grown students to scurry back to their rabbit hutches in Govan.

The University of West Scotia's unseemly enthusiasm for courting fee-generating Chinese students has led me to rechristen it the University of Beijing Outreach Annex, another joke that went down like a lead balloon. Definitely not one for Rettner and Donlevy.

There was a tap at the door which, out of habit, I ignored.

"Yes?" said Hutchison.

A worried little face, freckled and framed by red hair, appeared around the quarter open door.

"Dr Younge," it said. "Is this a good time?"

I sat back and folded my arms. You'd have to be desperate to take that as a sign of encouragement but that's what Logan did. He came in and hovered around my desk, too strung out to take a seat even if I'd offered.

"What?"

Logan nodded, as he did whenever I spoke. "I finished the report, the one on conditioning. For my final year project."

"That would be..." I needlessly checked my watch and creased my forehead as though calculating, "... six weeks after the deadline."

"I've had... there's been..." Again his head was nodding, no doubt at my sagacity. "Problems."

"And?"

"And so I hoped you'd make an exception. The university won't award me a degree if you don't mark this dissertation."

That was far from his only problem. With his multiple exam resits and crappy grades he needed the exclusive love of God if he was going to get anything at all.

"I emailed it to you this morning but, look, I even printed it out as well. I know you like it like that."

Paper had become as rare as cigarettes on university premises in preparation for it being outlawed altogether.

He shrugged off his backpack and delved in. Crumpled papers emerged and he put these gently on my desk, a votive offering to a vengeful god.

And then he did something clever—he was out of the door and gone before I could say a thing.

Hutchison had been watching this. He may look fresh off the boat but he's actually pretty smart. "That's a definite improvement."

"What do you mean?"

"The poor guy's a mess. He doesn't understand other people, he doesn't understand himself. That's why he's doing psychology. Old Logan would have stuck around while you turned him down. New Logan left it all in your court. He's depending on your inertia. Now you have to track him down and tell him to his face."

"Have you never heard of email?"

Hutchison smiled. "Have you, Dr Younge? Seriously, he's gaming you, albeit rather ineffectually. You've got to give him that."

"Even suckling infants know how to game their mothers, it's hardly a qualification for a university degree."

"But it's progress for him. It *is* a good sign."

I shook my head, trying to rid myself of this nonsense.

Hutchison hadn't finished. "I think you should give him a chance. So, what if he passes? It's not like it's going to have much effect on the world. After all, as you're never tired of saying, we produce far more psychologists than the country has any use for and that the most common qualification of bartenders is a psychology degree."

My weary, cynical old jokes keep coming back to haunt me. I wonder if the universe is trying to tell me something.

~~~

The department had five floors spread over four whole tenement buildings. Connecting walls had been knocked out almost at random. Stairs might take you up one floor, but then the next set might be a couple of tenements away. Sometimes to get up two floors you had to go up, then down, then up again. There was no rhyme or reason to the place and even second-year students, and not a few staff, could be found wandering dazed through the labyrinth looking for a toilet or an exit or a sharp object to end their suffering.

I can't help but belabour the blindingly obvious, but this messed-up building was so clearly an unintentional metaphor for how little we understood of the mind despite a hundred years of concerted effort. It was a particularly suitable site for an academic bastard like the Department of Metaphysics and Psychology.

Like the rest of the lifers, I'd got to grips with the absurd topology of the place, although even now the sudden closure of a staircase, say for repainting, collapsed the chaos down into a whole new level of disorder and everyone found themselves wandering around like the lost tribes of Israel.

The meeting room was near Donlevy's office, which was on the ground floor at the end of the corridor behind reception. Even I could find that. As I approached, I could smell fine blend coffee and imagined lavish mounds of pastries profligately displayed for the Dean's state visit. Rettner's own office was far away and high up on one of the gleaming towers that had risen up out of a block of demolished tenements like fast-forward stalagmites. I'd been there once and the view from Olympus out over the tenement rooftops of the West End had been a revelation for ground dwellers like myself who trudged through its sandstone canyons.

As I got to Donlevy's door, I was surprised to hear several voices. I'd thought the meeting would be just me, Donlevy and Rettner (note to self: the university is not all about me).

Three others were there already, their appraising looks like searchlights as I shuffled in. I nodded greetings and took a seat by a jug of coffee and poured its dense black contents into a cup.

Donlevy strode in. Tall, once blond but now balding, he must have been fifty but walked like he was twenty years younger. I can still remember the old days when life as a departmental head could be quite agreeable. Nowadays you had to be buzzing with energy or you were toast.

Donlevy affected a black Nehru jacket but with his tall lean frame he somehow carried it off. You couldn't doubt his nerve. In today's self-righteous times on campus, a white man wearing a Nehru jacket might be charged with cultural appropriation. I guess he felt that if it had been good enough for the Beatles it was good enough for him.

"Dai, William, Awang, Lucas, good of you all to come." He put down his laptop and flipped it open, the damn thing pinging brightly. "I guess we're all here then, apart from the Dean."

Immediately the searchlight beams of my colleagues' regard turned inwards, the scope of this meeting suddenly all too apparent. All four of us were ill-favoured. None of the departmental stars, shooting or rising, were at the meeting; nobody with grants more than half a million, nobody with recent stellar publications in stratospherically ranked journals.

We were the sick and the lame and we all knew it. This was an abattoir and the only thing missing was the plaintive lowing of the soon-to-be slaughtered cattle.

I tried to hide my own inner turmoil. "Got any plans for the summer, Ted?" I said as brightly as my leaden soul could manage.

Donlevy smiled gratefully and then told me God-knows-what while I nodded intermittently as though I was listening. Meanwhile I was on an internal dive to plumb the depths of my insecurities. I didn't publish enough, raise enough money, wasn't popular enough with the students (to put it mildly). I lived year to year, the coming of the summer break a barrier to the next academic year. If I made it past that then I could breathe easy for another few terms.

This year it looked like it would be 'close but no cigar'.

"... bit linkage broke." This brought me back to the here and now and I realised Donlevy was expecting more than a nod.

"What happened then?" I hazarded.

"No choice; grabbed her round the neck and throttled away 'til she stopped."

My mind went blank. The ball was back in my court and I didn't have a clue what he was talking about. Surely it couldn't be anything carnal?

"And was... everyone alright?"

Donlevy waved this away. "She was fine. Gave me a bad turn though, sitting there at the gallop with two loose reigns in my hand."

Horses, thank God! This day was already scary enough without dark unwanted insights into Donlevy's sexuality.

Awang Che cleared his throat. Indonesian, and no great fan of his home country, he had the most to lose if he were sacked. A shy, butterball of a man, his group dynamics course was a joke. It was supposed to be all about demonstrating leadership and effective group working, but he couldn't control his plethora of nervous tells, like scratching his ear when he was nervous, or rubbing his tummy when he hadn't a clue what he was talking about. His students used these to better guide their bullying.

"Can you tell us the nature of this meeting, Professor? The email was very... unclear." He sat back a little, already consumed by regret for implying Donlevy had been at fault in any way.

"The truth is, Awang, we didn't want to alarm you."

Nothing could be more alarming than that. Awang's mouth opened like a goldfish's but no bubbles came out.

Lucas Grimsrud was tall, thin and eczematous. Though he always looked rather run-down and bedraggled (which is why my cruel nickname for him was Pound Store Viking) he was made of sterner stuff. Fearlessly he asked, "Are we going to be canned, Ted?"

In his developmental psychology course, he'd dared to suggest that men and women thought differently and had provoked a remorseless campus campaign to have him sacked.

As a white middle-class male oppressor enforcing gender stereotypes, ever since then his coat had been on a shoogly peg *(Scottish, idiomatic—one's job is insecure).*

We both patronised the cafe in the Kelvingrove museum and I'd talked to him a few times over the last term. That men and women weren't exactly the same was so self-evident to him that he just didn't understand the problem.

"You've just got to cross your fingers and pretend," I'd said, only half in jest.

"I didn't get into psychology to pretend, Dai. I'm sick of being told what I can and cannot do, what I can and cannot say, what I can and cannot think. What happened to good old-fashioned liberalism? When did it morph into fascism?"

He'd sounded so hurt I remember shaking my head at his naivety.

Back in the here and now, Donlevy was shaking his own head. "Wouldn't be appropriate for me to pre-empt the Dean, Lucas. All will be revealed in due course."

Bill Steadman, old with unfashionably long white hair and possessing the wrinkled yellow skin of a lifetime smoker (a creature so rare amongst academics he should have been pickled in formaldehyde and exhibited at the Hunterian Museum), was looking only mildly perturbed, rather than aghast like the rest of us. He was past sixty and, even though his teaching was adequate, he'd been a big target for savings for quite a while. Promotions, ratchetings up during rare good times over a long career, had left him on a high salary. Dump him and downgrade his post and the university stood to save a packet.

Right now, he was tapping a yellowed finger on the desk in an annoying way, a classic example of passive aggression on which he had, in his heyday, written several impressive papers.

Donlevy turned to look at him as though about to say something when we heard the clicking of high heels far away. One could almost hear the squeaks as five scrotums tightened.

The Dean was short and wouldn't have been seen dead in flat shoes so the noise heralded her approach.

I could feel the panic in the room thickening into dread. Awang's eyes darted around as though looking for escape; Lucas was trying to play it cool but his eyes still widened; even Bill's ancient Adam's apple bobbed up and down in his scrawny throat.

And then she was upon us, a buzzing bundle of energy. "So nice to see you all. What a lovely day!"

Five seconds in and already she'd told two lies.

Professor Rettner's hair was bottle black, cut in a sharp line high across her forehead, then dropping vertically to collar level. It looked less like hair and more like a copper's riot helmet. High cheek bones, piercing blue eyes, she was attractive enough on first impression, but this never survived more than the briefest of contacts.

She was a social scientist of some distinction, serving on many national bodies which advised the government on the more dangerous social issues, from drug abuse to racism. That one day she would be Professor Dame Vera Rettner was a certainty. She sat on grant bodies and pulled in astronomical sums herself.

"Nice to see you, Vera," said Donlevy smoothly. I had to admit he was good. A number of years before, in one of the endless university reorganisations (or purges, take your pick), Psychology had been kicked out of the medical faculty and, having nowhere else to go, was snaffled up by the Faculty of Humanities and forcibly mated with the failing department of Metaphysics.

Psychology, although still successful in drawing in students, had been considered too touchy-feely for Medicine, appropriately enough as the new breed of GPs being turned out eschewed even seeing their patients in the flesh, never mind actually laying hands on them.

Donlevy's genius lay in making the best of a bad job, taking Metaphysics on board and coming up with the soul-searcher concept, the ramifications of which spread far beyond the few placard-carrying nutters at our door.

Like I said, gimmicks-r-us.

Although he'd managed to square that circle he still couldn't get out of being lumbered with a boss like Rettner. It never showed, and he never let on, but everyone was sure he hated her guts.

What she thought of Donlevy was a little less certain. Right now, she was favouring him with a megawatt smile. The redness of her lipstick, in my humble opinion, was definitely pushing the envelope of outright tartiness.

Psychology is often about the signs and symbols that people ignore but whose effects are profound. Red lipstick plumpens and exaggerates the lips and represents, at some deeper level, the blood-engorgement of the vaginal lips during sexual arousal.

Forget about 'empowerment' and 'confidence', it was all about 'fuck me, fuck me, fuck me'.

Perhaps by now you've gained insight into how I wound up on the department's shit list. Perhaps you're even thinking I shouldn't be allowed out in polite company, and you'd be right.

Rettner sat down and Donlevy poured her a coffee. "Milk and sugar?" he asked meekly.

"As it comes, Ted." She cast her gaze around the table. "Awang, how are you?"

Poor Awang! He had large dark brown pupils and we could see every tiny bit of them as his eyes widened in alarm.

"Lovely... I mean fine. Looking forward to next term."

Her hesitation was dagger-like.

"We'll get to that," she said after a couple of beats. "But first let me give you an overview of why we're all here."

Soon the conference screen was showing a multitude of graphs and all of them were heading down. If I'd had the nerve,

I'd have told her to cut the crap, we all knew the pandemic had sent the university finances into a nosedive. Coupled with that, UK relations with China had deteriorated. The net result was that the Chinese students who the university had so determinedly solicited had not returned in great numbers. Offered the chance of on-line learning, but still for the full exorbitant fees, most had declined, some not very politely. Besides, the tide was turning and China was surging ahead of us. Soon the UK would be sending our students to learn from them.

Rettner's pile-driving message was that spending needed to be reduced. Outsourcing, sending clerical and administrative staff to the dole, had all been tried. She made it clear that decimating academic salary costs was all that was left.

There were forty full-time academics in the department and the four of us made up exactly ten percent. That she was using the word decimate in the correct one-in-ten sense was scant comfort.

"Hard choices, gentlemen. We're going to have to let some staff go and that's the main reason we're here today. I'm sure you've worked out where this is heading but we're reasonable people..." and here she indicated Donlevy and herself, this time lying by only 50 per cent, "... so we'll give you a chance. Awang, you first."

"You want me to justify my existence, just like that, no warning?"

Big mistake! Even Donlevy's eyes widened in alarm.

Rettner's bonhomie and slickly reasonable tone vanished in an instant. She jerked forward, teeth bared. "You should *always* be able to justify why you're being paid. This isn't Oxbridge in the fifties. You don't have a sinecure. You're seventy years out of date, just like your lectures!"

"My lectures aren't—"

"And your student assessments. They think you're a joke! They run rings round you."

I'd seen this before with Rettner and felt as powerless now as I did then. She had two states, oleaginous when she wanted something from you, fearsome if you challenged her in any way.

If a man had bullied a woman like this, we'd have kicked the shit out of him, whoever he was, and he'd have been in big trouble. But when a single woman bullied a roomful of men then the basic rules didn't seem to apply. If we'd taken this up with the university authorities (of whom Rettner was one of the highest-ranking) it would have looked like a bunch of insecure more junior men with their noses out of joint picking on a single senior woman.

I reckoned this was why she never pulled this trick if at least one woman was in the audience. She could still be bracingly direct, but the brutality was dialled back.

I wouldn't quite pigeonhole her as a high functioning sociopath but was amenable to persuasion.

Poor Awang was now whining. "That's not fair. It's a difficult course."

"Fair! Fair! The pandemic wasn't *fair*. The university doesn't exist for your indulgence, Awang. We're offering you a generous severance package. A month's pay for every two years served."

"But that's only... six month's salary."

"If you're as good at your job as you say you are then it should be easy enough to find another one in that time."

She turned to Grimsrud. "Now, Lucas, let's hear your side of the story."

"My recent grants and publications are more than adequate..."

Rettner raised a warning finger. "I'm not talking about that; I'm talking about your blatant sexism and how uncomfortable you make your students."

Lucas was smart enough not to come out with the most obvious response. Rettner was showing very clearly that women, just like men, when given power can act in the most outrageous manner. When it came to abusing power there was complete parity between the sexes.

Instead, he sat back and I could tell he was forcing himself to relax. This meeting had already showed that Rettner was in no mood to take prisoners.

"I will formally apologise in whatever way you consider adequate. I'm still not entirely clear for what but I want to keep my job. All the universities have been hit by the Chinese exodus and there are no jobs out there to move to."

Rettner shook her head. "If you don't know what you've done wrong then how can you write a convincing apology?"

Lucas shrugged. "Then write it for me. Help me understand."

She shook her head, feigning sadness. "Not enough, Lucas. There has to be an element of punishment."

Super-duper new imaging systems are supposed to have revolutionised our understanding of the brain but, between you and me, they've done nothing of the sort. Our primary understanding still comes from what people say about what they think and feel, unreliable witnesses though they inevitably are when talking about themselves. Psychologists, whatever our faults, do listen to what people say. I'm sure all of us in the room (except for Awang who has slumped so far down in his seat he looked as if he was melting) picked up on the word 'element'.

For Lucas there was still hope.

He tilted his head slightly to the side. "What do you have in mind?"

Rettner looked at Donlevy; she didn't want all the blood on her hands. He sat forward earnestly. "Demotion, just for a while. You're associate professor now. Back to lecturer for two years."

Lucas licked his lips. "One year."

Donlevy couldn't help himself. They must have worked it all out beforehand but he couldn't avoid glancing at Rettner.

She looked exasperated at his weakness. "Eighteen months."

"And I get my old status back automatically."

"If you keep up your grant income and publications."

That wouldn't be so easy. Not many big money grants were awarded to lowly lecturers.

Lucas hesitated but then finally nodded.

Already numb I didn't even feel relief when her eyes turned to Steadman.

"Bill..." she said, treacly once more.

But Bill held up his hands. "What are you offering? A couple of years of pensions enhancements?"

"Sorry, Bill. In better times..."

He stood up. "You know, I don't care. This..." and he waved an arm to encompass us all, "... is disgraceful."

"Times change, Bill." Donlevy gave every appearance of being genuinely sad, but I wouldn't have bet my life on it.

"It's the end of an era. Our only sin was not appreciating what we had until it was taken away." Bill gave each of his fellow victims a crinkly smile then walked out, dignity intact, stopping only to clap a sympathetic hand on my shoulder.

Rettner turned to look at Awang and Lucas. "Thank you for coming, gentlemen. If you don't mind, Ted and I need to have a word with Dai in private."

Jesus Christ! They'd just humiliated some senior academics in front of their peers. What the fuck was so bad they needed to do it to me in private?

Awang and Lucas shuffled out while my mind reeled like a drunken sailor.

Rettner looked at me, put her hands together and took another great scoop out of the treacle jar. "Dai, we need a big favour from you."

I couldn't help swallowing loudly. Did they want me to put my own head on a plate? Did I have to supply my own garnish?

"What sort of favour?"

"It's all hands to the deck as far as finances go. We've all got to do our part."

Could I handle the sort of demotion they'd foisted on poor Lucas? Several years ago, I'd rented a rather a grand old Georgian flat on Park Circus with airy views over the city. I'd grown rather accustomed to quality accommodation, as I had to expensive liquor and Far Eastern holidays.

Rettner's empathy may have been minimal but Donlevy was made of more human stuff. My mental calculations must have been all too plain because he held up a hand, palm towards me. "No, Dai, we're not cutting your salary but we do want you to do some work for us during the summer."

The Dean of Sacking, as she was known by everyone but herself, was a busy woman and she no doubt had other futures to destroy. She shook her head irritably at Donlevy's emollience and tapped the desk with one long vermilion nail. "We're keen to rent out departmental faculties during the summer months. We've snagged a conference lasting a whole week, plenty of little side meetings so the whole place is booked. It's a significant bolus of income just when we need it. Of course, we'll need someone to liaise with the organisers while the conference is underway, to be here to deal with any unexpected problems."

"You mean like a caretaker?"

A narrowing of Rettner's eyes showed I'd almost triggered her. Donlevy sat forward again quickly: "Far more substantial than that. This could be an annual thing so we want you to charm them, make them feel at home. Just make sure things go as smoothly as possible."

"I don't remember hearing about any big Psychology conferences over the summer."

Donlevy waggled his hand. "It's a bit more fringe than that. Parapsychology more like."

"Koestler Chair stuff?" The writer Arthur Koestler had bequeathed a chair at Edinburgh University which had produced interesting although not entirely convincing results on clairvoyance. Fringe was right; the academic world still looked askance at anything to do with ghosts and ghoulies and anything that went bump in the night.

Donlevy couldn't quite seem to meet my eye. "It's less... academically oriented."

The only way universities ran academic departments of Parapsychology was if they received big-time personal endowments. Otherwise, they wouldn't touch the subject with a bargepole. Whatever would be nesting here for a week wasn't even as respectable as that.

I couldn't help myself; it just came stuttering out. "It's a nutters' convention, isn't it?"

This time Donlevy caught my eye then pointedly turned his gaze to the empty seats left by my badly mauled colleagues. Spookily, over the etheric sea, came the telepathic message: *Shut the fuck up, this is as good as it gets!*

Rettner tensed and this time it was my eyes that couldn't meet a gaze. Through gritted teeth she hissed: "If we're talking about academic validity..."

That statement wasn't going to end well and I knew this really was my last chance. I thrust my arms out as though embracing this wonderful new concept. "Love to help out as best I can! You can count on me."

The Dean's brow creased. Her lack of empathy made her poor at detecting irony but she knew what it was and often suspected it.

"Really!" I said, desperate to head off an eruption. "Desperate times and all that. More than happy to oblige!"

CHAPTER TWO

The meeting of two personalities is like the contact of two chemical substances: if there is any reaction, both are transformed.
Carl Jung

I sipped from my third glass of 18-year-old Glenmorangie. Sublimely sweet though it was, it did little to take away the sour taste of my lick-spittle grovelling.

"Serves you right, you precious little darling."

Mo Tarby was probably my best friend which is just as well. If anyone else had said that after I'd had a couple of drinks, they'd have found themselves kissing the pub's sticky carpet while I enthusiastically stove in their kidneys.

Both of us were medium height, medium build and on the cusp of forty; people had occasionally referred to us as the twins. Neither of us took well to that. While I still had all my hair, his was taking the Pony Express out of Dodge. Whilst I had a reasonably firm jaw, his was already showing the first faint sign of becoming submerged under nascent jowls. That's why I took offense at any comparison.

On the other hand, while my eyes were dark and pensive, his were blue and twinkling and somehow that seemed to make him luckier with the ladies. Dark clouds did not swirl around his troubled brow. That's why *he* was offended by the comparison.

A teacher in a down-at-heels secondary school, he simultaneously yearned after and detested my life as a university academic. It had come as a terrible blow to him when the old *reader* title at university had been replaced by the *associate professor* sobriquet. *Associate* was a qualifier meaning *still not really a professor* but I nevertheless could call myself a professor and that pissed him off no end.

"Some sympathy might actually be called for here," I said reproachfully.

Mo did a double-take. "I had to clear some sick off a desk today and *you're* wanting sympathy from *me*? I don't know why you're whining about being a caretaker for a couple of weeks. Teachers are caretakers their whole careers."

Mo represented one of the few failures of my name test. This was a psychological test I'd developed early on: a simple, rapid and extremely useful way of gauging people within seconds of meeting them. It was the only advantage of being lumbered with the name Dai Younge (as to why my parents would ever give their only child that name, don't worry, we'll get back to that).

Being introduced to someone elicited a number of responses which served to open them up like a frog pinned to a dissection table. These can be graded as follows:

Pleased to meet you: a weak response of an unconfident, reserved, boring person

You mean like someone who dies young?: insensitive, mouth runs far ahead of thought

You realise that makes it sounds like you're going to die young?: bottomlessly stupid and insensitive

Unusual name: arrogant, supercilious prick

Are you fucking having me on?: (Not a response I often came across in academic circles; more likely found in a Govan shebeen near closing time) —insecurity and anger management issues. Back away, keeping your hands in view the whole time

So you're Welsh then?: Can't face problems head on, resorts to displacement activity. A prevaricator (and, no, FYI, I'm not fucking Welsh. Thanks, Mum! Thanks, Dad!).

Some placatory, sympathetic response followed by a litany of other crap names to show I'm not alone—P. Nice, P. Brain, Ophelia Balls, Mike Hunt, I've heard them all: Not my favourite but at least we're starting to find some common ground.

You poor bastard: sensitive and empathetic, so maybe I could warm to them. Trouble is, those are the sort of people who rarely warm to me.

A loud laugh: insensitive but with a sense of humour—could be my kind of person.

The younger brother of Liv Fast?: Definitely warming to them.

Is that Younge with an 'e' (followed by a belly laugh)?: We're there!

And that had been Mo's response when we first met. Yet here and now, twenty years later, he'd turned out to be no damned use at all. So much for my elegantly effective test.

He was enjoying himself. "So, what is our esteemed professor going to do? A principled resignation, a dignified exit then genteel poverty, starvation and finally death?" Nascent jowls or not, Mo could still do a mischievous grin.

The Bon Accord is a pub beside and above a motorway slicing right through the centre of Glasgow before diving under Sauchiehall Street. Many years before at a city council meeting perhaps a single dissenting voice might have said 'Surely we're not going to cut such a large swathe through the heart of one of Scotland's biggest and most beloved cities?' to which everyone else on the council replied, 'Naah, fuck it!'

As if six lanes of motorway weren't enough, higher-level roads on its shoulders added even more tarmac. When one left the Bon Accord, one was immediately faced with ten road lanes between you and the titty bar far across the way.

Doesn't sound very appetising but somehow the Bon contrived to be the best pub in Glasgow. That it had some of the widest ranges of whiskies and real ale in the city may not have been entirely coincidental.

The only entry requirement was that you dress down. Striking up a conversation, you wouldn't know if you were addressing a Govan doxie or the Queen of Sheba, a pickpocket or the Procurator Fiscal (*Scottish term: not, as it sounds, a punter who procures prostitutes for sex, but rather the title of the public prosecutor*).

Not a few other academics frequented the place so, as it was both Friday night and the end of term, the place was heaving. There was some debate amongst my colleagues as to whether the pub had been repainted since the smoking ban or whether they'd just painted it browny-yellow to look like it had in the old nicotine-stained days. Whatever the answer, the decor rammed home the subliminal feeling that even if nobody was, they should all be smoking. I'd given up the habit fifteen years before but after an hour in the Bon I still found myself reaching unconsciously for a phantom fag packet in my breast pocket.

"Lost for words?"

I must have drifted away and forgotten to answer him. "Merely rehearsing a suitable response," I said, taking another sip of ambrosia. We were nestled against the bar, continually being jostled by punters ordering drinks from the gratifyingly attentive staff.

"I suppose if the choice is between penury and a mop and bucket, I really have no choice at all. It looks like riding shotgun on a bunch of witches and warlocks and what-have-yous, wiping their arses and mopping their hysterical brows all lies in my future."

Mo shook his head, disagreeing with me as usual. "It might even be interesting. I've often wondered if there's something in all that paranormal stuff. Didn't your mate Jung have some time for it?"

"Yes, my *mate* Jung did indeed publish a book called *Psychology and the Occult* before even you were born but it's now considered as archaic as spats and gaiters. We've moved on from that kind of nonsense."

"It's important to keep an open mind."

"It's also important to show some discrimination. People have been futtering around with the occult for hundreds of years and got absolutely nowhere."

"A bit like with science and our understanding of the brain, as you never tire of saying."

Nobody likes being hoist on their own petard so I ignored this and went back to my whisky.

Mo tapped the bar top with his finger. "Did I ever tell you what happened to my aunt? How when she was staying..."

I held up a warning finger and he faltered. "Whatever you're going to tell me, are there any photos or recordings or testimonies from independent witnesses, or is this just some anecdotal tale about something spooky?"

Mo waggled his fingers. "Well..."

"So, something purely anecdotal backed up by no actual evidence. Don't waste my time."

He looked displeased; he liked telling stories. "I may not have any hard documentary evidence to prove this, mate, but it's a dead certainty that you're a complete wanker."

CHAPTER THREE

Dreams are the guiding words of the soul
Carl Jung

What the hell was I doing on a bleak hillside? Swirls of mist swept over me, occasionally thinning to reveal a wild Scottish landscape far below. Glints from ripples in a loch filled the mist with sparks.

Something didn't feel right with my feet. Looking down I saw them intertwined with sodden yellow grass, my bare toes half submerged in the black mud of the hills.

I took a tentative step lest sharp stones lay hidden, but found the going nice and soft.

Except for the bone chill it would have been quite pleasant.

Why had I climbed a hill in my bare feet? Engrossed in trying to remember, I literally jumped in surprise when someone spoke.

"Are you lost?"

I turned around quickly. A figure was close but hazily indistinct.

"You startled me. I didn't hear you coming."

"It's the fog. It muffles, deadens, dissipates both sight and sound. Not unlike the approach of death."

Well, that was cheery. Lost and stuck up a cold mountain with a depressive. Why couldn't I have dreams where I was balls-deep in dusky maidens?

For an instant the mist thinned and I could make out the slightly stooped figure. He had all the sensible walking gear—stout boots, rucksack, even those long white socks with the top three inches turned over. From the knee down he looked like a courtier of a Georgian king, though they rarely wore bobble hats. His face was lined by wrinkles, like someone had recently run a rake over a Japanese gravel garden. Though I couldn't put my finger on it, something about him was vaguely familiar.

"What are you doing up here?" I asked.

He shrugged just as the milkiness obscured him again. It would have been good manners for me to step closer but something stopped me.

"The summit is only another few hundred metres. Perhaps I'll get above the mist; it should be quite a view all the way down Loch An Saol."

"I've never heard of a loch called that before."

I could hear, but not see, the scritching sound of his neck scraping over the fabric of his rain jacket as he shook his head. "Everyone's heard of it in one way or another. But why are you here?"

"I'm dreaming, obviously. The dead giveaway is the bare feet. I'd never climb a mountain like this."

"And naked as well. I think you may be onto something."

Somehow, when I'd look down to see by bare feet, I'd missed the fact that I was stark bollock naked.

Yup, definitely a dream.

I'm not vain or particularly modest so I wouldn't have bothered to cover my genitals with my hands but I did just that because it was suddenly so cold.

"How do I get down off here?"

The indistinct figure raised an arm, pointing up and to my left. "Come with me. We'll both get to the top and then I'll show you the way down."

The last thing I wanted was to climb even higher and get even colder.

"No thanks, I think I'll just head straight down."

And I did, leaving the already attenuated figure to be completely consumed by the mist.

CHAPTER FOUR

Thinking is difficult, that's why most people judge.
Carl Jung

I surfaced from the Land of Nod, poking my tongue through what felt like stapled-together lips and wondering what the hell that dream had been about. Those old codgers Jung and Freud set great store by the meaning of dreams, that they yielded profound insights into the workings of the unconscious, the part of our minds not accessible to rational thought. To them dreams often showed us things we hadn't consciously recognised, showed us what we really wanted not what we thought we did.

Bunkum! There are still some hangers-on to that hundred-year-old theory, but most experts now think dreams are just our way of breaking down and pigeonholing the memories of the day.

Assuming dreams mean anything at all, that is.

Mind you, being stark naked on a cold mountain would fit right in with good old Freud. He'd have said it was all about insecurity and maybe for once he'd have been right. I had much to be insecure about. It was two weeks since my meeting with the Dean of Sacking and the Soul Hunter but I wasn't feeling any easier in myself.

I pulled myself out of bed and headed for the bathroom. I lived in an old Georgian terrace converted to flats, resting on a hill overlooking Glasgow University and Kelvingrove Museum, another multi-turreted red sandstone confection springing from a laudanum fed Victorian imagination. I lived in Park Circus, a prestigious address not normally within the financial reach of academics. That's why rather than buying the place, I was renting at an extortionate rate. The untimely deaths of my parents, followed by several years of legal wrangling had yielded a significant sum but I'd piddled most of it away over the decades since.

Of course, my parents hadn't left an actual will; that would have made life just too easy for me. They'd died when I was only ten and in the following years of trying to get hold of their money, I'd learned far more about the law than any child should.

But the remnants of their money still helped me pay the rent on this place. Every time I came home and put a key in the door, I felt a tingle of pleasure because my parents, whose treatment of me was very much in the boy-named-Sue child-rearing methodology, had many times expressed a wish to burn through all their money so there would be nothing left for me.

'Stand on your own two feet' had been their mantra on the one hand while beating me down with the other. Though the beatings were only metaphorical, the effects were longer lasting.

Once I had moved in, I had just enough money for one important modification. In true Georgian form, while the public room was built on an expansive scale, the rest of the rooms were pokey, with the bathroom the pokiest of all. I like a shower but there was no room for a proper one so I'd had no choice. With a chunk of parental inheritance, I'd ripped out the old multi-generationally stained bathtub and installed a shower powerful enough to flense a bull.

This had been a decision not popular with my women friends. I'm no Lothario, but I was nearly forty and still a bachelor so there had been a trickle of bedfellows over the years. All but one, a hyperactive fitness trainer who did everything quickly, had complained about the lack of a bath. Sometimes I speculated that women needed a bath for some darkly secret feminine hygiene function, or perhaps it was so they could put candles all around it and pretend they were Cleopatra.

Naturally I'd made enquiries but had always met with the standard 'Stop being so intrusive and don't you dare try and psychoanalyse me!' indignant response.

Muggles feel exposed when they meet psychologists and psychiatrists; they think we have immediate and incisive insights into their characters and motivations.

But, of course, we don't so there's no need to worry. Not only that, but when it comes to studying the mind, it's a case of physician heal thyself. Without exception, all my colleagues had been mentally messed up at some point in their lives. They'd got into the trade to find out exactly in what way and by how much.

So, don't be intimidated by us: our feet are made of clay. You could make an amphora out of mine.

I put myself under the jet-powered Niagara of my shower and that got the blood once more trickling through my veins. Afterwards, I opened the single grudgingly small cupboard in my cramped bedroom (really, the Georgians were all mouth and no trousers) and tried to work out what an Associate Professor in Psychology and part-time janitor might wear for work.

Not that there was much choice. From a selection of dark clothes, I chose some black jeans, black T-shirt plus my usual blue bomber jacket, pre-scuffed by Marks and Spencers to make it look as if I might actually tinker with a motorcycle. In academic circles, suits had pretty much gone out even before the pandemic, but the lurgy had since seen off even jackets. Some academics had devolved to the sandals and shorts stage. One good flu epidemic and we'd all be wearing loincloths.

I wandered into my grand public room, a speck of dust in its galactic vastness, and trekked over to the window. Pulling back the high curtains brought the sunlight blazing in. To the right were the Gothic university buildings and the Kelvingrove Museum, but straight ahead were the gleaming titanium-clad flying saucer and armadillo of the conference centres down by the Clyde. Architecturally it was an uneasy mix of futuristic and retro and was like looking at the city through rips in time.

I made for the door out of my flat and checked myself in the hallway mirror. One too many drinks the night before showed in my bleary and unfocused eyes. I went out into the short communal corridor and pushed through the main door.

Kelvingrove Park was looking good as I made my way down the hill. Apart from a couple of little clouds, the sky was blue but the air still had a delicious hint of chill. It was an easy walk over the bridge across the river Kelvin then up the little hill and then across to the tiered ranks of tenements.

As I approached the department, I saw that already a bunch of people older than our usual student clientele and Christian protesters was milling around. Both of those groups had left for the summer.

A few of these newcomers were even smoking. Around here you had to be a determined student rebel to do such a thing nowadays. You'd need a rhino grade hide to withstand the withering disapproval of your self-righteous contemporaries. Clearly these folks didn't suffer from that sort of peer pressure.

A couple of the younger ones sported ill-kempt hair and gothic black clothing but the rest looked middle-aged and nondescript. Eyes turned to look at me as I nudged my way through and up the steps to the door. I was reaching for my little electronic fob to let myself in when someone said, "Excuse me, but are you Doctor Younge?"

I turned to find a woman in her late forties to whom time had not been kind. Polyfilla grade foundation had been applied to try to submerge them, but the deep lines across her face were still evident. Straggly blonde hair turning white hung either side of wide, brown, defeated eyes.

"I am." I shook the proffered limp-fingered hand.

"I'm Loris Tominsky, joint organiser of the conference. We'll be working closely together so please call me Loris."

Familiarity with these geeks was the last thing I wanted but there's a limit to just how much of a prick even I can be. "Pleased to meet you, Loris," I said as affably as I could. Wasn't a loris some kind of monkey?

"And what's your Christian name?"

"It's Dai."

Quick as a flash she reached out and touched my arm. "I feel your pain," she said earnestly.

This was a new and unwelcome response to my name test. I'd had sympathy before but this was way too forward. Being pitied by a nutter is never going to take pride of place in your curriculum vitae.

"Err... thanks." I pointed to the people loitering nearby. "It's a bit early, isn't it? Isn't due to kick off until ten and it's not even nine."

She smiled wistfully. Once she might have been a looker but something had knocked the stuffing right out of her.

"They're just eager," she said. "When you have unusual opinions then you're often on your own. Meeting up with like-minded people can be a comfort."

Funnily enough, that was academia in a nutshell. We all loved burrowing away in our own little fields, the papers we published like molehills showing our progress. But even we sometimes needed to play with others and that's just one reason why jetting off to conferences was so popular. Meeting members of one's narrow little tribe in far-flung places never got old.

"I'll..." I pointed at the door.

"Yes, please go ahead. I'll keep then occupied out here so they won't get in your hair."

My fob clicked me in. Rettner and Donlevy hadn't dumped this whole thing on my shoulders. Doctoral students had been drafted in to set the place up the day before, putting out chairs and tables. University catering staff would bring coffee and pastries in the morning and afternoon, domestic staff would come in the evening to run a cursory broom over the place. I didn't even have to act as bouncer as the organisers would have one of their own on reception throughout.

All I had to do was open up in the morning, lock up at night and be the point person if something went wrong. *The august face of the university*, as Donlevy had put it.

Wanker!

I unlocked the main door, turned on some lights and then ran out of things to do. Reception was a high bench behind which a few secretarial staff usually sat. I was pleased to see they had remembered to leave out maps of the department so the attendees would have a fighting chance of finding their way around.

Locking up at the end of the day was going to be my biggest problem for I would have to trawl this vast, convoluted space to shepherd out any lost souls. I figured I'd be able to locate them by their panicked, fearful gibberings.

"A bit complicated," a deep gravelly voice said almost in my ear. I turned to find a tall man with a narrow jaw and wolfish grin. "Telly Lemarck." He stuck out his hand.

This time the handshake was firm. "Dai Younge."

"Brother of Liv Fast?"

An old chestnut, but never so quickly and confidently delivered. Usually, it takes people several seconds to come up with that one and by then they're wondering if it's too obvious and stupid.

His chutzpah kind of won me over and I felt the faintest smile tickle my lips. "Yeah, the layout of this place *is* rather complicated. You'll have to send out the occasional search party. Pregnant women can't be allowed to wander off alone."

He nodded his head. "Afterbirth all over the carpet. Nasty! Not likely a problem here, though, the child-bearing years only a memory for most of the attendees."

"Young people not interested in..."

"In...?" He wasn't going to let me off the hook.

The hell with it; let's see if he can take as well as give: "... this crazy shit."

The wolfish grin broadened. "We need to have a drink sometime, Dai. You need educatin'."

"Don't we all. So how do you fit into all this?"

He shrugged. "I'm one of the organisers and I'm going to man reception for my sins, some of the time anyway."

We went over the arrangements. Lunch wasn't being laid on by the university but I assured him it was impossible not to find restaurants in this part of town. With the students and staff on vacation nowhere would be full so they'd be spoiled for choice. Especially in all the newly built Chinese restaurants and noodle bars, full of staff moping around waiting for their compatriots to return.

I left Lamarck and went for a wander around the building because that's how caretakers roll, right? Apart from checking the meeting room doors were unlocked and labelled, I wasn't sure what else to do.

Returning to reception I found Lamarck arranging rows of name badges in alphabetical order. I had the feeling this was a task disproportionate to his capabilities, not unlike an Associate Professor of Psychology playing the caretaker.

"So, educate me; tell me about this organisation of yours."

He smiled and nodded and I got the impression he was grateful to be diverted from his task. "The Paranormal Research Group, or PROG for short, is all about synthesis. The 'crazy shit' as you term it comes in all shapes and sizes: ghosts, UFOs, mediums, spirits, demons, clairvoyants, banshees, poltergeists. In fact, it's this menagerie aspect that makes people like yourself so sceptical. What the PROG is trying to do is explore the commonalities of these phenomena, to find an underlying explanation."

"A sort of unified field theory for all that goes bump in the night?"

He shook his head and chuckled. "Ah, the fabled openness of the academic mind."

"Fully open or fully closed, the extremes can sometimes be just as bad."

He shrugged and opened his hands. "I'm happy with half-way houses. What about you? You don't have to pay to attend. Are you going to come to any of the talks?"

I couldn't say 'no' without coming across as arrogant or dogmatically sceptical, so half-way house for me too. "Might pop in for a session or two."

"You'd certainly be most welcome. I'm chairing one in a few days' time." He looked at a timetable. "It'll be in room six."

I clamped down on my smile. To get to room six meant climbing one set of stairs, going down a long corridor, then up another set of stairs, taking a sharp right to what at first sight might be rest rooms, going through another door and down a half set of stairs. This was the only way to get into what we called the Annex, although it was simply another row of tenements at right angles to the main terrace, like a buttress. Your odyssey wasn't over, however, for then you had to go up another flight of stairs, then take the third door on your right. Your destination was a meeting room that sharks like Donlevy used if they wanted to put any outsiders on the back foot. If they came late or, even better, if they had to phone for directions, then they always arrived at a disadvantage.

A clairvoyant insight came sleeting down unbidden from the future: Lamarck's audience would not be large. Most would give up on their quest to find where it was and retreat to the coffee room for a natter with their chums.

"What's this session about that you're chairing?"

"Jung and the occult. Right up your street."

I must have pulled my head back a bit, as you do when you open your dressing table drawer and find a black mamba threaded through your smalls.

"One of yours, surely?" he said, apparently surprised by my reaction.

"Jung is to psychology as a penny farthing is to a Maserati. Something to look back on and laugh about."

Lamarck grimaced. "Really, I didn't know that. Seems to make a lot of sense to me."

I opened my mouth to deliver a scathing lecture but this was derailed by a woman bustling into the room. Her carefully styled blonde hair had been lacquered into immobility so that it hardly altered no matter how much she moved her head. She was dressed in a dark suit tailored very nicely to her trim athletic form. "Sorry, Telly," she said and was already consulting the membership list. "Call from work, even though I warned them I was going to be away."

Telly nodded, his eyes flickering over the length of her body. He formed a brightly brittle smile, not at all a look I'd expect from such an apparently robust individual. "Can't live without you, eh? Just like the rest of us. Sally, let me introduce you to Dai Younge."

"Get to fuck!" she said as her pale blue eyes swept up from my unpolished shoes to my no doubt already tousled hair. Again, a not unheard-of response to the Name Test and as revealing as they all were. It spoke of confidence and iconoclasm, while the smart suit and petrified hair indicated constraint. I was willing to bet she did a professional job, but burst out from her obligations like a firework in her spare time. I suppose dabbling with the mystical was marginally better than putting money on the gee-gees or mainlining heroin.

OK, I can see how this goes against my earlier assertion that those of us in the mind game can't instantly psychoanalyse people we meet, but that doesn't stop us trying. And getting it wrong most of the time.

Lemarck's smile turned rueful as he seemed to appreciate this outburst. "Dai, this is Sally Vale." We shook hands and I wasn't surprised at the firmness of her grip. "Dai is our university liaison."

That was at least better than janitor. "I like to think of myself as riding shotgun," I said.

She smiled. "I'm glad you're armed. Some of the characters who rock up at these things, well —as my mother used to say—*the things you see when you ain't got a gun*."

Telly laughed. "Now, now, Sally. Show some respect."

"God, you're an old fart, Telly. School's out. Relax!"

"Sally tells us all what to do," he said, looking at me. "And woe betide if we don't listen."

Sally was looking around. "Where's the coffee for God's sakes?"

I looked at my watch. "It should have been here by now..."

"So, what are you going to do about it, Shotgun?"

It was a close-run thing but, somehow, she got away with it. Obediently, I shuffled off to phone the canteen.

~~~

Later, Lemarck opened the conference in a room which was at least on the same floor as the main entrance so some sixty people made it. Sally was left to man reception. I had little to do now until someone complained about something so I took a seat in this, our biggest meeting room.

I was at the back and peering across rows of white-haired heads at Lemarck. It's not that everyone at this damned meeting was old but it was definitely skewed that way. Perhaps the older ones had believed in this nonsense all their lives. Perhaps they were old enough for loved ones to have started passing away at a more metronomic rate, an impossible to ignore intimation of mortality driving them into the arms of the charlatans.

The conference room had about as much charm as a used condom and the only decorations festooning the place were the numberless instructions from the university about how to behave. These earnest missives were full of terms like intersectionality, micro-aggression and the vaguely disgusting sounding gender fluidity. They assured us that the university was a safe space where triggering was condemned but transformation encouraged, where discrimination based on skin colour, race, gender, height and weight was absolutely and totally prohibited.

With the university determined not to offend or disadvantage its students, it was a struggle nowadays to fail anybody. Even young white guys who, although not part of a handily oppressed group, could rabbit on about the effects on their mental health, at which point the university would back away hastily. Firsts in Bachelors' degrees and distinctions in Masters had been as rare as hens' teeth when I was a boy, but it was very unusual not to get them nowadays.

Everyone was special, so nobody was any more.

Daring to even hint at this would have been enough to get me fired. At least my thoughts were secret, although not for long if Donlevy had his way. In the bowels of the building powerful machineries were working to decode the messages from electromagnetic activity in the brain and its blood flow. Psychology was turning into a geeks' paradise of detectors and computers. They promised a future where every squalid thought would be wantonly revealed.

Can't wait!

Lamarck was going through what conferences organisers called 'housekeeping'. No, there was no fire drill planned so if they heard an alarm, it was the real thing. Still not having grasped the magnitude of the department's convoluted layout, he failed to mention that if there was a real fire then they'd all be toast.

I suppose they could always follow me to safety but they'd have to run really fast. I didn't fancy the chances of those with canes, like the very large couple with American accents who were sitting next to me.

"... and, of course, you'll all get a chance to meet our guest of honour, Larry Price." As Lamarck said this, on the screen behind him appeared a picture of a robust-looking red-headed chap with a slightly hooked nose. This was greeted by an excited round of applause. "He almost didn't make it to Scotland. For a start he discovered an ancient Nubian tomb, reputed to be guarded by demons, not that that would stop Larry." At this the audience murmured appreciatively. "Then it was touch and go what with the Ethiopian authorities chucking him into prison for tomb robbing. Ill-advisedly, they released him on parole and he fled the country!" This time there was chuckling and shaking of heads. Evidently this Price guy was regarded as something of a card.

From there Lamarck started to reel off some program sessions. I was losing focus fast. *Transitions* seemed to be a big thing, *quantum mechanics* another. I guessed Schrodinger and his simultaneously dead-and-alive cat gave these nutters some pretensions of anchoring their crazy notions in 'science'.

Then the programmed talks started and I had to adjust my bigotry just a little. Some of the attendees were so out there you'd need a very long grapple to haul them back, but others were much more intelligent and thoughtful. These latter really were after the truth in what was a largely incomprehensible universe. People trying to make sense of it all yet not willing to swallow the establishment view. One talk essentially debunked some old poltergeist cases, another took a very dim view of aspects of spiritualism. Though nobody hissed their disapproval, it was clear this did not go down well with a substantial section of the audience.

So, I had to admit that at least some of the attendees exhibited open-mindedness and adhered to the critical methods of science. They were not all 'nutters', although that term was too easy a shorthand to discard for a cynic like me.

Even though the talks were quite interesting and nowhere near as idiotic as I had supposed, after a while my attention started to drift so I got up, squeezed by the arthritic knees and engorged thighs of the American couple and exited stage left.

I found Sally at reception. She was shuffling through some papers, raising her eyebrows as I leaned on the counter. "You look a bit stunned," she said.

"No, more like bemused."

She gave me a sweetly innocent smile. "Too intellectually rigorous for you?"

"According to what Telly said there's going to be presentations on Jung. Really? We psychologists put him to bed half a century ago."

She tilted her head back and frowned. "I happen to be a fan."

"Get to fuck, as someone once said."

"Well, that's dismaying. The only psychiatrist who made any sense, and here you are, a modern student of the mind and you're totally dissing his work."

"And for very good reason. Synchronicity, demons from the unconscious and what have you—not a shred of evidence for any of it. Genial and avuncular in a twinkly way, but Jung was a con man, a fabulist, a bullshit artist."

"Wow! I've heard it all now." She sat back, arms crossed over her chest. No doubt her stern look made others fade but I wasn't having any of that either, especially as one of her eyebrows was microscopically raised. I'm always a succour for irony.

I smiled as patronisingly as I could. "I think you're a deserving case, possibly even salvageable. Let me take you out to lunch and set you straight."

She shook her head. "God knows it's difficult to resist such charm but I'm kind of busy here." She waved her hand over papers and leaflets and badges. "Tell you what, though. We've put on a bit of a treat for the organisers and our special guest, a thank you for all the work they'll be doing. Nothing less than a vigil in a haunted swimming baths. It's tonight. Why don't you come along? Maybe we can set *you* straight."

I laughed out loud; I just couldn't help it. "And where are these swimming baths, exactly."

"Govan."

This couldn't get any better. Govan was bandit territory, home of that fictional rapscallion Rab C. Nesbitt. The denizens would eat these effete parapsychs raw. "Sounds like quite a show. I'm in!"

"I'll text you the details." I intoned my number and she started poking it into her phone.

"Sally! So lovely to see you. Give us a kiss!"

I turned to find that a tall, muscular red-headed chap had crept up next to me and was leaning over the counter, lips pursed.

Sally held up opened hands, warding him off. "Not on your life!"

By now I'd recognised this as the tomb-robber Larry Price. Beaten up aviator's jacket, cargo pants with pockets bulging, I realised I'd seen him on TV somewhere. As this came to me, I remembered I'd also seen Telly before, gussied up by makeup with the few extra pounds of weight TV always seems to add. I'd seen them both on the psychic ghetto channels you find on cable and satellite. The ones where minor spooky happenings are bulked out to an hour-long slot by people overreacting to trivial incidents.

Price straightened back up, rubbing his bristly beard. "Sally, my love, can't we let bygones be bygones?"

"Just stay away from me." No minutely raised eyebrow so no irony this time. I remembered the way Telly had looked at her, covertly and with yearning. I began to suspect shenanigans amongst the attendees and not just of a spooky kind.

Price, unfazed, turned to look at me. "Are you the new beau?"

I met his eyes. "Beau? Who are you? Queen Victoria?"

"Dr Younge is our university liaison," said Sally, tossing a name badge across the counter at Price. "So, play nice."

None of this seemed to bother the man. He picked up a programme and began to scan it intently. Already we seemed to have slipped from his consciousness. I found myself admiring his iron-clad self-absorption.

I looked across at Sally, who shrugged. She finished poking in my number and my phone pinged. She raised her eyebrows and I nodded. Who could resist a haunted swimming baths in the demi-monde of Govan?

~~~

But first I had to meet up with my fellow victims of Rettner's disdain. The day before I'd got a phone call from Awang Che asking me to attend a war summit with a view to mounting a joint defence against the appalling way we'd been treated. It was to be in Bill Steadman's office in the department.

I was lukewarm about this to say the least. I'd got off with the lightest staining from the shitstorm that had descended. OK, it was demeaning being a janitor but that was a country mile away from being sacked or demoted. I wasn't keen to poke the hornet's nest but at the same time I felt some solidarity with my colleagues.

So, I had reluctantly agreed and that's why, in the late afternoon, I made my way up through the department's intestinal convolutions to Bill's office.

When I knocked, I heard Bill shout, "Yup!" so I entered. Bill's room smelled of the tobacco fumes emanating from his pores like swamp gas from a marsh. He was often to be found out on the pavement puffing away with Elsie and her Christian friends, their addiction trumping their ideological differences.

Butterball Awang Che, Viking-gone-to-seed Lucas Grimsrud and skinny old Bill Steadman, conspirators against our demon queen, looked up at me guiltily as I entered.

"Gunpowder plot or what?" I said, to trying to lighten it up.

"Never mind that, what the hell is going on here?" asked Lucas, opening his arms as though to encompass the whole department. "Do you know?"

"Know?" I replied. "I'm the fucking ringmaster!"

They all blinked in surprise.

Bill was sitting at his desk and behind him the windows showed a view of the facing tenement which had been hacked about into making studios for the Media Studies department. Blackout curtains made the building look blind.

Awang and Lucas were in chairs to either side of the desk. The one in front had been left all for me and I took it.

"And is there an explanation you'd care to share?" asked Bill icily.

"*This* is my penance, Bill." I held up my big bunch of keys. "I'm a caretaker to a barrel load of nutters."

Now, my attitude to the parapsychs had softened a little but I didn't want the Guy Fawkes Three to know that. I felt I needed to lay it on thick because my punishment was pitiful compared to what had happened to them.

However, they all looked surprised rather than impressed at my suffering.

I filled them in on my exacting new role and watched their eyes widen, if not in pity, at least in surprise. When I told them I was going to some kind of séance or vigil or whatever in haunted swimming baths, they all blinked as people do when they hear something outrageous.

Bill, who'd always been sharp, caught on to the subtext quickly. "So, you're not going to help us, are you? This is just a slap on the wrist compared to what happened to the rest of us."

I shrugged.

"It's a bit more than that," said Lucas gruffly. "Rettner got away with it. From now on Dai's up for all the shit jobs imaginable."

That was a good point and one I hadn't thought of myself. What next, cleaning the offices in a maid's uniform with a feather duster up my arse?

Bill must have seen my expression change and understood (damn these psychologists!), because he sat forward. "Is being a caretaker in your job description, Dai? I'm betting not. You can get her on that at the tribunal."

"Hang on a minute, Bill. You're the one who seemed to take it the easiest, why're you suddenly so gung-ho?"

"It was an insult, after all my years' service. As for why I didn't let them know what I was thinking—I prefer to keep my powder dry." He sat back, arms folded.

Lucas was pointing a finger at me. "Sacking, demotion, caretakerisation..." He hesitated for a second at this neologism but then seemed pleased with it. Really, it wasn't bad for someone whose first language wasn't English. "Anyway, Rettner and Donlevy stomped all over due process. There are employment laws up to the wazoo about that."

Awang added his own insight. "Back in Indonesia, an employer could get hacked to bits with bukos if he went too far with his workers."

"What's a buko?" I asked.

"It's a long curving blade, sharp enough to take a cow's head off in one stroke."

By mutual but unspoken consent, the rest of us ignored this. Awang was manifesting depths none of us wished to plumb.

"Look," I said, "we've been around long enough to see how this plays out. Bringing a private prosecution takes big bucks and I doubt any of us has that kind of money. That means the union has to prosecute for us but the chances are they won't—"

"But we have good case!" Awang interrupted.

"It doesn't matter. Infamies like this are a dime a dozen in universities today. The union doesn't have the money to pursue them all. It cherry picks the best. Plus, no union lawyer in his or her right mind would want any case to do with a monster like Rettner. Nobody takes on Rettner without sustaining damage."

"You don't know for a fact the union won't help us, Dai." Lucas was getting angrier. "We've got to try at least."

"Yeah," said Bill.

"Definitely," said Awang.

Three pairs of resentful eyes bored into me. I sighed. "Oh, what the hell?"

CHAPTER FIVE

Everything that irritates us about others can lead us to an understanding of ourselves.
Carl Jung

I've never liked swimming baths. To me it's a human soup of lurking verrucas, with soiled sticking plasters floating like jellyfish and undulating their way straight into your face. Never mind the shrieking kids splashing about and the sudden underwater kick to the testicles that you never saw coming.

But when the damned pool is empty of people and water then it's even worse. In terms of end-of-the-world desolation there's nothing like a filthy cement hole in the floor.

Chucking things into holes must comply with some primal urge, for in the dim torchlight I could see a miscellany of objects, from traffic cones to sweet wrappers, strewn over the bottom. As I played my beam across the deep-end I made out a single training shoe, an orgy of empty plastic bottles and a ball of limp fur that might be a soft toy or a dead rat. Next to that was the inevitable condom and around it there were suspicious glints. I was too far up and the torchlight too weak but I was pretty sure the light was reflecting off sundry needles. Govan was to drugs what golf courses were to lawyers.

"I thought this place was always locked up. How did all this crap get in here?" Sally had come up beside me and she shone her own beam across the bottom, our circles of light playing around like searchlights seeking bombers across city skies.

"This is Govan," I replied. "Locked doors are a challenge. This'll be a happy hunting ground for the district's feral youth."

"Well, I hope they're not here now." She swung the beam towards the group bending over a pile of equipment at the far end of the pool and raised her voice. "Aren't you lot ready yet?"

"Patience, Sally, patience." The speaker was Sam Murray, who I'd been introduced to earlier. I was surprised to hear he was a physics professor (full not associate) at some obscure Midlands university. He was partly of Indian extraction but traces of a Thames Estuary accent suggested Home Counties. Trim, handsome and rather particular in dress, he was wearing an immaculate blue three-piece suit to visit this sump hole. Softly spoken and always smiling he seemed like a nice enough guy. When he'd been told my full name, his eyes had darted away in embarrassment.

"What's the problem?" Sally, even on short acquaintance, was proving to be rather impatient.

"We can't zero the magnetometer," said Loris, her innate expectation of defeat vindicated.

"Which itself may be significant." Larry Price's booming voice carried and echoed in the void.

"That would be jumping to conclusions, Larry," said Murray who, unlike Price, appeared to be a reasonable man.

"Apparitions need energy to manifest themselves, Sam old mate. There's always a backwash." Price had a set-in-stone delivery that was already rubbing me up the wrong way. I guessed that on TV if you wanted to sell this nonsense to the great unwashed, then doubt was a ratings loser.

"But nothing's manifesting yet, Larry."

"Just wait, Sam. Wait."

There was someone else here I'd only just met, although I'd noticed her making her stately, expensively-dressed way around the conference. She was called Maude and from her bearing I couldn't help thinking of her as Grand Old Maude. Tall, matronly with thick, plumped-up grey hair, she made an imposing figure. A slight over-bite only added to this impression of haughtiness.

"Oh yes." She was standing, arms outstretched over the pool. "The atmosphere is rich, pregnant. I feel so many presences." Even when I was introduced to her, nobody had mentioned her surname. A supposedly famous medium, she didn't need one apparently.

Lamarck was nodding. "Well, so it ought to. This is the most haunted swimming pool in the country."

The most haunted swimming pool in the country. To me that sounded not so much like small beer as an alcohol-free beverage.

"What does Telly do for a living, or does he make his money from TV?" I asked Sally.

She snorted. "Not many make money from that kind of stuff. Only Larry is a big enough name to be coining it from TV. No, Telly's a teacher. In fact, the head teacher of a primary school in East London. Lot of deprivation there so he has a tough job."

"What about you, Sally? What do you do for real work?"

"You don't take any prisoners, do you, Dai?"

"Do you?"

She didn't answer for a second. "I'm a banker in the city. Go on, off you go!"

"What do you mean?"

"Everyone's prejudiced about bankers. Come on, get it off your chest so we can move on."

"Can I get an overdraft?"

At least this made her smile. I guess it's not just psychologists who carry around a lot of baggage. Morticians, estate agents, sewage workers. Someone has to do all that stuff.

An electric-powered lantern suddenly illuminated the pile of equipment and I saw Telly Lamarck straighten. "Motion sensors are all checked." He pointed, starting at the top of the pool where he and the equipment stood. "North at this end, east to the right, south at the deep end, then west where Sally and Dai are standing. Camera's ready to be activated?"

Now was the turn of Andy Lister. Tall and very dark skinned he was supposedly a famous film director of the paranormal. Confident and voluble, he certainly could direct because, though this wasn't his equipment, he'd somehow taken charge of setting it up. He had arrived in stylish but tar-black leathers so in the dim light he was very difficult to make out. "Cameras operational, one on each side. Soon as something activates the sensors, the cameras'll track round to the side pinpointed. Watch the cables everyone! Easy to trip and do a header into the pool with only the concrete at the bottom to break your fall."

"That's right," chimed in Telly. "The lights are all going be turned off so no blundering around. Whatever happens don't move! I'll stay here with Samuel at the north end monitoring the equipment, Larry you sit on the east side with Loris, Andy and Maude on the south, Sally and Dai stay west. Sing out only if you see or feel something change. I'll let you know if we get any anomalous readings. Everyone OK?"

"What about the rights?" Price had a strong voice. Even though I was on the other side of the swimming pool it sounded too loud.

Lamarck put his hands on his hips. "What rights?"
"Book rights, TV rights."
"Film rights," chimed in Andy Lister.

"For Christ's sakes, guys," said Sally. "This is supposed to be for relaxation, for bonding, to get us in the frame for the conference."

"Yeah," said Lamarck. "Chill out! A couple of hours then we're off to the pub. Just enjoy yourselves!"

"Some of us are professionals," said Price snottily. "We're always on duty."

"Give me a break!" Sally was graduating from irritation to anger. I couldn't help feeling there was a lot of subtext shooting around to which I was completely oblivious.

Price was getting angry too. "It's like you people have never been on a paranormal investigation before. The essence of paranormal phenomena is their unpredictability, their mischievousness."

"Yeah." Lister was warming up. "How often do apparitions appear just after you've turned off the instruments? You're all seeing this evening as a sort of entertainment, not to be taken seriously. This is just when Spirit pulls out all the stops."

Now that was one bit of subtext I could decipher. The 'mischievousness' of their ghosts and ghoulies was their excuse for why they never seemed to provide convincing evidence. What a contrast: my physics colleagues rarely described gravity as being 'mischievous'.

Sally sighed. "So, what do you suggest as far as rights go?"

"Common rights to all the data, including pictures and sound from all that rented equipment at the far end. Sole rights for our own recordings."

"I agree," said Lister.

"I agree too," said Maude, although I couldn't imagine her waving a camera around like some paparazzi. She looked as if she'd be more at home sitting on an armchair while a man in a morning suit cranked up his daguerreotype camera.

Even from a distance and in the gloom, I could see Lamarck was looking mystified. "What do you mean your own recordings?"

"Well obviously we're going to record this on our phones," said Price.

"You're not recording me on your phone," said Sally vehemently.

"You've changed your tune. In fact, I'm pretty sure I have some footage of you on there right now. I could—"

"Don't you dare!" Sally was coming out of her seat and I grabbed her arm. It was too dark and there were too many cables to start rushing round.

"Calm down everyone!" Lister was waving his arms. "No using images and recordings of other people without their permission, OK? Otherwise, we record what we want."

"Agreed," said Price.

Sally and Lamarck agreed but still sounded grumpy. Sam Murray and Maude had said nothing and so they'd kept their dignity. They both just nodded.

"Whatever," said Loris.

Lister gave it a few seconds. "OK, take your assigned places. Make sure you're comfortable before you turn off your torches. No moving after that."

Sally and I installed ourselves on camping stools. I shone my torch around to make sure of the positions of the thermos and some store-bought sandwiches still in their wrappings. To our side was a camera stand, its cables snaking all the way around the pool to the stack of equipment at the north end. From this, another thicker cable twisted its way through a partly closed door to an office where a diesel generator was gently chugging away.

I'd been impressed when Telly had triumphantly opened the doors of his van to show it full of serious-looking equipment. I'd been less impressed when they'd made it clear I had to help lugging it all in. "Think of it as part of the bonding exercise," Sally had said.

I shone my torch beam around the peeling paint of the walls. The weak beam could just make out, far above, the broken panes of glass that must once have make a very impressive skylight over the whole baths. Now this had been boarded up in a futile attempt to keep out the rain.

Why in God's name was I here? I felt again for the reassuring bulge in my leather jacket where a flask of rather fine malt whisky nestled.

"Are you OK, Dai? Are you sure you want to go through with this?" Sally may have admired Jung but she was clearly no psychologist herself. In these circumstances, a woman asking a man that question is never going to get 'no' for an answer. The male ego is far, far too delicate for that.

"I feel just swell," I said.

Lamarck turned away from his equipment. "So, if everyone—" A peal of thunder exploded away whatever he said next.

"Jesus!" said Sally.

Suddenly, rain came hammering down on the panels in the roof above. I couldn't help flinching in surprise.

Lamarck gave it a beat then, voice raised, he continued. "As I was saying before I was so rudely interrupted, if everyone is ready, I'll turn off the lantern and you should do the same with your torches. Please don't move from your seats as it'll be picked up by the motion sensors. That'll set off the lights and cameras. Try to keep looking straight ahead. That way, if something is happening in the room and it has its own illumination, at least one of us will see it. Everyone set?"

There was a series of grunts and *uh-huhs* and the lantern next to Lamarck went off. We all turned off our torches, the darkness jumping nearer with each click.

I waited a respectable interval but, really, there seemed only one thing to do now. Slowly, carefully, I reached into my jacket pocket and took out my flask. Gently I unscrewed the top and lifted the flask to my lips.

Blasts of retina shrivelling light made me jerk in surprise and I felt expensive scotch splash chillingly over my legs. With each strobe flash the silver flask seemed to pulse in my hand like a living thing.

"Oh for fuck's sake," roared Price. "Who let this amateur come along?"

Lamarck was more emollient. "Dai, mate, the idea is to stay as still as you can. Just for an hour, then we're all off for a drink."

"And if you can't stay still for an hour then you should just fuck off." Price, the tomb robber, was showing himself to be a Grade A arsehole. What had Sally seen in him?

She seemed to agree because I heard her mutter, "Where's a vengeful Nubian demon when you need one?"

I put the flask away and the flickering shut off.

Sitting in the dark doing nothing is nature's cue to fall asleep and I could see this was going to be a problem. The drumming of the water on the roof was the only stimulus left to focus on but it too soon became monotonous and I felt sleep beginning its first gentle caresses.

I'd have given myself a shake but was afraid to set off that damned strobe. I limited myself to opening and closing my eyes very rapidly.

Just like too much stimulus, too little is a torture technique. Shutting people away in a dark, silent room can break you down just as fast as ear-splitting music. With nothing to focus on, the mind turns in on itself and all it can do is nibble away at the individual's self-belief. Doubts darted in and out like fish from the darkness of the ocean. *What am I doing here? Is this a cruel prank? Are these paranormal idiots ganging up to haze the muggle in their midst?*

Then I heard something, or at least I thought I did. It was so faint... I strained to pick it out. It was coming from my right. Was something creeping up on me? Why hadn't the strobes kicked in?

Jesus! Maybe it was a rat. A diseased, sewer-dwelling rodent out to savage my ankle.

Calm down I told myself, moving my foot just a tad so the vermin would know I was alive.

"Movement!" yelled Price suddenly. "Above and to the right of Younge."

I turned quickly just as the strobes kicked off. At first, I saw nothing in the nightmarish flickering.

"There!" someone else shouted.

And then I saw it! Streaking towards me like a missile.

I yelled in alarm, shooting to my feet, arms up to cover my face, dodging to avoid it. I took a few steps, my feet slapping down on the tiled surrounds.

Then my right foot suddenly didn't come down on anything and I felt myself falling.

A cold hand slapped me across the mouth, sharp fingers digging into my skin just as another grabbed me by the arm. I found myself swinging round, the hard edge of the swimming pool hitting me from head to groin.

The hands scrabbled at me, hauling me up, dragging me back to safety on the side of the pool.

The big lights flared. I looked up to find Sally leaning over me. "You nearly fell in, you stupid prick!" She stepped back then turned to pick up the two camp stools, which had fallen over in the kerfuffle.

"It was just a bat!" Price sounded triumphant, his views on me vindicated.

I got to my feet and sat down gingerly on my camp stool. Physically and mentally, I felt bruised and sore.

"Are you OK, Dai?" Lamarck's concern came echoing across the swimming pool.

I waved a hand. "I'm fine."

"Maybe you should dial the sensitivity back on the motion sensors," said Murray, "otherwise that bat's going to keep setting them off."

Lamarck shook his head. "I don't think it was the bat—it's too small. Maybe one of us moved just enough to set them off. If it keeps being a problem then fine, I'll turn the sensitivity down. Right, everyone. Stay still!"

Darkness again. I couldn't help thinking about that damned bat, twisting and turning through the air, flitting between us. I thought of its nasty little bacteria-covered teeth and my exposed throat.

"What are you doing," whispered Sally. "Why are you fidgeting?"

I realised I'd unthinkingly pulled my jumper up to cover my neck. "Nothing, just feeling a bit uncomfortable," I said.

"Get a grip!"

"Would you both shut up!"

"Shut up yourself, Larry," Sally hissed.

Swirls of rain pattered across the roof. Summer though it was, the damp and chill were beginning to penetrate. I couldn't believe this nonsense was their idea of a treat.

And it went on and on. The windblown flurries of rain stroking the roof were becoming too soothing and a couple of times I had to shake my head to keep myself from falling asleep and toppling off the camp stool.

I was sure it was getting colder and could feel goosepimples rising from my skin. Now and again, I thought I heard the tiniest of squeaks.

"Did you hear that?" said Price.

"It's just that damned bat," I said peevishly.

"No, no. That's not it. There's a presence."

"Oh my God," said Loris suddenly, both fear and anticipation in her voice. "I sense it too!"

I held my breath, straining to hear. Was it my eyes or was something moving across on the other side of the swimming pool.

Price's scream made me stand up so fast I felt dizzy. A loud thump told me something heavy had fallen into the pool. I'd put down my torch in case it fell from my nerveless hands, the clatter giving away that I had nearly fallen asleep. Now as my hand scrabbled across the floor, I couldn't find the damn thing.

And it seemed the others were having the same trouble.

"Put the lights on!" yelled Sally.

One torch did come on and its circle of illumination raced down the other side of the pool. I saw Price's toppled-over camping school. The beam flicked down into the pool and stopped on a mound writhing at the bottom.

By now my hand had knocked against my torch and I picked it up. Just as I brought it to bear, several others clicked on and then the big lantern at the end came to life. Only then did the strobes flicker to life. I could see Lamarck racing down the side of the pool. He stopped where Price had fallen in and bent down.

"Are you alright, Larry?" he shouted.

"No, I'm fucking not. Head feels like it's been hit by a hammer." By now there was enough light to make out that Price was prone, head to one side, one startled eye looking up at the world. His voice had lost its sharpness and he sounded quite bleary. "Turn those strobes off! My head hurts bad enough as it is."

I'd already had enough of Price. Enough to know that if I was at breakfast and saw him get squashed by a falling piano, that I'd keep right on eating. Unfortunately, I was hardly a disinterested observer here. He was the guest of honour at this ludicrous conference that I was supposed to be minding and he'd come a cropper in my presence. It hadn't happened on university property but would Rettner and Donlevy be charitable and understanding?

My guess was no. I had to do something.

I'd noticed a ladder down into the pool only a few feet to my right so I headed over and started to climb down, the barrel of the torch held in my teeth. When I got near the bottom, I took it out and played the beam over the bottom. Yes, here and there, needles glinted but there weren't that many and, with care, I could avoid them.

Gingerly I crunched my way across the rubbish strewn over the bottom and had soon got to Price. Closer now I could see the white of his teeth, his lips bared in a grimace.

"How do you feel?" I asked, lamely.

Price gave a bitter laugh. "Like I dived head first into an empty swimming pool."

I checked. We were halfway along the pool and away from the sharply dropping deep end so the height he'd fallen from could have been a lot worse. His brains may not be splatted all over the floor but that didn't mean we weren't stumbling through head injury territory.

He started to move and I realised he was trying to get up.

"Stay where you are!" commanded Lamarck from above. "You might have a spinal injury."

"I fell on my head, you wanker." Price seemed determined to get up so I helped him. As I got him upright, his head started to wobble and I thought he was about to pass out, but he gripped the side of the pool in both hands and steadied himself.

Lamarck and I played our torches over his head. Remarkably, there didn't seem to be any blood. By now everyone was clustered around looking down, except for Murray who was still hunched over the equipment at the shallow end of the pool.

Price edged his way along the side until he came to a ladder and started to haul himself out. I couldn't risk him losing his grip and smacking his head again so I cast propriety to the wind and cupped his buttocks in my hands and shoved him up the ladder. Other hands were reaching out and grabbing his arms and soon he was hoisted up onto the side of the pool. By the time I got out he was standing upright, firmly supported by Lamarck and Lister.

"What happened?" Lister asked.

Price blinked a few times, his head still wobbling a little. "I sensed something coming at me. Couldn't hear it but just knew something was there. Luckily brought my hands up to ward it off. Just as well because when the damned thing smashed into my shoulder, tipping me over the edge, my hands absorbed some of the force when I hit the bottom. Still fetched my head a mighty clout, though."

"We need to get you to hospital," I said. "You need a CT at the very least."

Loris sucked in her breath. "You don't need to be doing with that radiation, Larry."

Price gave another bitter laugh. "I know you're against modern science, Loris, but occasionally it can help. Better safe than sorry."

"I'll take you in my car," I said. "It's just outside."

"Shouldn't we call an ambulance?" asked Sally, who'd grabbed Price around the waist to support him.

"You've gotta be kidding," I said bitterly. "Price here is still conscious so he's all-singing and all-dancing as far as the emergency services are concerned. We'd be lucky to get an ambulance within four hours. Look, the largest Accident and Emergency Department in Scotland is little more than a mile away. I can get him there in a couple of minutes."

"I'll come with you."

"No point. It's going to take hours to get seen."

We manoeuvred Price along the side of the pool then through the changing room and out past reception and into the street. I'd been fortunate to get a parking space directly outside. By now Price seemed almost recovered and managed to get himself into the front seat unaided. I started the engine and we left the others behind waving desultorily. The evening hadn't turned out how they had expected and they probably didn't know what to do next.

I turned out onto the Govan Road and headed towards the Queen Elizabeth Hospital. Meanwhile Price was looking round at the interior of my little Mazda sports car.

His tone, as usual, was snotty. "So, what dreadful inadequacy are you overcompensating for?"

"What?"

"This car. I mean it screams bachelor. How old are you?"

"Hey, I'm taking you to hospital. Would you prefer to be tipped into the Clyde?"

"If it makes you feel any better, you can put anything I say down to my head injury."

What did that mean? Was it a sort of apology or was it just another insult wrapped up in extreme condescension? How had this guy lived so long?

Suddenly he pointed. "Are you taking me there? It looks like the Death Star."

At least in this he was correct. The new building had risen like an avenging hi-tech phoenix from the ruins of an old Victorian hospital called the Southern General (or Suffering General as generations of Govanites had called it). It was now called the Queen Elizabeth, sometimes referred to as Liz's Place but, more commonly, the Death Star.

"It's the biggest hospital in Europe," I said, though I don't know why as I wasn't absolutely sure it was true. He'd stung me and I was indeed overcompensating.

I turned into the grounds. All around the twelve-storey Death Star were clustered buildings in all shades of modern. With tinted glass and curved, hulking shapes, it made the place look like a moon-base.

Perhaps in a way that was true because for some unfortunates this was a launch pad into eternity.

There were drop-off spaces outside the entrance to A&E. I tried to help Price from the car but he batted away my outstretched hands. When he got out, he still looked a bit unsteady but wanted to make his own way in without my help.

"Look, the more easily you enter this place, the longer you're going to have to wait."

"What do you mean?"

"Ham it up, for Christ's sake! The more help and technology you need to get here, the quicker you're seen. The only sure way to get attention immediately is to arrive in something with rotor blades as standard."

"I've got a license to fly helicopters, you know." OK, so that wasn't quite a non-sequitur, but it was a slightly off-kilter thing to say. That really had been a bad fall.

More tellingly, he put an arm over my shoulder for support.

In Govan, A&E receptionists have literally seen it all. Even so, Price's Christmases came all at once. The receptionist, a bespectacled blonde with the detached chilly demeanour of a parking warden, did a double take when he told her his name.

"You're the guy off the telly! All that weird stuff."

Price opened his mouth, no doubt to say something that would take all his Christmases away again. I grabbed his arm in warning and leaned in to the woman. "My friend had a very nasty fall and he hasn't been acting right since. Bleeding on the brain is a real possibility."

Her professionally dead eyes swung to regard me. "You can dial it back a bit, sir. Monday nights are always quiet, especially now all the students have gone home and everyone else has flown off to Magaluf. Take a seat, it won't be long."

Triaged as also-rans, we did as we were told. Price cast a disapproving eye over his fellow sufferers waiting for attention. For a while he stared at a globular, red-faced guy almost certainly the worse for drink who was slumped in a seat in our row.

"Is he dead? He doesn't seem to be breathing."

"If you're worried, why don't you give him the kiss of life?"

"God you're a prick, Younge."

Now he turned his attention to an old couple huddled together. It was uncomfortable to see the fear on their faces.

Just then a younger couple rushed in, a toddler limp in the father's arms. I didn't see the receptionist do anything but theatre gowned staff and a trolley suddenly appeared, and all three were whisked away behind self-closing and self-locking doors.

I had been in enough A&E's to know that such poignant little vignettes were commonplace. Life at the sharp end when it all went suddenly wrong. They made my moans about teaching students look like the churlish whimperings of little Lord Fauntleroy.

Not something to focus on so I decided to take it out on Price instead.

"Double vision?" I asked.

"What."

I said the words slowly, as if I was talking to a child. "Have you got double vision?"

"No." He looked affronted and turned his eyes elsewhere.

"You know that the Coma Scale that's used around the world was invented here in Glasgow in this very hospital? That's why it's called the Glasgow Coma Scale or GCS."

"I'm not in a coma."

"Ah, but you might be slipping into one. How many fingers am I holding up?" I held up one.

"Fuck the fuck off!"

"My friend and I have invented an alternative coma scale. Do you want to hear about it?"

He turned to look at me as if I was mad. "NO!"

"You see, with the GCS they assess eye movements, verbal responses and motor skills to put a patient on a scale from one to fifteen. Fifteen means you're AOK, 3, the minimum score, means you're well and truly fucked. They can poke you with a needle, or ask you questions and you still won't open your eyes. Obviously, you're not quite there yet, but where exactly are you?

"You see my pal Mo and I have produced a scale corresponding to how much you've drunk so it's sort of the inverse. A score of one is one pint and essentially means no change. Five means five pints and your memory's going and you're slurring your words. Fifteen means you're unresponsive and you've drunk a bucketful and you're going to die from inhaling your own vomit. The equivalent in the GCS is when your brain swells so much it turns itself to mush and that's how you die. I mean, not right away. The GCS is a foreshadow of what is to come. It's a signpost."

"I think the word you're fumbling for is *prognosis*."

"Whatever. Let's see now. Your eyes are open spontaneously so I don't even have to poke you. That's four points right there so you're not officially comatose. Your verbal responses on the other hand aren't quite right. You've been using a lot of expletives..."

"So have you."

"Yes," I said patiently, "but I live in Glasgow. Plus, what you're saying doesn't quite follow on from what went before...

"Get to fuck!"

"Again, a little bit of an overreaction, don't you think?"

I might have been finding this funny but he wasn't. The skin on his face was nearly the colour of his beard. I continued: "So that's four points out of a possible five for that. Right, now for motor responses. Lift your right arm and make a fist."

Couldn't fault him there. Within an instant his fist was pressed against my nose. Not hard, but not softly either. "I'll give you the full six there," I said. "That gives you fourteen out of fifteen. Christ, that's barely the equivalent of a pint. Your prognosis is good."

I noticed a figure in hospital blues approaching but I was distracted because Price, almost scarlet now and shouting, started poking a finger in my chest. "You can take your Glasgow Coma Scale and stick it up your arse you snide, wanky little shit."

The man in blues looked a little taken aback, although I could hardly imagine angry people in a Govan A&E were entirely unprecedented. "Mr Price?" he asked gently.

Price stood up, still giving me a filthy look. "That's me."

"We'll have a look at you now. This way."

Price was led off deeper into the fortress and I was left wondering what would happen next. He could be there for hours. Should I leave? What was I doing here anyway? Why are we born to suffer and die?

Leave me alone without stimulus and my thoughts soon spiral down into the existential void. However, just as I was disappearing up my own metaphysical backside, my phone rang. It was Sally.

"How's Larry?"

"He's a bit of a prick, if you ask me."

"Very funny. His head injury. Remember?"

"They're looking at him now. I guess I'll wait and take him back to his hotel."

"That's very kind of you."

"Yes, that's what people tell me. All the time."

That at least got a laugh. "Phone me when he gets out. Let me know what the hospital reckons."

"You seem genuinely concerned. Are you two involved?"

Sally laughed again, this time rather sourly. "Yes and no. I'm worried about him because he's our guest of honour and he hasn't given his talk yet. And no, we're not involved but we do have history. A few years ago, hearing his skull clonk onto the bottom of that swimming pool would have been cause for celebration. Now, not so much."

That she'd consorted with a swollen bag of ego, wind and piss like Price dropped her a notch or two in my estimation. After a few more words we said our goodbyes and I again promised to keep her informed.

I noticed the guy who'd taken Price into the inner sanctum had come out and was making his way over to me. "I'm Doctor Pearson. Can I ask, are you a relative of Mr Price?"

"No, Mr Price is a guest at a conference at the university. I'm a sort of organiser. He doesn't come from these parts so he doesn't have any relatives in the city."

The man nodded. "And your name is..."

"Dai Younge." I spelled it for him.

He seemed too absorbed to pick up on my ridiculous name and just wrote it down studiously and then took my address.

"Is he OK?"

"He's clearly had a nasty bang on the head. We're giving him a CT now. You'll wait for him?"

I said I would and he left.

Two hours later, he emerged again but this time with a still angry-looking Price in tow. I could hear the celebrated parapsych from ten metres. "Well, that was a waste of time. Take two aspirins and have a good night's sleep! So much for modern medicine."

"We had to make sure there wasn't swelling or a bleed." Pearson caught sight of me. "Ah, good. Your friend's still here."

"This isn't my friend. This is some scabby half-arsed academic the university foisted on us. I wouldn't take another lift off him if you paid me."

I got to my feet. "Oh yeah, so would a kick up the arse do instead?"

Pearson interposed himself between Price and myself.

"Gentlemen please: this is a hospital!"

Price stood up straight, taller than both of us, and looked around. "Where can I get a taxi?" He must have seen a sign because he was off before Pearson and I could say a thing.

"Are you sure he's OK?" I asked as Price disappeared through the main doors.

The skin around Pearson's eyes creased. "Difficult for me to say. I didn't know him before he had a fall. Was he much different before it happened?"

"Not really," I conceded.

"If there's any signs of change just bring him back. We'll give him another going over."

I gave Sally a ring and gave her an upbeat report.

By the time I got outside Price was gone. It was nearly midnight so I wended my weary way home.

CHAPTER SIX

I am not what happened to me, I am what I choose to become.
Carl Jung

That is the kind of nonsense Jung spouted. I'm going to explain just how much nonsense by giving you a taster, an *amuse bouche,* of my upbringing.

Also, it lets me get my excuses in early.

It's not often two sociopaths fall in love. Where it does happen there's hell to pay and typically ends in a hail of bullets (Bonnie and Clyde, I'm looking at you).

Maybe before we start, we need to explain the difference between sociopaths and psychopaths.

The answer is—time and fashion.

Each medical generation loves changing its terms, and even its definition of whole diseases, to make it sound more knowledgeable than the previous one. They do it all the time to the point where mental illnesses come and go like will-o-the-wisps

For example, not so long ago the psychiatric profession classed homosexuality as a mental illness. Gay liberation was just starting up then and there was a huge pushback, so the psychiatric profession hastily regrouped and reclassified it as a mental illness only if the 'sufferer' was troubled by it. They gave this a fancy new name—homodysphilia. A few years later that moniker became passe and was dropped in favour of ego-dystonic homosexuality.

'Neurosis', that twentieth-century mainstay, is now not considered a separate condition at all. Neurotic depression is no longer neurotic and isn't considered a depression. At one hysterical meeting of the international cabal of psychiatrists that tries to work out what is and what isn't currently an illness, hundreds of new conditions like PTSD, anorexia nervosa, bulimia and panic disorders suddenly appeared and 'grew empires of sufferers' overnight.

This cabal (called the DSM) literally votes previously unimagined conditions into existence. Not many other scientific fields identify phenomena by voting. Referring back to our old and rather more respectable friends the physicists, they could vote gravity out of existence all they wanted but, if they took an incautious step, it'd still squish them like a bug.

So, there is no difference between sociopaths and psychopaths except for a restless need to change terminology by a group who, in my humble opinion, actually knows very little about mental illness. The only difference between DSM psychiatrists and witch doctors is that the former cast ballots rather than knuckle bones.

Mom and Dad were psychopaths and it gave them pleasure to fuck people up. However, they were smart, smart enough at least to make sure they never wound up in jail. They figured that if they were going to mess with people it had to be in such a manner so as not to leave scars.

Let me think: what profession allows you to do that and get away with it?

Psychiatry, of course! In a profession that can eradicate or create scores of mental illnesses on a vote, which in the past lobotomised and electroshocked at a whim, how is anyone going to even notice a couple of malevolent charlatans in its midst?

But surely, some naive readers might think, wouldn't their lack of success in curing people be noticed?

To such readers (who I envisage as big-eyed and pig-tailed, wearing tutus and a tiara and with big lollipops in their mouths) I'd like to gently point out that psychiatrists don't cure anything. Sure, they can sometimes use drugs to suppress symptoms for a while but there's no permanent remedy.

So rather than making patients well, the best even legitimate psychiatrists can do is produce patients slightly less fucked up than before.

Spotting when a couple of maverick psychiatrists are producing patients a bit more, rather than a bit less, fucked up is always going to be tricky.

And my parents weren't stupid; they didn't deal with the florid conditions, the psychoses like schizophrenia or bipolar disorder, where even benevolent intervention can send patients off the deep end with messy headline-grabbing results.

No, Mum and Dad stuck to the lower end type of neurotic conditions (for want of a better word since the DSM snatched that perfectly adequate old one away). You know, the hypochondriacs, the over-anxious, the mildly depressed. The sort of conditions the poor just have to live with, while the rich can afford to waste money using highly qualified witch doctors.

In other words, Mum and Dad messed only with the rich, like Robin Hood used to do. They worked their patients like marionettes and had a good laugh about it over the dinner table every evening.

In those days we had a nice old bungalow in the affluent area of Bearsden, its covering of ivy over the front turning to a beautiful crimson in the autumn. A real butter-wouldn't-melt-in-its-mouth type home. From the outside, anyway.

Mum was tall, reaching almost six feet in her high heels. Dark hair, stylishly dressed but with cold, cold eyes her effect could be intimidating. She tried to disguise it with a lot of lipstick to emphasise a wide, smiling mouth. Only I knew how artificial that smile was, how quickly it dropped when she got home and closed the door.

Joviality was something Dad also never understood at a fundamental level, but he could mimic it well enough. Mimicking other people's reactions is how psychopaths get by in society and you have to watch them closely for a long time before you realise that sometimes their reactions are always just a little bit off.

The thing that makes us understand others rather than just mimic them is empathy. That's what lifts the rest of us out of psychopathy, and that gives our personality texture. It also makes us vulnerable and it softens our hard edges. It makes us human in a way that allows people to love us for our weaknesses and not just our strengths.

Without that empathy we become more of a mechanism than human. We become two-dimensional, cartoon-like.

So, at home I was a three-dimensional person stuck in a two-dimensional world with cartoonish characters. And I was powerless to do anything but watch the story unfold.

Dad was big and bear-like with a full head of dark hair and a luxuriant beard. I noticed how women, and not a few men, felt the need to pat him as if he was some sort of furry toy.

Mum and Dad appeared comforting, upbeat, articulate, well-off and well-dressed. The trouble was, this powerhouse duo ganged up on me, a scruffy, tongue-tied kid. I never stood a chance.

For some strange reason nobody believed me when I told them that my parents were crazy as the proverbial shithouse rats, a perfectly adequate description the DSM has yet to warm to.

And truth be told, according to the shifting sands of modern psychiatry, they really weren't mentally ill. The prevailing theory goes that mental illness can change with time or with therapy. Psychopathy is considered a different beast altogether. It's hard-wired into the brain and immutable. Nothing can change it.

Ergo psychopathy is not a mental illness. It is what it is, and those who possess it are simply a subset of humanity. Get over it.

Getting over it is tricky when you're confined to a house with two prime examples. Paediatricians worried about my early lack of thriving, how I was thin as a rake until I was ten years old. I can't tell you all the things they stuck in my mouth and up my backside to make sure it wasn't a problem with my digestion.

What actually took my appetite away was listening to my parents discussing their sport over the evening meal. Cannibals at a feast poking away at the remains of their victims.

Post mortems might begin like this:

"Constance has had a dream," Dad might say as we cut into our fish fingers (psychos tend to be sybarites, self-indulgence being everything to them but, strangely, neither of my parents gave a toss about food. We could have afforded caviar but instead our luxury was steak mince).

"Constance, the little blonde who works for that charity?" asked Mamma, dipping a chip into ketchup.

"That's the one—played doctors and nurses with her younger brother."

Patient confidentiality was a courtesy my parents had little time for, at least between themselves and my unwilling ears.

"Handy," said Mother. "Wide open, inviting."

What she meant by this was that such a relatively minor childhood transgression constituted, to these two, a crack in the facade. Where a proper psychotherapist may have tried to fill this with pharmaceuticals or at least some kind of neuro-analytical Polyfilla, Mum and Dad saw a weakness to be exploited.

"What's her problem, again?"

Dad waved his fork in accompaniment as he answered. "Same old, same old. Minor neuroses, has too much time and money on her hands. Has all the illnesses under the sun, real Disease of the Week stuff. Uses these to explain away her not getting a proper job."

The lids narrowed over Mother's cold eyes. Mum and Dad had both come from families at the lower end of the social spectrum. They resented the well-off, although that's what they had become themselves, their private practice salaries jet-fuelled by neurotics like this Constance.

"So, hypochondria, but what else?"

Dad gave a little grimace. "Incipient paranoia. Thinks people at the charity she works for are talking behind her back and making fun of her."

"Which they probably are."

"Of course. Self-indulgent, dressed head to toe in Armani chic, wafting around the offices of a charity for malnourished kids. When she's at work that is, what with her neuro-condra-myelonic-megamorphism, or whatever the disease du jour is. Of course, people are talking behind her back. It's only natural."

"Inevitable. So, what are you going to tell her?"

"Well, the dream she had a couple of nights ago was the old naked-in-company one." (Mine too, unsurprisingly.)

Mum sat back and laughed. "Revelation," she said. "Jungian dictates from the unconscious, suppressed but active, manifesting themselves in disease and doubt. The imperative to get it all off her chest for the sake of her health."

"Bingo!" said Dad, waving his fork again. "Full disclosure to her workmates about her diddling her brother. Set the record straight. Start again from scratch."

I have to admit I kind of think that what Constance needed most of all was a good slap (I am the son of my parents after all) but I could see that Dad's advice would be like tossing a ship onto rocks.

"Leave her alone!" I found myself saying.

Two eyes weren't good in this household but four eyes were definitely bad, and they were all staring at my ten-year-old self.

"Is that your professional opinion, son?" asked Dad.

Mum sniggered.

"She needs... she needs..." I began but already didn't know where to go with this. Gentle reassurance or a good slap? Tranquillisers or anti-depressants? To be honest, even today and after a PhD in psychology, I still don't know the answer.

Dad, who would have given her a full lobotomy if he could have got away with it, put his cutlery down and steepled his fingers. He raised his eyebrows, waiting for my words of wisdom.

Fully clothed, I still felt naked.

"You know nothing about psychology, Dai, yet here you are offering advice. Why is that?"

My eyes darted to my mother. No help there.

I looked back at Dad. "I just picked it up. Listening to you two every night."

Dad nodded as though in appreciation. "Then give me some examples of Jungian archetypes."

My ten-year-old mind immediately went blank.

Dad smiled. "Well, at least tell me the difference between psychotic and non-psychotic conditions."

"I'm not saying I have exams or anything..."

"Qualifications, I think you mean qualifications."

"But this Constance, you're just going to make her embarrass herself. That can't be good."

Dad leaned forward across the table. "Truth is everything, son," said the lying bastard. He could be so earnest when he really tried. Poor fucked-up Constance didn't stand a chance.

Mum chimed in. "Dai's growing up, Stan. Time for him to put away childish things."

Dad nodded. "You're right, Laura. The fledgling will soon leave the nest."

At ten?

"We need to ease his way. What's called for is..."

"...a camping trip!" they both cried in unison.

~~~

Rannoch Moor: blasted heather encrusted moors broken only by black water pooling in bogs and small lochs, sun-browned grass on the otherwise barren hillsides and all under a leaden sky.

"You don't want to step into any of that water, son," said Mother as our jeep slalomed around the bogs. "Slurp you down as quick as that." She snapped her bony fingers.

"Please take me home," I said as clearly and as reasonably as I could.

"And snakes," she said. "Tap out your Wellington boots before you put them on. Just in case."

"In case of what?" I said, my voice suddenly weak as water.

"In case one has crawled in overnight."

"A snake," I said faintly. "Are they poisonous?"

Dad gave an insouciant wave with the hand not holding the steering wheel. "Some are, some aren't."

By now we were several miles from the last house and that had been overgrown by straggly brown grass and looked like, if it was inhabited at all, it would be by trolls.

"But if I'm bitten, I could die. How would I get help?" This was in the days before mobile phones and, even if it hadn't been, my parents would never have allowed me one.

"Adder bites are rarely fatal. Sore, mind you."

I watched the backs of their heads nodding away in agreement.

"I don't want to spend the night here," I wailed.

Mum turned around to look at me, putting her arm across Dad's shoulders. I struggled to imagine how they could still bear to touch each other. "Think of it as a test of manhood, of leaving childish things behind. Cultures all over the world do it."

"That's right," said Dad. "In Borneo, boys like you are locked away in a Spirit House for six weeks, then witch doctors slash their bodies with razors to give them scars that make them look like crocodiles. Some of the kids die from blood loss."

Mother was getting into this too. "In Ethiopia, the boy has to stand naked in front of four bulls. He has to jump onto all their backs three times. A lot of the boys get stomped to death.

"And don't get me started on the Sambia tribe in New Guinea. At seven, the boys are tied to a tree and sharp sticks are stuck up their noses for ceremonial blood-letting. Then the men of the tribe beat them black and blue to toughen them up."

Dad waved his finger. "Not to mention making them take all the men's willies in their mouths to gain strength from the 'man's milk.'"

Bear in mind I hadn't even been taught about the birds and bees, so that image was frighteningly bizarre, incomprehensible and viscerally disturbing.

"And as for those Mardudjara Aborigines—" I could hear the relish in Dad's voice, "—a boy your age would have a tooth knocked out and his septum, that's the strip inside your nose that separates your nostrils, that would be pierced. Then the boys are taken out into the wilds like this and circumcised with a rusty knife. To top it all they then have to eat their own foreskin."

I felt my own foreskin shrivel. "You're not going to…"

Mum, still looking at me, enjoying my reactions, shook her head. "You're just going to camp out overnight. I mean, seriously, compared to all that you've got it easy."

"Mind you, the ritual circumcision thing has considerable historical precedent," said Dad, still in full stride.

"With Zulus it was done by a hallucinating old witch doctor with a spear or even just a sharp rock. I bet that didn't always work out so well."

Anything to do with my genitals scared me so I was glad when Dad finally veered off the subject. "One tribe called the Matis drip venom in kids' eyes, inject them with frog poison to make them sick and slap them with stinging nettles. Another lot weave bullet ants into gloves and make the kids wear them for ten minutes. Even one bullet ant sting feels like being shot, you see where the name comes from, and the kids, the ones who survive anyway, tremble uncontrollably for days afterward."

Mom had kept her trump card for last. "And the Maasai, they kick the kids out of their huts and tell them they can't come back until they've killed an adult male lion with just a spear. Compared to that, how can you possibly complain about going on a little camping trip?"

She turned around to face forward, as though in disgust at my weakness but I was pretty sure she was just hiding a smile.

By now I was so deep in shock that my vision was blurred, there was ringing in my ears and uncontrollable little spurts of urine were being soaked up by my underpants. I hardly noticed when they finally stopped the car and got out.

While Dad rummaged around in the back for the tent, Mum gently pulled me out of the car.

"My brave boy," she said. I looked at her, our eyes barely a hand's breadth apart, in complete incomprehension. She smiled. "I put a Mars Bar in with your fish paste sandwiches. You'll like that."

Dad knew as much about tents as I did and the erection that rose had a misshapen appearance, the Caliban of Camping. Its triangular entrance, to my fucked-up mind, looked like a mouth waiting to gobble me up.

Dad clapped me on the shoulder, Mum rubbed a hand down my back and before I came out of my dwam (*modern Scots noun—a state of dreaminess, but less of an enchantment and more of a stupor*), they'd got in their old Jeep and were heading back to civilisation. I ran after them but it was half-hearted and I gave up after a few steps.

I watched as the vehicle made its haphazard path through the bogs until it shrank to the size of a pea then disappeared. Turning back, I picked up the Tupperware container, prised off the lid and crammed the fish paste sandwiches into my mouth.

Haven't been able to touch the stuff since. Classic association.

Swallowing the last big bolus of gluey bread, I looked around for something to drink and realised the idiots had left me with nothing.

There's a spectrum of our misdeeds that goes from malevolence through insouciance and finally reaches stupidity. At what point on this spectrum does my parents leaving me overnight in summer without anything to drink actually lie?

Dunno.

I cast a glance at the nearest pool of water. It was five metres across and the water was peat-black because that's what it contained. This no doubt was where the bogles (*Scots noun— an ugly or terrifying ghost or phantom*) did their business.

I turned around, surveying the vast emptiness, and knew I was going to die there. I was reasonably confident (say around 75%) that my parents would come back but there was the little matter of how they would find me. There was barely a track to follow, no distinctive big rocks or trees (in fact, no trees at all). Even with the best will in the world, which they didn't in any event possess, how would they find me again? Like the business with the water, I doubt it was something that had crossed their minds.

Then I remembered the snakes and literally jumped into the air, trying to get my welly boots clear of the heather and scrubby grass amongst which countless venomous reptiles were no doubt lurking.

Gravity of course brought me right back to earth. I wailed.

~~~

Sometime in the evening the midges came upon me like a biblical plague. In my mouth, up my nose, mating with my eardrums, they forced me into my gargoyle tent. I quickly zipped it up behind me, left inside only with the thousand or so midges I'd brought along. All evening, they filled their bellies with my blood. No matter how hard I flailed and slapped and scratched, they took their turns like bikers at a gang bang.

Finally, I could take no more and decided to make a run for it. Didn't know where I was going, didn't care if I was sucked down by a bog (at least it would keep the midges off). I pulled down the zipper and flopped out into air which was suddenly much cooler than in my fetid tent. As though by magic, the midges fled and I felt the night air caressing my skin.

As my awareness opened out from my internal agony, I saw the night sky. For the first time it wasn't submerged by the wash of Glasgow city lights. An infinite multitude of tiny sparks looked down upon me.

For a city boy to find himself alone and surrounded by an eternity of nothing was a profound experience. I seemed marooned on an empty planet lost amid the myriad suns of the Milky Way, its lens stretching from horizon to horizon.

I sat there on the ragged grass and perhaps I might have become one with the universe were I not so bothered by the thought of snakes. I couldn't help but imagine them slithering towards me, their jaws open, their fangs dripping with green venom as they zeroed in on my tender flesh.

I shivered for hours, the Milky Way wheeling in slow motion across the firmament, not a sound disturbing the stillness of the moor.

Somehow, despite my dread of the snakes, I must have fallen asleep. My childish brain, trying to process the horrors of the day, made my dreams teem with slithering, flying, biting monsters that chased me through a never-ending bogland from which the skeletal arms of the long-drowned reached up to catch my ankles.

Something, some sharp animal sense previously buried by the bustle of the city, jerked me awake. I opened my eyes to find a bright star moving fast but soundlessly across the firmament.

Was I dead, was this an angel come to take me to heaven? I placed my hands down on the ground, the snakes momentarily forgotten, and pushed myself to my feet.

The angel was getting closer, it's light blinding. And then I could hear it, the sound rising quickly as it rushed towards me. This was no gentle voice of an angel, rather the roar of a devil. I felt my legs weaken and tremble as the beast bore down on me, its mighty breaths beating me down, whipping up the straggly grass, sending my tent tumbling away.

I opened my mouth and screamed as the creature thundered to earth.

~~~

And what followed was my one, and so far only, flight in a helicopter. My rescuers, day glo tabards covering their flight suits, treated me gingerly, as if I was an unexploded bomb. If they'd had enough cotton wool, they'd have wrapped me up in it.

Even as we rose, and the ground disappeared below into a uniform blackness, they were inspecting me, their fingers gently running over my body, the beams from their muted head torches sweeping over me, looking for traces of blood. One of them shouted a question but it was sliced away by the roar of the rotors.

Outside, the first faint lights were appearing as we cleared the moor. Rising still further revealed a man-made starfield scattered around the black artery of the Clyde.

I could make out the moving dots of cars as we zipped over the expressway. Crossing the river, we lost height rapidly. I could see the flashes of an ambulance waiting by a huge illuminated 'H'.

Strong arms cupped me and, to my surprise, I found myself lifted like a doll, out of the copter and across the circle picked out by the lights and to the open door of the ambulance. As these slammed shut behind me the ambulance took off and went a ridiculously short distance, it couldn't have been more than a hundred yards, before stopping again. I had a chance to glance at the guy who had carried me, but I only got the impression of a big nose with flared nostrils and an explosion of beard from the neck of his flight suit. The doors opened and I found myself carried once again, but only the short distance to a trolley. Its wheels rattled and a succession of grimy fluorescent light fittings whizzed by above my head.

I hadn't a clue what was going on but I was beginning to appreciate the drama.

The rattling stopped and a worried-looking guy in a white coat shone a little torch in my eyes. I felt my shirt being opened and the cold touch of a stethoscope on my chest. Then I felt a coarse blanket being laid over my shoulders.

"What's your name, little man?" said the doctor (by now I'd worked out I was in a hospital).

"Dai Younge."

Did the doctor, just for a nanosecond, give a little smirk? I may only have been ten, but I'd grown used to the effect of my name.

"Where am I?"

"The Southern General Hospital." Maybe I looked blank because he added: "In Glasgow."

"Where's my Mum and Dad?"

The doctor glanced away, as if he didn't know what to say.

And no one could. For days, despite me asking the same question with increasing degrees of puzzlement.

~~~

Not long after leaving me, when they were almost off the Moor, and no doubt laughing their heads off at the predicament they'd left me in, Dad had probably taken a wrong turning and driven the Jeep straight into a small but surprisingly deep loch. The beaten-up old vehicle had more holes than a sieve and filled up fast.

It had made quite a splash going in, enough for a cyclist, miraculously passing on the nearby road, to hear. But for the prompt actions of the emergency services, and the keen eyesight of the pilot who had followed the tyre tracks back through the dirt and mud, I'd probably still be on that damned moor.

Psychos, as a general rule, do not commit suicide and I have no reason to think that is what they intended. Post mortems revealed that after they'd dropped me off, they must have stopped for a good swallow. Again, as a rule, psychos being into self-gratification, if they have a taste for alcohol they don't know when to quit. They certainly drank a lot, so I wasn't surprised an empty whisky bottle had been found in the passenger foot well.

There was certainly evidence that they'd tried to escape from the Jeep. The windscreen was starred where Dad had booted it, presumably in a bid to get out. Trouble is, kicking out a windscreen is difficult, just as opening a door can be, when there's water on the outside pressing in. Apparently, in that predicament, the idea is to wait until the car is almost full of water, so the pressure is more or less equalised, and then you can open the door or kick open the window and escape.

But drunk and panicking, perhaps they didn't think about that, or perhaps they'd never heard that advice. In the event, Mum hadn't even managed to undo her seat belt.

I think they would have returned later that night after having a boozy meal somewhere. If they really had left me overnight there's a fair chance I would have wound up dead. That would have been difficult to explain away. They'd have come back a few hours later out of self-preservation, not out of love.

What can I say about foster care? After a few false starts (it's difficult to develop a relationship with a kid who is near catatonic) I wound up with a couple who could at least put up with me. I know I'm trying to pull at your heartstrings here but I can't in all honesty complain too much about them and my treatment. No abuse, certainly. The only charge I can make is one of faint indifference.

To get back to my original point, which was Jung and his idea that we *choose* what we become. How can you go through that experience on the moor, plus ten years of living with demonic parents like mine, and not be profoundly affected?

Did I choose my subsequent fear of snakes and midges? I think not.

Not that these were the only consequences. I became obsessed with trying to work out why my parents did what they did to me. Anything, perhaps, to explain away their fathomless inhumanity. And that's why I 'chose' the study of psychology. To try to understand what had happened and make sense of the senseless.

[SPOILER ALERT—it didn't work]

CHAPTER SEVEN

Be grateful for your difficulties and challenges, for they hold blessings. In fact... man needs difficulties; they are necessary for healthy personal growth, individuation and self-actualisation.
Carl Jung

I'd passed this place many times and it looked like any old-red brick public office building. On one side was the Palace of Art and the rising ground of Bellahouston Park, to the other side down in a dip was the thrumming M8 motorway.

Now, jammed in the back of a cop car, I got a chance to better appreciate the anti-terror accoutrements of the Helen Street Police Station.

Dragged from my pit at 6 a.m. by the insistent ringing of my doorbell, and finding two heavily built plainclothes Glasgow coppers on my doorstep, I'd found myself accompanying them down to their station for a chat. If I'd been wide awake, I might have put up some resistance but that state was still several cups of coffee away.

The birdies were chirping in the trees and the sky was ocean blue as they'd led me to their nondescript car, the inside smelling of a jasmine scented air freshener which wasn't entirely effective in camouflaging more human odours.

After a twenty-minute drive we were at the cop shop, a gate in the razor wire topped fence opening for us. Inside the compound I could see dishes and antenna climbing up the walls and across the roof like hi-tech ivy. Scattered around were a miscellany of vehicles including a mesh windscreen riot van and one of those incident caravans that appear when something dreadful has happened.

None of this was doing much for my peace of mind. "What's this all about?" I heard myself saying and not for the first time.

"You'll see soon enough, Mr Younge." DI Philban, but for an extra twenty kilos, bore more than passing resemblance to Clark Gable even down to the thin moustache. Once upon a time he must have been catnip for the ladies.

I always bristle when people try to fob me off but coppers in Glasgow are never insubstantial creatures and you mess with them at your peril. Shutting the hell up until I found out what was going on seemed the sagacious thing to do here. I'd even baulked at telling them my title was Professor, the first time they called me mister. Now if I tried that I'd have looked spineless for not mentioning it in the first place.

By now, I was trying to guess what I'd done wrong. In my day I'd smoked dope and dropped acid and drunk earthy teas of magic mushrooms but that had all ended well over a decade ago. I hadn't hit anybody or anything when driving and then done a runner. I hadn't taken any bribes because nobody had offered me any. The porn I downloaded on the internet was vanilla and my taxes were automatically extracted from my university salary. I didn't belong to any subversive political parties, never mistreated animals and took my turn sweeping the communal stairs where I lived, like any good Glasgow wifey.

I'd never been lifted by the cops so I'd never had to think like this before. Now that I had, I was taken aback by my unsuspected saintliness. It wasn't just the porn; it turns out *I* was vanilla as well.

And with this sudden awareness of how embarrassingly guiltless I was, came the self-righteousness of the aggrieved.

The locks on the car doors clicked open and I stepped out into the yard. DS Kendrick, no more than five feet six but built like a gun emplacement, held out his hand in front of him like a maître d' showing me to a seat. "This way, sir," he said, his accent more Aberdonian and sing-song than Philban's gruff but functional Glaswegian.

Philban had produced a lanyard from his pocket which he wafted over an electronic reader by the very plain-looking door. Was there a grander entrance somewhere else where members of the public could get in? The place looked so low key from the road that I'd never even noticed it.

Inside it smelt like an office except for people who didn't wash much. The coppers led me down a long corridor, stopping at a reception desk to sign some documentation. A sergeant was manning the desk but he didn't even spare me a glance.

The interview room they showed me into had a large desk holding compact recording equipment and around it were four chairs. I was sat down facing a wall-mounted camera.

Philban pushed a button on the recording equipment. "Interview with Mr Dai Younge on Tuesday July…"

"Whoa, whoa, whoa!"

Philban clicked the button again and they both sat back in their seats, arms folded.

I held my hands out, palms up. "What's this about? Do I need a lawyer?"

"Why? We haven't arrested you."

"I guess that means I'm free to go?"

Philban shrugged. "Of course."

I was beginning to wish I'd paid more attention to all those police procedurals on TV. 'I know my rights' was a common cry of people in police stations. I was realising that I knew no such thing.

"And if I tried to walk out…"

"We'd arrest you. One way or another you're going to talk to us."

"At least give me a hint."

Philban pushed the switch, "Interview with Mr Dai Younge on Tuesday July…"

After he'd got the preliminaries out of the way, he pulled out his phone, poked at it a few times then held it towards the camera before turning it round so I could see. "Do you know this man?"

I realised right away it was Larry Price lying on a bed but I was surprised at the red hat he was wearing with something grey like a feather lying across it. As sometimes happens in my life, my unconscious recognised the full truth before my conscious mind managed to. I was forcing myself back in my chair in revulsion before I'd really understood what I was seeing.

Something had split open Price's skull. It wasn't a feather lying on his head but brain tissue exposed by the gash. Price's eyes were wide open but all life had fled.

"Jesus fucking Christ!"

Only then did I realise just how intently the two coppers were looking at me.

I could only hope they'd spotted the genuineness of my reaction.

"Do you know this man, Mr Younge?" Philban repeated.

"Yes, it's Larry Price. What happened to him?"

"And how did you know Mr Price?"

It took a while as I explained the ludicrous circumstances but to little reaction from the two cops who sat like statues throughout. At one point my phone rang and I went to answer it but they shook their heads and told me to turn it off.

"And when did you last see Mr Price?"

Belatedly, I began to choose my words more carefully. "At around ten o'clock last night. At the Queen Elizabeth A&E department."

"And why were you both there?"

"Because Price had banged his head when he fell into an empty swimming pool. I mean he didn't look like that." I pointed at the phone. "There wasn't even any blood."

"And how did he fall into the swimming pool?"

This interview had started out badly but now it was about to really go south. "He reckoned a demon pushed him," I found myself admitting.

That was too much even for these stone faces. They struggled to contain their smiles.

"And do you think a demon did it?"

"Of course not. Price and his cronies are nutters. I was just there as their university liaison."

"So, you don't believe in demons and ghosts and whatever."

"Probably as much as you do." Judging from the way Philban's caterpillar eyebrows lowered this didn't go down well. These guys were used to sitting in judgement on the dregs of humanity from high on their horses. They didn't like any implication that they were on the same level as the rest of us.

"What sort of relationship did you have with Mr Price? Were you friendly?"

I really didn't like where this way going. By now even I realised the coppers weren't looking to explain an accident but to catch a murderer.

When on the back foot, come out swinging.

"I didn't like him at all. Opinionated, arrogant, deluded and so far up his bottom he could see out of his own mouth."

Kendrick leaned forward a fraction. "So, you didn't wish him well?"

"Please, I'm asking you again, what happened to him?"

Kendrick said nothing: all take but no give.

Philban, however, was more forthcoming. "Someone hit him with something sharp. An axe maybe. Do you own an axe?"

"I'm an academic living in a Georgian terrace in the heart of a city. Of course I don't own an axe."

"Did you get into a fight with Price?"

"No."

"Yet harsh words were spoken at the Queen Elizabeth, according to witnesses."

I couldn't help laughing. "I bet harsher words are spoken there every single night."

"Victims of assault are there every single night as well, Mr Younge. Usually the two are related."

I held Philban's eye. "I did not assault Price. I did not hit him with anything. The last time I saw him he was well and truly alive, albeit a little dented."

I'm not entirely naive but some part of me had hoped that my earnestness would touch them so I was taken aback by the hint of a smile on Kendrick's lips.

That's the thing about psychology: it's full of nicely described theories about how the mind works and why. The trouble is, when exposed to real situations like this, sharply defined ideas smear out and the theories become next to useless. I met a physicist once who said pretty much the same thing about his field of mechanics. Theories, underpinned by beautifully elegant equations, fell apart when exposed to reality. Friction, air resistance and a million other confounding factors eat away at these pristine underpinnings and bring the soaring idealised equations crashing down.

In other words, just between you and me, when it comes to understanding the workings of other people's mind, I'm as clueless as the next man.

The more they questioned me, the more I wished I'd paid attention to those cop shows on TV. Had they enough to put me in a cell? I'm sure there are parts of the UK where a night in the cells might not be too unbearable, but this was Glasgow for Christ's sake. What sort of bear might I end up with as a bedfellow?

They kept asking me the same questions, especially about the conference, about which they gave the appearance of knowing nothing, and my movements after I left the Suffering General. There was not much I could say that pleased them as I'd gone straight home to bed alone. They kept mentioning the ubiquity of CCTV cameras that might give the lie to my story.

What was particularly chilling was they kept saying how closely Kelvingrove Park, over which my flat commanded spectacular views, was dotted with CCTV. Although they wouldn't tell me where Price had died it sounded as if it must have been close by. Had Price been staying at a hotel near my flat?

We're comfortable in our own surroundings but when we're taken out of them our confidence evaporates. By the time I had convinced myself that anal rape in a dingy police cell was the only thing that lay in my future, Philban suddenly said I could go.

"But don't leave Glasgow, and keep your phone with you at all times."

"Can I call a taxi to get me? Will they pick me up from here?"

"We're south of the Clyde not south of the Limpopo."

I suppose it had been a stupid question. It hadn't been a pleasant morning for revelations and I was still shocked.

It turned out there *was* another way out of the cop shop and I soon found myself out on a normal urban street. I realised I could now add 'murder suspect' to my resume. It sounded kind of flash. I contemplated calling Mo; he'd be impressed.

But then I thought of the conference. Had it been cancelled? Did Sally and the others even know what had happened to Price?

Sally and Lamarck had both given me their contact numbers and I dialled hers first.

After a few rings, she answered, her voice hushed and I got the impression she was leaving a meeting room where someone was talking. "Dai, what happened to you? We had to phone your Estates department to get someone to open the place up."

That she led with this didn't bode well and I realised I was going to be the bearer of bad news. There had once definitely been something between Price and her. Just how deep this had been I was about to find out.

"I take it you haven't heard about Larry?"

"I thought you said he was OK and the hospital let him out."

"He was and they did but I'm afraid something terrible happened to him afterwards. I'm sorry to have to tell you this but he's dead."

There was a long pause then: "Naah."

"What do you mean 'Naah'? I'm telling you the truth."

"But... he can't be... how did it happen?"

Someone hit him with an axe didn't seem the most sensitive response. "He sustained another head injury," was the best I could do on the spur of the moment. I thought that was quite good, though a little clinical.

"How?"

Aw, fuck it! "Someone hit him with an axe."

"Is this a joke?"

"The coppers who spent the last two hours questioning me didn't seem to think so."

"Why were they questioning you?"

"The last time I saw Price was at the hospital. We didn't part on the most amicable of terms. A staff member witnessed it and he had my contact number. After Price was axed, he was taken back to the same hospital, still barely alive but not for much longer. That's how the cops got onto me. They didn't seem to know about the conference until I told them so I'm guessing they're heading your way even as we speak."

"So, you're, like, a murder suspect?"

Hearing someone else use that term didn't make it sound so flash after all.

"Look, I'd better come back to the university. You and Telly need to work out what you're going to do next." That the conference might be abandoned was suddenly the silver lining in the dark cloud of the murder of a fellow human being.

But one that I could live with.

~~~

The taxi dropped me off at the department. Stressed out parapsychs were standing on the steps smoking and gossiping, looking both stricken and excited at the same time.

Someone on reception I didn't recognise told me that Sally was in one of the smaller meeting rooms and setting it up for interviews. The cops had phoned and told the conference organisers to do this and make sure nobody left the vicinity.

When I found Sally, incredibly, she was smoking a fag. Indoors and on university premises!

This sight was so wild I almost swooned. Thirty years ago it would have been commonplace, now it was outrageous. My surprise must have been all too evident.

She raised an eyebrow. "You disapprove? Try to stop me!"

"Not me, guv. In fact, I admire your bravado," I said, taking a seat on the other side of the table she'd pulled into the centre of the room. I'd have shown solidarity by asking for a cigarette but I'd given up years before after a mighty struggle. I knew from bitter experience that even a puff would instantly enthral me once again to that seductive but demanding mistress. "How do you feel?"

She took a meditative drag and puffed out a cloud of toxic but fabulous-smelling vapour. Why does smoking still look so cool? In times of stress like this, it gave you the appearance of being in control. It was displacement activity, of course, and so a form of deflection, showing you weren't really coping at all.

I tried not to huff up the smoke too obviously.

"I can't believe he's dead. He was so... *vital*."

"So you and he were...?"

She gave me a weary-eyed look. "Now's not the time for anyone to get circumspect, least of all a grump like you. No, as I said before, we weren't in a relationship. Once upon a time we were. He had a sort of glamour which, by the way, actually means magical enchantment. If that's what it was, it wore off pretty quickly. As a psychologist you may not be surprised to hear that beneath that bluff, aggressive demeanour, the man was a bubbling fountain of insecurity."

Grump? Sure, it was true, but that didn't mean I liked to hear it. I tried to keep my face as cool and impassive as my police chums. "So, you're the one that called it off?"

"Yes, and it annoyed poor Telly no end. We'd also had a bit of a fling and he'd got it onto his head that Larry had seduced me away from him. Yet when I dumped Larry, I didn't go back to him. Telly couldn't get his head around that."

So, Telly must be suspect number one. I'd keep that in mind in case I needed to keep Philban and Kendrick off my back. Telly seemed a nice guy but if I needed to throw someone under the bus...

"But they both seemed on good terms with you."

Another weary look. "Men who find a woman attractive never quite shut the door. Just in case."

I was used to the cynicism of bitter old men like Mo and myself but hadn't come across it before in someone like Sally. Then again, attractive women wield such power over men it was naive not to assume it wouldn't breed cynicism under those beautiful exteriors.

"Well, the door has definitely shut for poor Larry now." Weird that I was using his Christian name when I never would have while he was alive.

"Yeah." She stubbed her cigarette out on the fag packet and put it back in with the fresh cigarettes. At least she was preserving some proprieties.

A thought struck me. "Of course, to you and your friends he's not really dead. Are you going to hold a seance or whatever? See what Larry has to say for himself."

Her pale blue eyes regarded me unblinkingly. "Don't try to pick a fight. I'm not in the mood."

I shrugged. "I'm serious, or at least I'm trying to take all this seriously. Maybe you could get his spirit to tell you who killed him. Anything to get me off the hook with the polis."

"Polis? Oh, right, police. Come to think of it, here I am alone in a room with a murder suspect. I'm quite a-flutter."

"You don't look it."

Again, the steady blue eyes. "Don't downplay it, sunshine, if you know what's good for you."

What did that mean? I was about to ask when there was knock on the door behind me. I could hear it opening immediately. I turned in my seat to find my old pals DI Philban and DS Kendrick regarding me with God-like indifference.

"Mr Younge," said Philban.

"Officers," I replied.

"We'd like to talk to Ms Vale so, if you don't mind..."

I turned back to her. "I'll call you later." Then I got up and edged by the coppers and out the door. I could feel their eyes following me.

~~~

Not sure what else to do, I went for something to eat then came back and hung around in the little staff room in the department. Through the window I saw other coppers troop in. Now and again, they came to me asking to commandeer rooms for interviews, for lists of delegates and for coffee.

I wasn't so happy about being treated like a barista but, for once, I didn't make a fuss. Lecturer, caretaker, barista—was there no end to the strings I had to my bow?

Though nobody came right out and said it, it seemed that out of respect the program had been abandoned for today at least. Delegates wandered in and out, some teary, others with eyes bright with fascination at the turn of events, and all gossiping avidly.

As the day wore on, in dribs and drabs they had all eventually left. Those who hadn't been interviewed were given strict instructions to come back the next day. I set the snib on the door so once they got out, they couldn't get back in. Soon the building only contained me, the cops, Sally and, it turned out, Telly who wandered in looking a little stunned.

He hardly even said hello as he made a bee-line for the coffee. He came back to my table and pointed at a chair. "Do you mind?"

"Of course not," I said, a little surprised he'd bothered to ask; I thought we were way beyond that. I don't get on with a lot of people but something about his easy manner reminded me of Mo.

"Nice of you, sharing a coffee table with the number one murder suspect," he said.

"Naah, I'm the number one murder suspect. Coppers are gagging to slap the cuffs on me."

"Why?"

"Last one to see Price alive. Last one to call him a cunt in front of witnesses."

Telly's eyebrows rose in what looked like welcome surprise. "So, I may yet smell the sweet scent of freedom."

"Why are you in the frame?" Although, from what Sally had told me, I already knew the answer to that.

He hesitated then shrugged. "Love rival."

I nodded sagely, just like any eminent psychologist to whom the depths of the human mind were familiar, well-travelled territory. Someone to whom no act of human nature could ever come as a surprise.

"Was she worth it? Or was it a he?"

"Yes, and it was a she. Love of my life, to be perfectly honest."

As an eminent psychologist, I knew when to let sleeping dogs lie. I would need to get to know Telly a whole lot better before I could start taking the piss out of his love life.

I held up my coffee cup. "To Larry, may he rot in hell." Our cups chinked.

"Did you mention good old Larry's tomb-robbing proclivities?" I asked. "I mean, maybe the cops'd make the Nubian demon their number one suspect."

He looked at me wearily. "Sure, that's just the sort of thing two hard-bitten Glasgow coppers would go for. I'm not that stupid."

"So, what now? A special plenary seance to communicate with the freshly dead shade of Larry Price?"

Telly had a long firm jaw and there was something almost vulpine about his quick, wry smile. "Oh, I'm sure there'll be impromptu little affairs all over the city. What else have the delegates to do now that today's been cancelled? Mind you, something less impromptu, more organised might be in order."

I dangled a little hook. "Is Sally out of the frame, do you think?"

He looked away. "Don't let it go any further but Sally was the final point in our little love triangle. Those coppers must have wormed it out of her because they came for me next. She'd dumped Larry, quite a few months ago in fact, so she definitely ranks below us as candidate for a charter flight to the chokey. Besides which an axe isn't likely to be a woman's weapon—according to the cops, that is. Between you and me, that's doing Sally a disservice. She's a damned sight more athletic than me. You too, I'd guess."

"Thanks. Have to tell you, one mad axeman to another, I don't like to have my thunder stolen by a weak and feeble woman."

"Don't say that to her even in jest unless you want to spend the rest of your life on a ventilator."

My phone rang. I couldn't help swallowing when I looked at it and saw *Dean of Sacking*. I'd tried to phone her earlier to let her know what had happened but she hadn't been available so I'd left a message with her secretary.

I held a finger up to Telly. I should have stood up and left so I could take the call in privacy, but I was just too weary.

"Hold for Dean Rettner!" said a bright and preppy voice; a voice used to telephone dealings with people already at a disadvantage and who might even have already piddled themselves a little bit.

Rettner came on dismayingly quickly, as if she'd been ready to pounce.

"What the hell? Is this your idea of looking after things?"

"It didn't happen here, Vera," I said, reasonably confident of this as I hadn't seen any SOCOs in full white burkas doing fingertip searches through the department. "I can't be a bodyguard to all of them when they've left the university premises."

"However you cut it, Dai, this happened on your watch. Have the press been in contact yet?"

"No."

"Well, if they do then don't say a word. Not a word, Dai. Are you hearing me?"

"I am." I imagined what this would look like splashed all over the papers: *Man Slain by Axe at Uni Nutters Conference*. Tasty!

I guessed she was imagining something similar. "The lawyers tell me we can't shut this down without incurring liability. So, you've got to shut it down for us, one way or the other. We want this circus out of town."

"And how do I do that, exactly?"

"Use your imagination, man!"

And she hung up without even a goodbye.

"Bad news?" asked Telly.

"Yes, from a very unpleasant person in a very powerful position. Do you think the conference will be cancelled?"

Telly shrugged. "Jury's out, though maybe that's not a very happy expression at the moment. Depends if Price comes through."

"What do you mean?"

"If he comes back from beyond the veil at any of those impromptu seances we were talking about. Who knows what he might say? In fact, I've decided I'm going to hold a seance this evening. I need to take the temperature."

"What if a ghostly Price appears and points a shaking, skeletal finger at you?"

"I didn't kill anybody. I'll be fine. Do you want to come along? Have Larry point his finger at you?"

I shook my head. "I'm too feart, as we say up here."

We agreed I should come over to open up the department as usual the next morning, then he left.

I felt reasonably content: surely either the cops or dead Larry would want this farrago shut down and I'd be off the hook with Rettner.

~~~

I took my coffee to reception, then checked as much of the old building as I could be bothered with. As far as I could tell only Sally and the coppers were still there. The cleaners could sweep up the bones of any who remained undiscovered.

It was getting late before the coppers appeared, gave me a brief nod then left. Sally followed a few moments later.

She still looked stunned, although redness about her cheeks suggested mortification or, more likely, anger.

"Do you people have anything to drink in this godforsaken country?"

"I've heard tales," I said, picking up my jacket.

"Then let's see if they have any substance, or are you otherwise engaged?"

I shook my head. "No. Anyway our police chums told me not to leave Glasgow. May as well make myself comfortable."

The Dram pub forms an equilateral triangle with the Department and my house. I was confident that even if I made myself very comfortable with drink, it was within staggering distance of home, albeit via an incline that got more aggressive the more I imbibed. The pub was frequented by students so Mo wouldn't have been seen dead in it, preferring the aged polecat redolence of the Bon Accord. Sally, I decided, would be more at home in the former.

I led her to one of the big windows looking out on the road. "What do you want?"

"You people make a big song and dance about whisky, right? Ditch water, actually and metaphorically if you ask me, but this is your chance at justification."

Not a little affronted, I nonetheless bought her an eighteen-year-old Dalmore, a florid, operatic whisky that was as far from ditch water as you could get. I also bought her a Bruachladdich for contrast.

"Try that one first," I said pointing to the Dalmore.

I'd bought myself the same and savoured the soothing Dalmore trickling down into my guts. Even just that first taste took the edge off a brutal world.

Judging by the look on her face it had worked its magic with Sally as well.

"Ditch water?" I asked.

She took another sip. "You make a compelling case." She relaxed back into her chair like liquid metal flowing into a mould.

"How did it go with the cops?" I asked.

"Other than making me feel like a whore, it went just fine."

"What did they say? They were icily polite and professional with me, though somehow conveying that they didn't believe a word I said."

"Oh, they were like that with me too, it's just their questions. Who I'd fucked, where and how often."

"Really?"

"Well, not quite as blunt."

"So, they know about Telly. Sounds like he might have pipped me to the pole position. Do you think he might have done it?"

"Give me a break!"

"How can you be so sure?"

"Because I know him. Wouldn't hurt the proverbial fly. But you—" a long sharp nail was aimed between my eyes, "—you have more than a touch of the night about you."

Maybe there's something in this psychology business after all. From the way she said that I just knew I was in with a chance for I sensed a potentially delicious hint of perversity. I may not be the prime murder suspect, but I was definitely in the running. Yet here she was drinking with me in a pub. She should be eyeing me suspiciously and backing away, not sharing a convivial dram.

Of course, she was a murder suspect as well. I should have been backing away too and, believe you me, I would have done if she hadn't been so attractive.

Don't look at me like that. I'm just a man.

I noticed her Dalmore had led a short but glorious life. I pointed to the Bruachladdich. "Try that one now."

She took one sniff and recoiled in disgust. "I thought poison was the woman's weapon of choice."

I didn't say anything but watched her take a tentative sip. She grimaced. "Seaweed and iodine, redolent of poultice."

"That's a fair description."

"So why did you buy me this mouthwash?" She took another sip.

"I chose these two just to show you the range of malt whisky."

"Sublime to the ridiculous." She took another sip. I was confident she'd drink it all. People almost always did. Some even came to like the peaty whiskies more than the warmer, sweeter comforters.

"So how did you get into this paranormal nonsense?"

She grimaced. "It's always nice to meet someone with an open mind. But, if you really want to know the truth, it's because of guilt."

"What, are you haunted by the shade of someone you wronged?"

"Many a true word is spoken in jest so, yes, you've got it."

"So, you've actually seen this apparition?"

"Oh God! The high and mighty psychologist bringing his fearsome analytical tools to bear on a poor victim of superstition."

Wow, 'high and mighty'. If I was going to get her into bed, she'd soon put the lie to that.

She leaned forward, the tip of her forefinger flicking the end of my nose. "But I don't believe in ghosts. What I saw did not come from without but from within. As for all the other people attending the conference, with their poltergeists and banshees and UFOs, with their fairies and angels and demonic possessions, their clairvoyance and astrology and crystal gazing, all of it comes from within themselves."

She stopped and looked in surprise at her empty glass. "That went down more easily than I expected."

"Another? Honeyed kisses or seaweed poultice?"

"Something in between."

I brought both of us back a Macallan. It had its eulogisers but it was pretty average in my book. "So, you're saying that the stuff being talked about at this conference is basically all in the delegates' heads."

"Yeah, and in fact I was supposed to be giving a talk on just that but, of course, it's up in the air now. The thing is, and you'll be surprised by this, people interested in the paranormal are actually very open minded in that they'll listen respectfully even to opposing views. The complete opposite of you in fact. In the end it may all be water off a duck's back and they'll keep right on believing, but at least they'll give me a hearing."

"Hey, what am I doing right now if not listening to you? What's the title of this talk?"

"Jung and the occult."

She'd said she was interested in Jung but I hadn't realised it went so far as lecturing about him.

"You've got to be kidding!"

She shook her head. "Nope, seriously. Jung may not be the flavour of the month with you psychologists, but he pretty much explains everything about the paranormal."

"Jung was a shaman and a showman. A twinkly-eyed con artist who kidded the world he was a serious scientist but all he was peddling was metaphysical bullshit entirely unsupported by evidence."

She clapped. "Thanks for proving my point about open-mindedness. Game, set and match."

I sat forward, faking earnestness. "It may not be too late for you. You need a kind and gentle hand to set you straight on modern psychology, to wean you off the ancient, muddled thinking of Jung and Freud. But that would take time and we're drinking expensive whisky at pub prices. My flat's not far, there's lots of good whisky there and so I think you should come back for the learning experience."

She finished her dram in a oner. "So patronising! I think I'm going to have to mess you up a little."

CHAPTER EIGHT

The erotic instinct is something questionable, and will always be so whatever a future set of laws may have to say on the matter. It belongs, on the one hand, to the original animal nature of man, which will exist as long as man has an animal body. On the other hand, it is connected with the highest forms of the spirit. But it blooms only when the spirit and instinct are in true harmony. If one or the other aspect is missing, then an injury occurs, or at least there is a one-sided lack of balance which easily slips into the pathological. Too much of the animal disfigures the civilized human being, too much culture makes a sick animal.
Carl Jung

"This place is huge. And you're the only one who lives here?"

I handed her a Glenmorangie Quinta Rubin (another honeyed operatic whisky). "It's not quite as it appears. In fact, this is the only big room, the rest are pretty small."

"Cold in the winter too, I imagine," she said, tapping the single pane of glass and sounding slightly appalled.

"Just one of the downsides of living in a conservation area."

She came and sat beside me on the sofa, a fawn leather affair that didn't quite match the Georgian ambiance of the room. On the other hand, it was durable and easy to clean.

A bit like me, really.

She pursed her lips and narrowed her eyes a little as though in intense thought. "If you did kill Larry, why would you have done it?"

"Can we focus for a moment on how outrageous what you've just said is?" I'd thought her notion that I was a killer had been a sort of perverse come-on but now I wasn't so sure. "Look, to be perfectly clear, I didn't kill Price, OK?"

The sides of her lips turned down as though she had heard something dubious. "You might have done but you just don't know it."

"What are you talking about?"

"Jung says..."

"Oh fer..."

She held up a hand, palm towards me. "No, let me finish! Jung says we are almost entirely motivated by unconscious but longstanding patterns of behaviour. These make us do things for reasons we don't understand but we then use our intelligence to provide a spurious retrospective rationale for what we've just done. For example, we might take an immediate and instinctual dislike to a person, then we use our intelligence to look for reasons to justify that."

"Jung and Freud and the unconscious—give me strength!"

Sally wagged a finger. "But it makes so much sense. If we were rational beings then, presumably, we would agree on pretty much everything. There'd be no political parties because there'd be nothing to disagree about. Instead, different parties ring different instinctual bells in all of us. Sometimes, even when there's a consensus, nations go on to do terrible things. I mean look at Hitler, or Stalin or Mao. Look at Cambodia and Pol Pot. In all of those countries people murdered their fellow citizens in the millions. Even if they weren't involved in the murders, most were complicit in some way. Ten million murdered in both China and the USSR, a fifth of the entire population in Cambodia. You need a lot of help from your countrymen, actual or implicit, to murder that many."

"So that's your explanation for all those massacres. Jung and the unconscious."

"Yes. I mean it's not even as if it was racism as these were people killing their fellow countrymen. Germany was considered the most civilised country in Europe at the time yet they degenerated into the worst kind of barbarism. In the old days they'd say people there were being plagued by demons. And, in a sense, there *are* demons but, rather than coming from Hell, Jung is saying they come from our unconscious. What other explanations could there be for such horrors? Are you perhaps saying a cloud of evil orbits the Earth and occasionally descends on random countries. If so, you should be the one speaking at this conference."

"Whoa! Now you're just getting nasty for the sake of it. But let me try and get this straight. First thing this morning I was as innocent as a lamb. By late afternoon, in the pub, you had me down as a murderer, conscious or otherwise. Now, in the evening, you're lumping me in with mass killers like Hitler. Look at me, does this really make any sense to you?" I held my arms wide; boring old me, on my comfy sofa and in my comfy house.

"Wolf in sheep's clothing." Her smile was warm but there was definitely calculation in her eyes.

I shook my head and stood up. "Maybe you're right. I mean, look at me now pouring you another glass of expensive whisky. Is there no end to my evil?"

"I'm not condemning you for the workings of your unconscious."

"Like hell you're not."

"You wouldn't even know you'd done it yourself."

"I wouldn't know I'd murdered someone! Really?"

She held up a finger, taking time out for another sip. Her eyes closed but I saw the bulge as her pupil rose under the lid in a transport of delight. I'd seduced another person into the love of the dram.

Hardly a crime but even so it was the most criminal thing I'd done in years, despite what this crazy woman might think.

She opened her eyes again. "It's like with all the believers in the paranormal, in fact it's the thesis of my talk. The instinctual behaviours make us act but, because they arise from the unconscious, our rational mind doesn't realise it all originates from within. Sights like 'ghosts', and sounds such as voices from people who aren't there, are considered by the rational mind to have just appeared out of the blue. What is actually happening is that all of those paranormal phenomena plus stuff like poltergeists and banshees and whatever, come from within ourselves and not from outside."

"You know, you may actually have a point there. You're saying it's all in their heads. A lot of people would agree with you. But I don't see how hearing voices that aren't there could lead on to me murdering someone and then it somehow slipping my mind."

"Don't tell me you've never heard of a fugue state. A dissociated, amnesic condition where the subject is fleeing from an unbearable situation. It can last for weeks or months, never mind a few hours."

"What unbearable situation?" I'd come round to thinking this was all an elaborate wind-up but I was getting less and less sure. After eight generous measures of the Water of Life I was guessing that neither was she.

We were just a couple of feet apart on the sofa, facing each other, both our arms on the back of the sofa but not quite touching. It's difficult to spot arousal after a few whiskies as both bring a high colour to the cheeks. "If you think I might be a murderer then why did you come to my flat? Why have you allowed yourself to be alone with me?"

A fingernail traced a not so gentle path down my cheek. "I can take care of myself," she said, almost under her breath.

~~~

I'd like to say we retreated to the bedroom where we made tender love but that would be a lie. There was, a little later on, a gentle interlude when I demonstrated the effect of pouring just a little whisky over a woman's nipple. It puckers the aureole and raises the nipple (be sure to try this at home!).

However, everything else was just plain ferocious, and not on my part. Sally was a strong woman with a prop forward's power in her thighs. Even though at the end I found myself on top, it was all I could do just to hang on.

It was arousing and delightful but (and I'd better whisper this) just a little bit frightening.

~~~

That same old bastard was there again. The same white socks, the same bobble hat. The same vague feeling of familiarity.

I looked down. Yup, I was naked again on top of a high chilly mountain, the cold wind nipping my genitals.

"For God's sake what is going on?"

The old man shook his head. He was closer than before and I noticed the wrinkles on his face were so deep I wondered how he cleaned them. It must be like degrouting the tiles in a shower. "You can't escape this," he said with the sort of august inarguable tones producers pay actors good money for on TV ads. The sort that can sell you anything.

"Escape what?"

"Decision."

"I really need to wake up."

The old man grabbed my upper arm, firmly enough to teeter on the edge of painful. "You must come with me," he said and I found myself being led further up the mountain, my bare feet squelching in black mud.

"Who are you?"

"You know who I am."

"No, I fucking don't."

A sudden gust of wind chilled me to the bone. "Do you have any spare clothes in your rucksack?"

"You don't need them." Again with the venerable tones.

"Yes, I do. Do you need yours? If not then give them to me."

He stopped then turned to look at me and gave a big sigh. "The clothes are a metaphor. Obviously."

I threw a punch but he ducked under it then came up quickly, both his arms round me, pinioning my own arms by my side. I would have head butted him but he jerked his own head forward, pushing mine back so I couldn't. For an old guy he was really flexible.

Then I was lifted clear off the ground. I struggled with all my might as we climbed higher, the old man not even breathing hard. Our faces were so close I could smell his breath. Old people's breath can smell of death but the only fragrance from him was of flowers.

I hate being trapped by anything or anybody. My breathing was as fast as his should have been as the panic rose in me, submerging my racing heart and filling my lungs with fire.

I yelled in fear.

Light flared around me and I thought I was having a stroke. But then, faintly at first, then with shocking clarity I found the mist dissolving and far, far below I saw the floor of the glen and the vivid blue waters of a loch. Just ahead of us the mountain ended in a sheer drop. The old man was heading towards it.

I renewed my struggles but his grip got inexorably tighter. Just as he seemed about to hurl us off the edge he stopped and released me. I fell only a few inches but I almost lost my balance and went over the edge.

He stood back, arms spread. Now the only way back to safely was through him.

"Jump!" he said.

"Are you out of your mind?" I'm not great with heights and with my back to the drop, it already felt like I was toppling over.

I rushed him but he turned and drove his shoulder into my chest. It was like hitting the edge of a well-bedded tombstone. Winded, I staggered back, the heel of one foot coming down only on air.

Somehow, I didn't fall. I punched again but he warded me off, as if he was swatting away a fly. I tried a feint with my right fist, my left a roundhouse that should have landed on his jaw but somehow didn't.

"Don't fight it!" he said. "Jump!"

"Make me, you evil old bastard!"

And that's what he tried. He came at me hard, his hands outstretched. I dropped to the ground, my body catching his shins, pivoting him over and sending him flying into the void. By the time I'd got up and looked over the side he'd gone, my eyes only catching the faraway movement just as he hit an outcropping of rocks, bouncing off in a rag doll cartwheel before thumping down into the turf.

He lay there spreadeagled, like a tiny crucifix.

"Gotcha you old shit!" I screamed, so loud it made my lungs ache.

~~~

Something was shaking my shoulder. "Dai, Dai for fuck's sake!" The woman's voice was right in my ear and urgent.

I opened my eyes and sat up. I was vastly relieved to see my same old bedroom, although now it looked more like a sexual battlefield, clothes strewn around like the limp bodies of the slain.

Sally was beside me wide-eyed. Her hand that had been gripping my shoulder let go to brush the sweat-slicked hair back from my forehead. "What the hell were you dreaming about?"

"What time is it?" I looked for my alarm clock but it too had been a victim of our struggle, a flailing limb having sent it flying off the nightstand. Its face lay buried in some underwear, as though from shame.

"Early, probably. I was fast asleep when you started screaming like a baby. When I tried to stop you thrashing around you punched me, you fucker."

I realised the knuckles on my right hand were sore. "Oh God, are you OK?"

"Yeah, yeah. You hit me on the shoulder. It's fine, I did worse to you last night."

And I realised she was right. My body felt as if it had been on the losing end of a fight. Even so, what I'd done to her appalled me. "I'm really sorry."

She lay back and put her hands behind her head. "So, what was the dream about or have you already forgotten?"

That I went ahead and told her shows how off guard I was. I'd forgotten about her interest in Jung. Because the workings of the unconscious aren't accessible to our rational minds, the only evidence of the unconscious come from three things. Firstly, we can make a guess from the things we do; secondly from the myths which resonate with us. Mainly, however, they come from dreams because then the rational mind retreats and the unconscious comes out to play.

She listened to my stories of the old man. When I finished, she shook her head. "Emblematic or what?"

"What do you mean?"

She came up on one elbow, the sheeting slipping down to reveal a breast. This was sufficiently distracting that the following reported conversation may not be entirely verbatim.

"I know that psychoanalysis isn't the flavour of the month in your profession but those dreams are absolutely gravid with meaning."

"Dreams are just dreams," I said.

"Oh, please! Your unconscious is sending you a letter and you're pretending you can't read."

"Jung was a mumbo-jumbo merchant. A con. Dreams mean nothing."

"They mean everything."

"Fine Dr Vale, psychoanalyse me." Somehow a fingertip strayed across her exposed nipple but she batted my hand away.

She lay back again, covering herself with the sheet. "Climbing a mountain clearly represents your path towards knowledge and personal enlightenment."

I snorted.

"Just for once try to keep an open mind," she said, annoyed. "The old man is a classic Jungian archetype, in this case representing wisdom and I don't mean the wisdom of the intellect but rather the wisdom of the soul."

"Dressed like a hill-walker?"

"Why not? A man properly attired to climb the mountain of truth. Which is why you were naked in your dream because you're an idiot and not equipped to climb anything."

"You don't think my nakedness simply implied insecurity. I mean look at how I've been demoted to caretaker. My future looks more than a little uncertain. No wonder I feel naked."

"Oh, so now you do believe dreams mean something?"

"Yes, but they can mean just about anything."

She turned over on her side to look at me. "The old man is wisdom and he's asking you to take a leap of faith. The path up the mountain is false, something planned out by your rationality. Soulless, unmoored from the depths of the unconscious it's a false way. The old man is showing you there is another way. Do you really not see where I'm going with this?"

As she said this there was a flash of something in her eyes, that strange fire I'd glimpsed the night before.

"Just tell me. You're going to anyway."

"It's this conference," she said earnestly. "The paranormal is a challenge to your whole way of life. That's the leap the old man wanted you to take. Out of fear you killed him, just like you killed Larry."

"What!"

"You heard me."

I should have laughed in her face; I should have told her to leave. And the only thing stopping me was that look in her eyes.

Her hand wormed its way under the sheets and found my thigh.

This time I was ready for her. I reached for her, matching ferocity with ferocity.

Even so, if it had been a fight, she'd still have won on points.

CHAPTER NINE

Until you make the unconscious conscious, it will direct your life and you will call it fate.
Carl Jung

As if my life wasn't already spinning out of control, now I found myself at a real seance.

Early that morning I'd got a call from DI Kendrick, no less, perhaps realising that when it came to the conference, I was the only responsible adult in the room. Apparently, the cops didn't think there was enough evidence to warrant shutting the whole thing down; Price's body had been found elsewhere, after all. The most likely explanation was a mugging gone wrong. Even so, Kendrick made it clear that neither I nor the conference organisers should leave Glasgow until further notice, but even that stricture had seemed half-hearted.

That meant Telly, Sally and Loris. Kendrick's prohibition was wider, though, and included people who'd been at the swimming baths so Andy Lister and Sam Murray and Grand Old Maude were also still in the frame. With me, that made a total of seven sort-of suspects.

"What about all the others at the conference? Any of them could have done it," I'd asked.

Kendrick had sighed. "There's a limit to how many we can keep in Glasgow unless we find substantial evidence of their involvement. Besides, if we let the conference proceed then most will stay here for a while anyway. We can take another crack at them if further information emerges."

So, I'd trundled in with Sally and opened up the department. Even though they hadn't been told what was happening, at least a score of delegates had rocked up first thing anyway, lonely marginalised people looking for the like-minded. Moths to a flame.

Then Telly arrived and the conference started up again after a fashion. While they were setting things in motion, I checked a local newspaper. It was a big relief to find that although Price's murder had made second page news (a local football derby marred by sectarian violence had filled the front page) as 'Macabre Murder of TV Psychic', the reporters hadn't made any connection with the university.

I was reflecting how that might at least keep Rettner from falling on me like a ton of bricks when Sally entered and gave me a big smile. She came over and trailed a finger across the shoulder of my jacket. Although we'd been violently intimate, this was the first sign of actual affection she'd shown. I was immediately on my guard.

"That big Georgian sitting room of yours, it's really nice."

"Uh huh," I allowed.

"In fact, it would be perfect."

"For what?"

She sat down next to me, leaned in eagerly and put her hand on top of mine. "A seance!"

"Bugger off!"

"Come on, Dai! We need to hold one somewhere. Everyone says so. Well, everyone at the conference anyway. Nobody had a chance to say goodbye to Larry."

I pulled my head back in disbelief. "Say goodbye to Larry? What the hell are you talking about?"

She shook her head, clearly believing this didn't merit an answer. "Plus, we can ask who killed him. Who knows, it might even get you off the hook."

"Or push me further on." Did she really believe I was the murderer? It was obvious the concept had spiced things up between us. Was that just some sort of fetishistic wind-up? I'd given considerable thought to this notion over the early morning but still hadn't found an answer.

"Look, you kind of owe us."

"I don't owe you anything."

"Well, the university owes us and that means you."

"How? We contracted to provide you with facilities and you've got them. The university didn't kill your precious pal Price and neither, for that matter, did I."

She snorted. "Facilities? This architectural abomination. People can't even find where they're supposed to be going. Every session gets serially interrupted with people turning up late in dribs and drabs."

I shook my head. "You should have done your homework. Checked the place out before you hired it."

"We did. Your chap Donlevy showed us round and he did it so smoothly and with such charm we didn't realise how complicated this warren was. Bastard must have practised the route so he could do it blindfold."

That was more than likely true but I wasn't going to admit it. "Not our fault your delegates can't find their way out of a paper bag."

She poked a finger into my lapel. "Look, sunshine, there's a lot of ill-feeling here. This is your chance to smooth things out, head off the stampede. I mean, you wouldn't want us to make a big fuss about this to the press."

That was shrewd but unfair. In my relaxed, post-coital state I'd perhaps alluded to Rettner's and Donlevy's discomfort at any association with the parapsychs, itself an abbreviation she had not warmed too.

And, to cut a long story short, that's why later that rainy night, a motley crew made its wet-footed way to my door.

I'd inherited a large dining table from Ma and Pa, which had been put in storage for years until I grew up and owned my own place. They'd occasionally given dinner parties where they'd toy with the guests, provoking fights, shattering marriages and reducing people to tears. The parties were unsurprisingly few and far between as, once bitten, people never returned.

As you might imagine, I gave few dinner parties myself so I'd hardly used the table. Its light wood had barely a scratch although it must have been fifty years old at least.

Darker wood would have been better, more gothic. As it was, we looked as if we were at a community council meeting rather than explorers venturing into the netherworld. Candles had been brought in and provided wavering illumination.

There were a dozen or so attendees. I noticed all seven of the pseudo-suspects were here. Lister had already been told to put away his phone so he couldn't record anything. Murray was next to Loris. She was obviously distraught and he was comforting her. Sally was next to me, Telly on my other side.

Maude was to be the star of the show. Matronly, stiff backed, with bouffant hair, her manner as grand as ever. Earlier, Sally, to my surprise and dismay, had been fluttering around her like an acolyte.

Although we had drawn the blinds, outside the notoriously changeable Glasgow weather was trying to batter its way in. Gusts of wind sent rain squalls lashing at the windows.

Grand Old Maude cleared her throat and the conversations ceased abruptly. "Good evening, everyone. As you know, we are here tonight to communicate with our friend Larry."

She hesitated. "Larry has only recently crossed over; his spirit has had little time to adapt to the land beyond. So terrible was his death that his shade will still be experiencing a tempest of emotions. Unquiet spirits are a challenge to deal with for they may echo the violence they have recently suffered."

All around heads were nodding sagely and, despite myself, I felt some trepidation. Price had been a bastard even when things were ticking over. Now he really had something to kick up a fuss about.

Perhaps Grand Old Maude sensed this for she looked directly at me. "Professor Younge, I understand you are sceptical of much that we hold dear. Please try and quell your doubts during this seance as negative emotions can act as a damper on any communication."

She looked around the room. "Whatever happens, we must all remain for the duration of this seance. If you are uncertain, or feel in any way worried, then please leave now."

Everyone looked at everyone else but somehow all their eyes ended up on me, the weak link in the mumbo-jumbo chain. I shrugged as nonchalantly as I could.

Maude inclined her head ever so slightly in acknowledgment. "We will extinguish all the candles but for this one before me."

Several people licked their fingers, reached out and extinguished the flames. I'd seen this done once or twice before at dope-addled parties in my student days. Yelps of pain had invariably followed but tonight nobody even flinched. Candle snuffing was apparently an art well practised in spiritualist circles.

Candles may be mundane things but I couldn't doubt their power at times like this. The dark that had been held back suddenly advanced upon us to leave a single warm sphere of light. This globe flickered as though it too could so easily be extinguished. A powerful metaphor for life and death and the fragility of the veil that separates them.

Random slaps of wind and rain against the windows were beginning to jangle my nerves.

I felt myself being submerged in the silence that followed. So much so that I twitched when Maude suddenly said, "Larry."

We waited as a thousand drops of rain pattered against the window.

"Larry, are you there? Your friends are waiting for you."

Someone gave a stifled cough and I almost jumped again. *Get a grip!* I told myself.

"Larry?"

I looked around at the pale faces revealed by the flickering frame. All other eyes were on Maude. She slowly closed her own.

Rain smashed against the window. Then again. Then once more, as if someone was slamming their palms against the glass.

"Larry?"

The room felt suddenly cold and the candle flame swirled, although I felt no draft.

Once more rain slammed against the window. I licked my lips. Around me, as much as I could see in the low light, all the others looked tense and expectant.

But such a state can last only so long. As the seconds lengthened to minutes, and the minutes stretched one into the other, I felt tension draining away to leave boredom.

I'd long since lost track of time. I was supposed to meet Mo in the Bon at ten. The seance had started at eight. Had as much as an hour already gone by? My hands were on the table so I couldn't even check the time on my phone without everyone seeing.

There was a sudden squeak and I felt the table move and its legs rumble over floorboards. I heard the collective intake of breath.

My hands had been touching the table so I knew it hadn't moved far. The candle on it had barely flickered. I peered into the gloom, just as there was another squeak and shudder.

This time the candle did move, skittering across the top and nearly overturning.

"Lar..." began Maude but something stopped her.

Her features froze for a moment but then began to slowly change, to melt. It was as though a mask was slipping from her face.

Hairs rose on the back of my neck. The audience gave a sigh of gratification.

I felt my scrotum tighten in alarm. I tore my eyes away from Maude, looking for fear in others but all I saw were rapt and votive expressions.

I sat upright, ready to do a runner but Sally's hand suddenly grasped my wrist.

Maude's face drooped like heated wax, lengthening her jaw, her jowls melting. Shadows cast by her hooked nose on her cheek disappeared as her nose straightened.

"Oh, my God, it's Larry," whispered Loris, sitting forward.

Maude's eyes blinked open but then slowly closed.

Loris, her voice tremulous with excitement asked, "Larry is that you?"

Maude's mouth opened but only a strangulated gasp emerged.

"He can't work her vocal chords. Larry, tap with your hand, once for yes, twice for no."

One of Maude's hands twitched as if it was being worked by a drunken puppeteer. It thumped down on the table.

"Larry, is that you?"

The hand rose and slapped down.

Another sigh came from the audience.

"Larry are you well?" An unusual question to ask someone who was dead, I thought, and almost giggled.

The hand rose and fell twice, each thump in this dark silent room had the finality of a death knell. It was only then that I realised the rain had stopped battering against the window.

"Your soul is not at peace?"

Thump.

"Because your killer has not been apprehended?"

Thump.

"I wish we had a Ouija board. Did anyone think to bring one?"

Before anyone in the audience could reply, Maude's hand, like a dying fish thrashing on a fishing boat's deck, slapped down twice.

"No?" Even Loris was puzzled. "Do you mean they're not needed?"

Thump.

"I'm not sure I understand. Wait, is your killer here in this room."

Thump.

"Can you point them out?"

Thump.

"Point them out, Larry."

Maude's hand rose, the forefinger opening jerkily, like the blade from a rusty flick knife. It turned to point directly at me.

Awkward!

~~~

"For fuck's sake," said Mo, leaning forward on his barstool as avidly as Loris at the seance. "How did that go down?"

The buzz of the Bon Accord went on as usual. The clientele, indeed the whole of the rest of Glasgow, Britain and the world, went about its business unconcerned at my predicament.

"Not well. Of course, they believed every word of it. As soon as I was fingered, they pretty much all fled, giving me black looks as they went. Disapproved of in my own house! Have you any idea how that feels? Even Telly, who I thought I'd made some connection with, was a bit offish. And as for Sally..."

"Who's Sally?" I hadn't seen him since before the conference. So, I told him more about my arrest on suspicion of murder and about Sally and the effect this had had on her. Not all the salacious details but enough that he sat further and further back until I feared he would topple from his stool.

"Jesus! You lead one of the most boring lives I know but I turn my back on you for a couple of days and all hell breaks loose."

That stung. "I'm not boring."

"Yeah, you keep telling yourself that."

"I'm not!"

"Whatever. Let's work this through slowly. First off: I don't believe you murdered anyone," he said with mock earnestness, resting his hand on the back of mine.

I flicked it away.

He waved his palms at me. "Sorry, I'm not taking this as seriously as I should. Let's do this properly. Firstly, the only reason you were taken in by the polis was because you were the last one to see this chap Price alive. That's what they do. The fact they haven't interviewed you since suggests they've found bigger fish to fry. This Telly chap definitely had a motive and so did the gorilla you went to bed with."

"She's meeting me here later. I'm inclined to tell her you called her a gorilla and watch as she makes you eat your barstool."

"Yes, OK, that was uncalled for and I'm a bad man, but I thought we'd established that many years ago. Anyway, my point is that it doesn't sound like you're even still in the frame for the killing. So relax."

I'd worked that out for myself but it was still reassuring to hear someone else say it. It was also reassuring that he'd assumed I was innocent, not that I'd admit that to Mo.

Then again, I felt slightly offended that he thought I was incapable of murder.

"Let's move on to the seance," he said. "Surely you don't believe any of that nonsense?"

"Yeah, it's easy to sit in this warm well-lit pub and pontificate but in a dark candlelit room on a stormy night and someone's face melts..."

Mo snorted.

"What?"

"That's a trick as old as the hills, even I know that. Flickering candles cast shadows, enhancing any changes to facial expression. It sounds as if this Maude is a real pro. She probably practises in the mirror to buggery. I mean that's how fraud works in this whole paranormal game. It's like with illusionists, they go to extreme and elaborate lengths to make their tricks work. Punters see it and don't have the imagination to figure it out."

"Yes, I think you're probably right."

"Probably?"

I sighed. "If it *was* a trick, it was really well done. But I guess Maude's matronly blue stocking persona may just be a cover for a Barnum and Bailey showman. If you'd been there though, I don't think you be quite as certain."

"As for the table moving, I—"

Sally bustled in. She'd been back to her hotel room to freshen up and she was wearing a white coat over red shirt and trousers. She seemed suddenly taller and I realised that for the first time tonight she'd put on high heels, a red pair. She looked spectacular and vastly overdressed for the Bon.

Once again, I sensed my luck might be in.

I introduced them. Introducing women friends to Mo always had a civilising effect. The misanthropic cynic vanished until he got to know them better and then would shyly reappear.

Tonight, however, after all that had happened and all that I'd told him, polite small talk just didn't seem to be on the cards.

"Ah yes," he said, shaking her hand. "You're one of the mumbo-jumbo brigade, as my axe murdering friend here calls you."

She glanced at me. "Your friend is just as charming as you said."

"Would you like a drink?" Mo beat me to it.

"Dalmore, eighteen-year-old, please."

Mo sat up a little straighter on his stool. He liked operatic whiskies too.

I dragged over another stool to form a triangle and we sat facing each other. By then our three Dalmores had arrived and we took our first meditative sips.

Sally closed her eyes. "Mm. If that doesn't cure the ills of the world, then I don't know what does."

Mo was looking back and forth at the two of us. "I've got to say, you're punching below your weight here, Sally. What on earth do you see in him?"

Sally narrowed her eyes and tilted her head to one side, appraising me. "I think it's his magnanimity and lightness of spirit."

Even I had to laugh. "We were just talking about the table moving at the seance. Mo was about to expound."

"It's a con," said Mo. "Anyone can make a rattly old table move with just one finger.

"Naah," said Sally.

"'Naah'! Is that the best you can do?"

"Well, if you insist, Mo, I can give you a more detailed explanation but you'll need to concentrate really hard. Can you do that?"

"Maybe just this once."

Sally took another satisfying sip. "Have you ever heard of Michael Faraday, a physicist from a couple of hundred years ago? Famous for his laws on electromagnetism. Well, he investigated table turning in a rather ingenious way. He first covered the table top in layers of cardboard loosely glued together. The layers got slightly larger the higher they were in the stack. He marked the position of each layer on the underside of the one above. Then the seance began."

Mo was nodding his head. "That's clever. I guess if it was ghosts or whatever causing the table to move, all the cards would move together. If it was people doing it then only the top layers would move. So, it was a con!"

"Naah."

"What, but you just said..." Mo sounded petulant but I could tell he was enjoying this. He liked women who gave as good as they got.

"You're neglecting to take into account the unconscious. I realise you're only a teacher and hardly as au fait with psychology as the august Professor Younge here, but Jung had much to say on the matter."

"I may still be rubbing sticks together to make fire, Sally, but I do know that the august Professor Younge here thinks Jung was a bunkum artist. So I ask once again, what do you see in Dai?"

Sally waved this away. "Jung made a study of the paranormal. He felt that like dreams and myth, the paranormal was a way to study the unconscious which was otherwise, by definition, inaccessible to our rational minds. He felt our unconscious was part of the collective unconscious which connected us all together. That this allows us, at an unconscious level, to be aware of things not accessible to our rational minds.

"With table turning, what we are seeing are small unconscious movements by the participants. Each is unconsciously responding to the questions put by the medium. In the case of what happened earlier at Dai's, the collective unconscious included Larry's unconscious and made itself felt by unconscious movements. Larry was in a sense present and so the table moved to show this. The people did move the table but it wasn't a con."

Mo grimaced. "Sorry, that's too much of a stretch for me. What about the face melting?"

"Well, if we're going to continue with the Jungian theme, then Maude was simply manifesting her unconscious which, via the collective unconscious, was linked to Larry's unconscious."

"Even though he was dead."

"Jung's view towards the end of his own life was that the collective unconscious encompasses the whole universe and all knowledge. The rational mind is cut off from this, constrained as it is by its bag of skin. This idea of a sort of universal library isn't just found in Jung. Many believe in something called the Akashic records which is essentially the same thing. Christians might even think of it as God's Ledger."

"Wait a minute!" said Mo, who was wide-eyed by now. "If you're saying this represents real knowledge, that it's written in God's ledger no less... then it's saying that Dai really did kill this Price chap."

The ends of Sally's lips turned down like a judge pronouncing sentence and she nodded.

"Oh yeah, he definitely did it," she said.

CHAPTER TEN

People will do anything, no matter how absurd, to avoid facing their own souls.
Carl Jung

But not Ted Donlevy. Not only did he want to face his own soul, he wanted to hunt it down and wrestle it to the ground.

And what exactly *is* a soul? The immaterial essence of a human being? The principle of life? A spiritual spark? The emotional aspect of human nature where dwell all feelings and sentiments?

A little nebulous but all those definitions are sort of within the same ball park, and that raises two immediate questions:

Is the soul immortal? Christians and Hindus say yes, but in Judaism it's disputed.

Is it just humans who have a soul? *Yes* say Christians, *no* say Hindus and Jains who believe even bacterium have souls. In Shintoism even apparently inanimate things like rivers and mountains and rocks have them too.

Though searching for the soul had in recent decades fallen out of favour in the scientific community, not so long ago the search for it drove many of the advances in neurology and cardiology. Until a couple of hundred years ago, everyone believed the soul resided in the heart, as did the Ancient Egyptians. They left the heart in the body after death while taking out the viscera. They thought the brain was just head stuffing and didn't bother saving it at all.

Judaism for some reason thought the soul resided in a bone at the top of the spine.

Despite all this, modern science rumbles on as though the idea of soul is absurd. Apparently, we're just chemically reacting molecules and electric currents because that is all we can detect and examine with our increasingly elaborate instruments. Nobody can prove the soul exists and therefore it doesn't.

Yet on the quantum mechanical frontiers of that most quantitative of disciplines—physics—whether someone is observing an experiment or not changes the outcome. Something about the human mind would appear to be absolutely intrinsic to how the universe operates. Hard to believe a couple of kilograms of neuro porridge (or 300 grams of cardiac muscle if you subscribe to the Egyptian view) could do that.

On the other hand, if your brain or heart was the seat of the soul, what happens if it's messed up by disease or injury? Evidence from brain injury suggests that sometimes peoples' behaviour does change. Some head injury patients become disinhibited, some become angry and violent where before they were passive. If the soul was really immortal and separate from the body, then why should it be affected by damage to the husk?

Perhaps one answer to this can be found in the analogy of remote surgery, where a surgeon miles away operates using a remotely controlled robot. If the robot becomes damaged, say it over-amplifies the surgeon's movements so the robot scalpel cuts deeper than intended, the patient may die but the nature of the surgeon is not changed. He can still go on to operate on another body later, a little sadder, a little wiser perhaps, but ultimately still the same surgeon.

So, whether the soul exists or not, and whether it survives death is a mess of conflicting ideas and beliefs and no matter how much mainstream science may pretend it's not a problem, the issue just isn't going to go away.

And that's where Ted Donlevy's genius came in. The forcible mating of the lacklustre metaphysics department and the ill-favoured department of psychology was a disaster akin to a selective breeding experiment run by one of those head injury patients. But old Ted turned it around and presented it as a once in a lifetime opportunity to answer these age-old questions.

And he was lucky, in response to global epidemics and market crashes and wars etc, the world was going through a period of existential self-doubt.

He struck a chord and money fell from the sky. Expensive new imaging technologies began to accrete in the basement and extremities of the department (these instruments were so sensitive that a student thinking impure thoughts would set off alarm bells. Only kidding, thank God!). Even some physicists were employed on this quest, despite the only thing they had in common with philosophers and psychologists was that their specialities all began with 'p'.

With three competing academic terminologies, the department became a tower of Babel. As a psychology lecturer I'd been dragged into this. Where once I'd talked of the unconscious, now I was expected to understand functional magnetic resonance imaging and existentialism, superconducting quantum interference devices (SQUIDs) and Socrates and his shadows on the wall of a cave.

Over time such arcane terms tripped from my tongue but impinged little on my day-to-day practice. To me, interrogating the soul with extremely strong electromagnetic fields would be like examining a mouse with a sledge hammer and chisel. After a few drinks, I was known to suggest that all this hi-tech would wind up killing the souls of its student volunteers and turn them into zombies.

The only trouble was—how would you tell?

So how did they use all this multimillion-dollar equipment? Basically, the researcher would stimulate the subject, for example by showing them disturbing pictures. Parts of the brain might become stimulated and so electrically excitable and increase its blood flow. MRI would pick up the latter, SQUIDs the former.

But so what? Correlation isn't causation. Not only that but some bits of the brain lit up whatever you did, like the amygdala. Did that really mean it was the seat of the soul?

It seemed to me that if the soul existed it probably would be incorporeal. Maybe the brain just reduced all those life experiences into some form that could be transmitted to the incorporeal soul. Maybe the brain was just some sort of aerial.

Whatever. The bottom line was that Donlevy the Soul Hunter hadn't found what he was looking for, had provided nothing new for the few remaining philosophers in the department to incorporate into their abstruse theories. The grant bodies were starting to understand just how much of a waste of time this had been and sooner rather than later the purse strings would be pulled tight.

One unfortunate corollary of all this was that Donlevy had offended the deeply religious who felt he was straying into the territory of God. If you could prove a soul existed then there would be no need for faith. And faith is at the heart of religion.

Some of the more militant Christian fundamentalists took such exception to this that death threats were made.

The worry was that Christian fundamentalists like Elsie and her mates who picketed the department every morning of term, visible but harmless, were just the tip of the iceberg. That grimmer, more determined forces were gathering to slay the heretic.

I had watched all this over the years, bemused at all the heat and vitriol and appalled by the waste of time and money.

If I was forced to come off the fence, I'd say that all this high-tech effort to detect the soul was a complete waste of time.

That there probably is an underlying spiritual structure to the universe but it will take a long time, if ever, for our materialist science to get a handle on it. At this stage it's sort of like using a microscope to study the heavens, or a theodolite to analyse dreams.

Despite what everyone says, I'm a hopeless romantic at heart.

CHAPTER ELEVEN

But what a dreary world it would be if the rules were not violated sometimes!
Carl Jung

"Oh, please!" I groaned.

Same deeply wrinkled old man, same old mountain, same knowing I was dreaming but still unable to wake up.

"You didn't have to kill me," muttered the old man who, despite being squished, was whole and back on the mountain top.

"I didn't mean to. Anyway, it was you trying to kill me. You just tripped and fell."

"I was trying to release you, trying to make you fly."

"Give me a break!"

And with that I turned my back on him and strode off down the mountain.

~~~

"Oh for fuck's sake," I found myself saying out loud as I woke up.

Even back in reality, Groundhog Day continued. Again, a bedroom that looked like the aftermath of the charge of the Light Brigade. I wouldn't have been surprised to find a dead horse under my bed.

Sally was lying beside me on her elbow, her head perched on one hand. "No screams this time, just muttering. What happened?"

It didn't take much recounting. When I'd finished, she shook her head, obviously very unhappy.

"What?"

"That's not good. Surely you see that?"

At the moment there was no end to what I couldn't see. I couldn't see why everyone thought I was a killer. I couldn't see how Sally and I had wound up in bed again.

Well, the answer to that one wasn't entirely unclear. If an attractive woman makes it apparent that she wants to go to bed with a man, then you don't need Grand Old Maude to tell you what's going to happen next.

"You turned your back on the wise old man archetype. You should have jumped, like he said."

I exhaled loudly, looking up at the ceiling and the elaborate cornicing over-painted in white so often it looked like an icing-covered wedding cake. "Spell it out for me, Dr Jung."

"You're not resolving whatever the issue is. It could mean..."

"What?"

"It could mean you'll kill again."

I turned towards her, lifting myself on my elbow with my head in my hand, so we were regarding each other like a pair of bookends. There was a lot going on in her beautiful blue eyes but, for the life of me, I couldn't see any fear.

"What are you doing here, Sally? You give every indication of actually believing what you're saying, so what on earth are you doing in bed with a murderer?"

I remembered poor Mo's reaction in the pub. Louche enough to bend with most blows, he hadn't been able to cope with what Sally had said. He'd left soon after but not before giving me a wide-eyed pleading look.

She pursed her lips. "Can't you even work out the answer to that?"

I hesitated, but the time for being circumspect had expired with Larry Price. "I can think of some reasons but none of them are good."

Again, the grimace. "Well done that man!"

"Is it purely a sexual thing? Putting yourself in harm's way, the ultimate vulnerability, do you find it sexually stimulating? Or is it deeper than that, that you want to end your life but you can't do it yourself so you put yourself at the mercy of a murderer?"

She lay back. "All my life I've heard other people talk about themselves. It soon becomes clear they haven't a clue what they're talking about. When it comes to themselves, they can't see the wood from the trees. I'd be delusional if I didn't think the same thing applied to me. There may be some truth in what you're saying but can I suggest a third explanation? Mountain climbers risk their lives all the time but somehow society accepts this."

"Do they? I think mountaineers are about as crazy as you can get."

"I've always led an unconventional life. Some would call it daring, always pushing the envelope. I mean just recently I raced the rapids in Patagonia, took ayahuasca in the high Andes of Peru. I crawled through a tomb that Larry was pillaging, shooing away the venomous serpents with a stick. I race stock cars in my spare time where one good bash can tear open metal panelling and sever your jugular quick as you like. As with mountain climbers I risk my life because, for brief moments, it makes it taste so much sweeter."

I'd read a paper once comparing mountaineers to soldiers back from intense wars. Hyper-stimulated by what they'd done and experienced, normal life was dull to the point of suffocation. Often the only way to cope was drink, drugs and an early death.

"I hate to rain on your parade," I said, "but I really didn't do it."

She laughed. "Maybe, but I like to think you did."

~~~

I had much to reflect on as Sally and I made our way to the department that morning. My weakness was number one on the list. I should have kicked Sally out of my bed but instead we'd re-enacted the Battle of Borodino. There'd been mass casualties but we'd both somehow emerged as victors.

I couldn't rule out the possibility that I was just as messed up as she.

The early summer light glinted off a galaxy of dew drops clinging to the grass. The river Kelvin burbled happily away as we cut through the park. On the wide footpaths bleary-eyed owners were being dragged along by their mutts, and around them zoomed bicycles driven by students and earnest, ambitious academics. Above us at the top of the hill, the skeletal tower of Glasgow university was fingering the sky.

Birdsong is rare in cities but here in the park they were having a high old time.

The world, it seemed, was in a good mood.

Me, less so. I'm not a law-breaker and despite my bohemian ways I didn't like being suspected of anything by the police. I was sure of my innocence but I'd heard too often of miscarriages of justice. Innocent men hung or imprisoned for a lifetime. Despite the glory of the day, I couldn't rid myself of a feeling of deep unease.

Today the program was back in full swing and even though I got there at nine, Sally hanging back on the final incline up to the university so we didn't arrive together, a bunch of attendees were already waiting.

None of them would meet my eyes. The jungle drums must have been beating throughout the night and they'd all heard of Larry's accusation by proxy. And, unlike any rational person, they'd believed it.

I'm not sure I'd blushed in the last twenty years but I felt myself doing so now. I fobbed my way into the department, letting the door shut behind me before they could charge in.

I wandered through the shambolic building, checking the right doors were unlocked, then stood for a moment or two to regain my composure. I was on my colleague Bill Steadman's floor and I noticed his door was slightly ajar. I knocked and pushed it open. Bill was in his chair reading the parapsych conference programme booklet. He looked up at me with eyes round with surprise. "This is... this is..." he stuttered.

"Barking, demented, absurd, grotesque—take your pick," I supplied helpfully.

"Rettner and Donlevy are out of their minds allowing this stuff on university premises."

"More like desperate, I guess. No Chinese so no money."

Bill's had the lined face of the long-term smoker and his skin was sallow like an old pub ceiling on which a generation of nicotine had been deposited. He held the programme up and shook it. "No wonder they kept quiet about this. Talk about embarrassing!"

"Look, Bill, about this action you're trying to take against the university. If you push them too far then they'll never back down and you'll never get a settlement. You know what Rettner's like."

"It's grist to the mill. I'm going to dig around, see what other bodies those two have buried."

Bill had clearly got the bit between his teeth and I just hoped he didn't wind up being buried along with the other bodies. "What are you doing here anyway? Why aren't you somewhere where the sun is shining?"

He shook his head. "I've been canned, remember? Vacations can be any time I like from now on and the sun's always shining somewhere on this planet. No, I want to see how this case pans out first. Need to know where I really stand."

"Awang and Lucas?"

"Lucas is around. Poor guy has a lot of work to do if he's going to get grants with his reduced status. As for Awang, he's gone dark. Won't answer calls or texts or emails."

"Any idea why?"

Bill crossed his arms. "A bit of a softy is Awang. I don't think the thought of going up against Rettner was helping his bladder control. I'm guessing he's either done a runner or a header into the Clyde."

Bill and I weren't exactly close so there wasn't much more in the way of chit-chat and soon I went back to the entrance and opened the door and held it while the attendees trooped in. Again, none met my eye except for Sally who had arrived by now and gave me a secret little smile.

She manned reception while the others went off to the coffee room. Rather than mingle with people who thought I was a killer, I wandered down the front steps and sat on the little wall out front. I was looking up at the blue sky and not really thinking of anything when my phone rang. I looked at the screen and saw 'Dean of Sacking'.

Today was a slope leading only down. "Hello, Vera."

"I've just checked my in-box and it's a war zone. Six separate complaints." Her voice was tense but at least she wasn't shouting. Not even an 'hello' first.

"About what?"

"About you. From people at this damned conference. They all think you killed this Price character. They don't want you involved anymore."

Rettner's read on other people had never been great, one of the disadvantages of borderline psychopathy, and I got the impression she thought I might object.

"Sounds like a good idea to me," I said.

She gave a little grunt of annoyance. "Not so fast! The university isn't going to be pushed around by a bunch of charlatans. This conference was a bad idea from the start and shouldn't have been allowed to go ahead."

Events of the last couple of days had made me understandably paranoid, but I'm certain there was reproach here. Rettner was trying to slide out from under any blame and needed someone to take her place, no matter how innocent.

There was no point spluttering about how letting this thing go ahead had had nothing to do with me. That would just get her mad. I did feel the need to put her on the spot, though.

"Do you think I killed Price, Vera?"

To give the old bird some credit there were no emollient protestations about my innocence, instead there was a second of silence as she gave the issue some serious thought. Then:

"No," she said.

Again, I felt the obscure annoyance at being thought incapable of such a crime. Asking her why she felt this way would just have sounded weak and needy so instead I just said, "Thanks, Vera."

"Don't worry about it, Dai. Any more trouble from this lot and you just shut it down. The whole thing's becoming more trouble than it's worth." To my surprise there was almost a warmth there, as if for the first time ever she might actually be on my side.

After we'd said goodbye, I sat staring at my phone in wonder. Had I got her wrong?

Out of the corner of my eye I saw someone approaching. It was Telly and he had his hand outstretched. We shook and I must have been giving him a questioning look.

"I want to apologise," he said, ending the firm handshake. "I got a bit carried away yesterday at the seance. All those theatrics... but I've had a chance to think about it more carefully and I'm sorry I harboured doubts about you."

"Maude did sound convincing. I almost believed her myself."

He gave a reluctant grin. "She's good but it wouldn't be the first time she got a reading wrong."

"Besides," I said, sounding even to my ears a little churlish, "what happened to the vengeful Nubian demon hell bent on punishing Price for his tomb-robbing? Your chums seem to flip from one crazy idea to another in the blink of an eye."

He shrugged and looked so embarrassed that I changed the subject, although necessarily to one that was no more comfortable. "How'd it go with the coppers?"

I noticed lines around his eyes that hadn't been there before. "They haven't been in touch since yesterday. You?"

"Nothing."

"Do you think we're off the hook?"

"Who knows? After Maude's *coup de theatre* I reckon I'll have replaced you as Number One suspect."

"How would they have heard about it?"

"Well, at least a half dozen of your lot sent emails to the Dean of my school accusing me of murder. I don't imagine they were shy of telling the coppers the same."

"I'm very sorry about that. I can assure you that I wasn't one of them. Like I said, sense has returned."

Behind Telly I could see more attendees arriving. "What's on the menu today?"

"Well, there's a film on UAPs..." he hesitated, "... that's UFOs, unidentified flying objects, in old money. In the afternoon Sally's giving her talk on Jung and the unconscious. I've seen it before and it's good, though most people here don't find it comfortable."

"Ah yes, Jung's single metaphysical explanation, explaining away the thirty or more separate paranormal phenomena. Sort of like Occam's Razor. The simplest explanation is usually the most truthful."

"Exactly! Sally's talk is a very elaborate way of telling the delegates that all the stuff they believe in is coming from the depths of their own minds."

"I'm surprised she seems so popular."

He shook his head. "She still thinks all the phenomena we deal with are yielding profound metaphysical truths. That we are some of the few granted access to the all-knowing collective unconscious. That makes us pioneers, a beguiling concept. That's why so many at least tolerate her and, to be honest, they reckon Sally is telling the truth about most or all of the other phenomena. The only exceptions being the ones they believe in themselves."

I pulled my head back. "I wouldn't have put you down as being so cynical."

"Hey, I try to keep an open mind. Sally and Jung may be on to something but I don't think it explains everything."

"So, what's your take, which bit of this compendium of beliefs do you go for?"

He shrugged. "I try to keep an open mind but, occasionally, I'm sure the dead have talked to me. Maude reckons I have mediumistic tendencies, though underdeveloped. I think something is going on here, I just don't know what it is."

"The dead talk to you?" I tried to keep my tone neutral but I doubt I succeeded because he grimaced and shook his head as if he didn't want to talk about it.

The street was unsettlingly empty. No hungover young men slouching by, no groups of gossiping young women clutching folders or laptops to their chests, no shell-shocked foreign students still trying to make sense of this strange country. Like all the students, I would have fled abroad when the summer came if I could so I wasn't used to neutron-bombed Glasgow during the summer break.

Telly had been saying something and I realised I'd drifted away.

"What was that again?"

"The MRI, the tour that's organised for tomorrow. Could you take me through it at some point today, just so I can make sure everything's OK? Due diligence and all that."

This week had been such a helter-skelter of events that shouldn't have happened, that the MRI tour which had seemed safely in the future was now upon me. Incredibly, tomorrow was the last day of the conference. Things should be winding down, which seemed strange when everything was so up in the air.

"Right. I need to check on a few things but I'll do them this morning. How about I take you around during lunch? I'll meet you at reception at one."

"Sounds good. I'd better be off. Some of the UAP footage is spectacular. Sure you won't come along?"

"Not right now, but I'll see you later."

Telly almost bounded up the steps.

He'd been kind and that's why I'd agreed to be helpful but nevertheless his request was no small thing. The MRI was a dreadful beast crouching in the basement, like a savage hippo lurking in a swamp, its energies spreading out around it like ripples.

I hated it. To me the MRI was to psychology what a firearm was to a nursery school, stuff that should never be brought together. The postdocs who dealt with the monster, supplicating it and protecting outsiders from its potentially lethal embrace, weren't due to come in until tomorrow. They'd have to ride shotgun on the parapsychs, shepherding them away from harm. All I would have had to do was tag along.

Then again, if it was just me and Telly, what could go wrong? Locked doors would make sure nobody else stumbled in.

In the end, after futtering around doing admin jobs, I went to see the film on UAPs. I took a back row seat. The lecture theatre was full and the audience very appreciative. The speaker, Andy Lister no less, gave a rather thoughtful analysis of the footage. Not always grainy in the way these things usually are, it had been obtained from US military aircraft, and had already appeared on TV. It showed what looked like Tic-Tacs zooming around at unconscionable speeds, and small globular objects skimming over wave crests.

Carefully, Lister went through the possible explanations, giving each a genuine chance. He was so even-handed about it, I couldn't work out if he believed in Little Green Men or not.

I was almost convinced myself. Some of these sightings manifested during a US naval exercise employing the most advanced radar techniques available. The displays showed objects dropping straight down at phenomenal speeds then decelerating at rates that would liquidise flesh.

I was warming to the whole thing when I felt a hand on my thigh. I'd been so entranced I hadn't noticed Sally leave her seat and come to sit next to me.

"You don't believe all this old twaddle, do you?" she whispered.

"Er..."

"Oh my God, you do!" Even in the dimmed room I could see her shoulders shaking.

The implication that I was turning into a parapsych made me squirm in embarrassment. "Well, those things aren't your Jungian projections from the unconscious because they've been caught on film. That..." and I pointed at a dancing Tic-Tac gadding about in the sky without visible means of support, "... definitely come from without and not from within."

She patted my leg and smiled patronisingly. "Yes, you're right. Those things are real, made of metal or wood or sealing wax or whatever-the-hell."

"But you don't think they're aliens from outer space?"

"Of course not. Have you any idea how far away the nearest star is? It'd take thousands upon thousands of years to get here. Nothing organic could live that long and even if it did then something in the spacecraft would be sure to break down irreparably and everything would die."

"Suspended animation? Faster than light drives, like in Star Trek?"

"Ouffle dust, magic wands, the Wicked Witch of the North. Maybe that's it. Someone or something on Alpha Centauri wished upon a star and wound up in Texas."

"So cynical," I said but not without admiration. "So, what are those things?"

"Well obviously it's all secret military technology. Don't you know nuffink?" She flipped the tip of my nose with her forefinger.

"Apparently not."

"The US spends more on military research than it spends on all other research combined. Remember when the world first became aware of the stealth bomber? It suddenly appeared, all-singing and all-dancing, at a press launch. Black and sleek and like no aircraft we'd seen before. It looked like something out of Star Trek which was the SF *du jour*. Yet its prototypes must have been flying around for decades, generating who knows how many sightings of UFOs.

"Remember Roswell in New Mexico in 1947? How an alien spacecraft was supposed to have crashed and non-human corpses found in the wreckage, but then all the evidence mysteriously disappeared. How an obvious cover story was put about of a crashed weather balloon which was taking dummies aloft?"

"I have heard about this. So, what did happen?"

"I'm open minded enough to admit I don't know but I'll give you a much simpler and more believable explanation. A prototype stealth aircraft crashes. It's found by a farmer who tells other people. The army sends in squaddies to pick up every scrap of wreckage as the secret of stealth technology is all to do with the radar absorbing cladding. The alien bodies were simply airmen who had lain in the heat of the desert for four days in the heat. Even you wouldn't look so cute after that, or even human at all." This time she ran a hand through my hair.

Stirred but not diverted by this show of affection, I pointed again at the screen. "And what about the Tic-Tacs?"

"Drones obviously, except ones that the military has been developing in secret for decades using scads and scads of cash. Did you know they were using drones as long ago as the Vietnam war? Imagine how much they'll have developed since then, what with all that money being thrown at them."

I had to admit that didn't sound entirely unconvincing. For the first time I began to wonder if I should grant Sally temporary parole from my 'nutter' category. Then again, I remembered how she was consorting with me, a suspected murderer. Perhaps she belonged there more than anybody.

"Are you coming to my talk this afternoon?"

"Sure, I'll try not to be late. I'm doing something at lunch. Telly wants me to take him through the MRI visit first. Like a dry run for tomorrow."

Sally nodded. " Magnetic Resonance Imaging." She rolled the words around as though savouring them. "I wish I could come myself but I'll be rehearsing my talk."

I didn't tell her I wouldn't have wanted her to come even if she were free. The whole secret of safe visits to our electromagnetic hippopotamus was to keep control of the environment. Controlling Telly might be difficult enough, but controlling an enthusiastic Sally was, as I knew very well, impossible.

The questions which followed the talk were gushing rather than critical. The only exception was a snaggle-toothed old gent in a tweed suit who claimed what we had seen were Nazi space ships venturing out from their base at the South Pole. Apparently, there was a huge cavern there where an immortal Hitler still directed the development of advanced technologies.

Even this audience had trouble swallowing that. Lister wearily rubbed his eyes.

I wandered back to reception. Loris was there looking as harried as ever, although nobody new was checking in. The conference had started with nearly a hundred badges laid out for collection and now just five remained. We were near the end of the conference so it seemed unlikely anyone fresh would turn up now.

"How are you doing, Loris?" I asked, coming round the desk to stand by her.

I hadn't meant to creep up on her. The look of panic on her face when she realised she was alone with me would have been comical under normal circumstances. Eyes open and mouth wide, I could see a skeins of saliva stretched between her upper and lower teeth.

"Chill, Loris!" I said, my hand raised in reassurance but this only made her flinch.

Though startled, she recovered quickly, visibly hardening her resolve. Her eyes narrowed.

"Larry Price was a genius. He had so much to give. He didn't deserve to die," she said with quiet force.

"Uh huh." I knew that sounded half-hearted but it was the best I could do as I just couldn't bring myself to agree with her. Dishonesty, I've always found, just took too much energy.

In silence we regarded each other across oceans of fear and disgust (hers) and contempt (mine). The silence dragged; changing the subject or making small talk would look weak and neither of us wanted to go there.

The funny thing was, the longer this went on, the more I came to respect her. I had put her down as a neurotic jelly, believing in everything and so knowing the truth of nothing, but beneath it all was something altogether steelier.

"Dai, are you ready?" I had been so engrossed in our staring contest I hadn't heard Telly come up behind me.

"How can you sleep at night?" said Loris, but too low for Telly to hear.

Maintaining my dignity, such as it was, I turned to Telly. "Yup, let's go."

Without a backward glance at Loris, I led Telly towards the first set of stairs leading down.

"Watch your back, Telly," she shouted after us.

"What's her problem?" I asked when we were out of earshot.

"All the women had the hots for Price. God knows how many he's been through over the years."

"Even Loris?"

"She's had a difficult personal life. Once she turned heads, including Larry's."

"Really?"

"Yeah, she was into sex magic."

"Do what?"

"Sacred sexuality is a thing. Aleister Crowley, Ira Craddock, The Ordo Templi Orientis, they were all into it."

"What does this sex magic involve?"

Telly chuckled. "Seriously?"

"Does it involve... I don't know... costumes for example?"

"Don't let your imagination run away with you, Dai. It's about releasing energies and to do that you have to treat the process with respect."

"But it's all grunting and groaning and pawing. Or is that just me?"

This time his laugh was frank and loud but he didn't seem inclined to take the conversation further. Maybe he was into sacred spooky sex and didn't want me making fun of it.

I held open a door for him. "So, if Loris had a sexual relationship with Price, then she should be a suspect too. In fact, if you're telling me old Larry got around, then there may be a bunch more here today. Did you tell the cops any of this?"

We'd been descending three flights of stairs and had come to a doorway. This was the basement and it was where our electromagnetic hippo dwelt. Telly stopped and gave me a little wink. "I may have mentioned it in passing."

I let the door swing closed behind us. This might explain why the cops hadn't been back today even though I'd been expecting them. Too many suspects to interview. Too much like hard work. Easier to put it down to a random stranger mugging someone walking through the park. There were certainly plenty more crimes easier to solve in Glasgow and easier ways to keep their detection statistics healthy.

Then again, what did I know of the police? Certainly not enough to take such a cynical view. All my life I'd led a middle-class existence where the only crimes I'd experienced were those perpetrated by my parents.

At last we arrived at the MRI department. Warnings were peppered over the doors and windows as if a horde of graffiti artists high on meth had been set loose.

"Looks forbidding," said Telly.

"Yeah, the extremely powerful magnet's always on. Metal can't be allowed in to the high field area but I'll make sure you're safe to take in. Tomorrow a bunch of postdocs will shake down the people coming on the tour."

I fobbed us into an ante-chamber where there were a bunch of lockers. I picked a clipboard and checklist from a pile by the side. This listed a long series of no-nos that would stop people going into the high field. Neither I nor the postdocs tomorrow had any intention of actually taking any of the parapsychs into the room where the field was so high that it was actually dangerous, but we still had to do this. Besides, it was a nice piece of security theatre and would give the parapsychs a *frisson*.

But it turned out Telly had neither a cardiac pacemaker nor a metal IUD. He'd never picked up shrapnel during the war nor had fragments of metal in his eye. He'd never had an aneurysm clipped nor any surgery.

"You haven't lived," I said.

I got him to empty out his pockets into a plastic tray that I would lock away. As usual with MRI ingenues, Telly went along with everything until it came to his mobile phone.

"I'm expecting an important call," he said, unconsciously clutching the phone with both hands as though I intended to wrestle it away from him.

"That's what they all say. Nowadays people would rather give away a kidney than their phone. The field in there is so strong, the phone would be torn from your hands, or ripped from your pocket, and would be reaching a speed of over a hundred miles an hour before it hit the magnet. It's not called the ferromagnetic missile effect for nothing. Not that the university gives a toss about your phone, but they might get a bit sticky if your missile phone damaged their million-pound magnet."

Telly reluctantly yielded his phone to me as if it was his first born and I was the Pied Piper. I then went through the checklist for myself. I'd volunteered for MRI studies before and had been taken through it each time. A tonsillectomy, a couple of crowns and a broken arm, had not excited any concerns amongst the staff who manned the unit, so I knew I was OK.

I put all my stuff in a tray and locked Telly's and mine away in lockers and then used my non-magnetic fob to get us through the next set of locked doors into the control room. A large window showed us the beast for the first time.

"It's big," said Telly.

Many times larger than any real hippo, even the hole through the middle was big enough to take a small one of those. Not only that but the magnet room, with walls and wooden furniture painted surgical white, hardly resembled a mud-hole.

"So, what's going to happen tomorrow, exactly?"

"Your lot will come down in groups of four. More than that would form a herd and they're never controllable. None of them will go into the magnet room itself. We'll run some scans to show how it's done but we'll use student volunteers we've already checked thoroughly. We'll put them into the magnet and you'll see the scans of their brains come up."

"But we can't go into the actual magnet room."

"No."

"That seems a bit of a gyp. The university promised we would see some scans being performed, like for the Austen study. Instead, we're going to see it through a window. We may as well just use YouTube." He seemed genuinely peeved.

"Well, for a start, onlookers don't stay in the magnet room during a scan anyway as the sound reaches a hundred decibels. As for the Austen study it was performed in the dark with nobody around to distract the mediums... hang on, is the plural of mediums media?"

Telly looked away as though embarrassed. "We say mediums, whether it's the correct Latin or not."

"It's not. Anyway, these mediums were in the dark inside a magnet so they wouldn't be distracted when they tried to communicate with spirits, though how they did that with the MRI making a sound like a submachine gun in their ear is an interesting question. Anyway, even if we set it up like that, there'd be nothing to see."

"But what do you think of that study, Dai? Don't you reckon that proved that the mediums did have powers?"

"No, I don't." Incredibly, the Austen study had actually been published in *Nature*, to the disgust of everyone in the Department. "True enough, when the mediums reckoned they were communing with the dead, a small part of their brain 'lit up' on the images. It's called the anterior cingulate. Trouble is, it lights up in just about any cognitive study, whether it's recognising faces or reacting to pictures of atrocities. Just about any thinking or feeling can set it off."

"And are you an expert in MRI, Dai?"

He had me there. "No, I don't hold much water with this new-fangled high-tech approach to psychology."

"So, you don't think the anterior cingulate is the seat of the soul?"

"I'm not even sure there is such a thing as a soul."

Telly shook his head. "That's sad." I saw a mischievous twinkle in his eyes. "Sounds like the university sold me a pup. This was supposed to be a proper demo. Donlevy made it a big selling point."

No surprise there. I could well imagine Donlevy promising just about everything, and leaving it up to minions like me to make it so.

"Well, I'm sorry about that but I'm not sure..."

"You can make it up to me."

"How so?"

He waved at the brute through the window. "I've always been fascinated by high-tech. Take me into the magnet room and run a scan. I want to hear this thing roar."

I shook my head. "I can't even begin to list all the Health and Safety regs that would breach."

The devil, had such a being existed, was shining in his eyes. "More than your job's worth, eh, Dai? Your man Donlevy sold me a pup. I'm gonna have to complain."

Great! Donlevy had oversold but I had a pretty clear idea who'd end up carrying the can.

"Fine, I'll take you in but I'm not running a scan because I haven't got a fucking clue how this thing works. Your anterior cingulate will go unimaged."

He looked genuinely disappointed. "OK, but at least take me into the room and load me into the magnet. I mean I can see the controls on the side of the hole from here. One's got an arrow pointing in, one pointing out. Surely even you could work that."

This was annoying. Even I, a member of the department, wasn't allowed into the room unsupervised. The door was kept locked but the little locked box where the key was kept was just above the control console. It was level with both our eyes, as was the box's label, which read 'Magnet Room Key' in big letters.

Anyway, it should be safe. None of the MRI staff were due in until tomorrow and the locked doors would keep everyone else out. Why not indulge him if that would make the problem go away?

The hell with it! And while we were at it why not just have a little bit of fun? The MRI staff had shown me a demo when I'd volunteered. They'd enjoyed doing it because it got such a reaction, even from me. It had literally taken my breath away.

"OK, but I'm doing this under duress. First pat yourself down just to make sure you really have removed all the objects from your pockets."

He did this then shrugged. I got the key and opened the magnet room door. As soon as I did, I felt the cold. The magnet room was highly air-conditioned, mainly because the electromagnetic fields very slightly heated the subject. Ironically the innards of the magnet were bathed in liquid helium at minus 270 degrees Centigrade which was within a ball hair of being as cold as anything in the universe. However, the innards of the brute were encased in a high-tech version of the sort of vacuum flask people kept tea and coffee in. The subject's body might only be within a few feet of the supercooled liquid but wouldn't freeze.

But, when the magnet wasn't scanning, you could hear the refrigeration system—a rhythmic twittering sound. "That's a funny noise," said Telly on cue. "What is it?"

Not as well disposed to Telly as I had been, I shrugged. "A budgie must have got loose from the neighbouring tenements. Nobody's ever been able to catch it. If you find it's in the tube with you, swat it away before it craps on your head."

He didn't seem to know what to make of this but I didn't care. Now that he was in this strange environment, the hulking magnet and the pristine whiteness making it look like some sort of temple to alien technology, he had lost his bumptiousness. He pointed down at some ellipses painted on the floor. "Are these some sort of warning lines. Can I cross them."

He made to step over but I raised a hand quickly. "Not yet!"

He froze mid-stride and I tried to hide my smile. Mess with me, would you? "Let me show you something first."

I went outside to a cupboard where I knew they kept the pillow and brought it back in.

Telly frowned "What are you going to do? Smother me!"

"Tempting, but no. Just watch."

I stepped to within a couple of metres of the magnet and held out the pillow.

"Ready?" I asked.

"What for?" he asked.

I let the pillow go and he gasped in shock. I'd seen this before but I couldn't help but be startled again. The pillow moved so fast it was like teleportation. In an instant it had fired into the magnet like a bullet.

"What the hell?" I was gratified to see his stunned reaction.

"I'll need your help. You can cross the lines now. We're going to pull the pillow out."

It was good to see him so freaked out. He crossed the lines as if he was in a minefield. We got either side of the patient bed at the entrance to the magnet, then reached in and grasped the pillow. I saw the amazement on his face as he started to pull. It was like trying to move a car with your bare hands, not some feather-light cushion.

It took both of us fighting against the titanic but invisible forces to get the damn thing out and back across the lines.

"What... the... fucking... fuck?" he said when we got safely back to the door.

"This is why we make sure all the metal is off your person. You see why it's called the ferromagnetic missile effect? The magnet is always on; anything ferromagnetic brought near it will take off at an acceleration over twenty times that of gravity, reaching speeds of well over a hundred miles an hour almost instantaneously."

"Metallic... but it's a pillow full of feathers."

"Nowadays pillows are made from foam. However, there are some special pillows that provide extra support by having metal springs in them. The springs are very fine and weigh only a few grams but, as you saw, they make this pillow take off like a jet fighter... actually that's wrong, no plane takes off as fast as this."

"Doesn't it damage the magnet?"

"It's a well-padded pillow, so no."

He nodded. "Then I can have a go."

I should have seen that coming. Had to admit, though, that I wanted to see it again as well.

Telly took the pillow and walked forward. Even though I was watching as closely as I could, when he let go, I couldn't see the pillow move. It just went from his hand to the middle of the magnet in no time at all.

We wrestled it out of the magnet again. "Another go," he said but I took the pillow and put it back in the cupboard.

"Shows over," I said. "Time to lock up."

"Hang on, hang on. I want you to load me into the magnet. You said you would."

"Why do you really want to do that?"

"I just do."

"Haven't you ever had an MRI scan before?"

Telly shook his head. "Hale and hearty me. Never had a day off sick in my life."

I glanced at the couch controls. They did look straightforward.

"You're nuts. Most people would pay good money never to have to get in an MRI."

"Don't be such a pussy. It's not a big ask."

"It *is* more than my job's worth."

He snorted. "Come on!"

"What is this need to be fed into a hole. Trying to crawl back into the womb?"

"Now you're just getting nasty."

"Fine, if you insist, I'll load you in but then I'm pulling you right back out."

He held up a hand. "Not so fast. I want a chance to meditate in there. Right in the centre of that colossal magnetic field. Imagine what it'll do to my thought processes."

"It doesn't do anything, you dick. I've been in there myself. Believe me, you're not going to reach nirvana any quicker in there."

"How do you know? Are you a trained meditator?"

"How long are we talking about? Hours? If so, you can forget that."

He shook his head. "Fifteen minutes."

"Five."

"Ten."

"Seven -and-a-half."

He grimaced. "Fine. Good job I can get into the zone quickly."

The couch was quite high but could be lowered to let people on, but before I could find the proper control, Telly hopped on easily. Still upright, he brought his legs up and laid them on the couch.

He looked at me with a smile of triumph. He opened his mouth but, instead of saying anything, he hesitated and his eyes darted to something behind me.

Everything changed.

Something hard slashed across my shoulder. I flinched in pain as I heard a sickening thud.

And Telly vanished in an instant.

With a hissing sound like a giant serpent, a white cloud exploded out of the magnet bore, bathing me in its freezing breath. Blinded and shocked, my legs turned to jelly and I fell to the floor. In my panic I tried to crawl away, my shoulder erupting in molten agony.

The cloud billowed around me. All I could see was my hand in front of me, ghost white and rimed in frost. My lungs burned with the cold.

Within the featureless white was a hint of darkness over to my left. The magnet room door! Painful though it was, I started to roll towards it. Each time my shoulder touched the floor it was like being slashed again.

The freezing cloud was dissipating. Within seconds it had vanished completely and I found myself almost at the door. Groggily I levered myself up with one hand and got my knees under me. Holding onto the big handle of the door I pulled myself up and turned to check if Telly was OK.

What I saw didn't make any sense. I blinked and blinked again, as though it was an hallucination or a nightmare. Not believing what I was seeing I lunged at the end of the couch, catching it with my good hand. Holding on for support I managed to shuffle forward on my still nerveless legs.

The cloud that had burst out of the magnet had almost gone by now but what was revealed still didn't make sense. I could see the hair covering the top of Telly's head but either side of this were the soles of his feet. He was bent completely double.

"Telly!" But my voice was so scratchy that what came out was nonsense. I cleared my throat. "Telly!"

Pushing my hip against the couch for support I leaned in and grabbed his foot and shook it. "Telly?"

He wasn't making a sound. I had to get him out. I pulled at his foot but nothing happened. Finally, stupidly, I remembered the couch controls and pushed the out button.

The couch moved, and I almost lost my balance. It slid out dutifully but Telly was left behind, still horribly contorted. As the couch came out from under him, his feet dropped and I saw something embedded in his abdomen. His whole body was pivoted over the object. I stared, trying to focus, and finally realised what it was.

I almost threw up with the horror. Darkness closed in from the corners of my eyes. I turned and staggered away, out through the magnet room door. The blackness was now filling half my vision, as if I was wearing blinkers.

What I was looking for had a big red notice above it but I just couldn't find it. I took a deep shuddering breath and at last I saw it. Staggering forward I jabbed at it but my fingers bounced off something smooth. Closer now I saw the plastic shield covering the big red button. The room was spinning faster but I just managed to flip the shield up.

I jabbed again and felt the button smack against its casing. Something mighty came to life with a roar like an approaching train. Too dizzy to stand I took my finger from the button and tried to grab the side of a nearby console. I touched it but couldn't get a hold. Toppling like a felled tree I just managed to get my hand in front of my face before I crashed to the ground.

Everything was spinning and stars were appearing. I was tumbling through a galaxy and spiralling down into the black hole at its centre.

CHAPTER TWELVE

God enters through the wound.
Carl Jung

For a few seconds nothing happened, as if the screen had frozen. The camera was aimed at the back of the department and the extension that housed the magnet.

I was about to complain when, on the screen, the fire door flew open and a black clad figure slipped through and dived into the shadows.

"Shit!" I said.

"Keep watching!" said DI Philban gruffly. He thrust the iPad closer. So close I couldn't focus so I had to push it back, but gently.

Nothing was happening on the screen, although the fire door was now swinging open.

Then a cloud like a nuclear mushroom rose out of the MRI building. It was so dense it was like a bright white balloon that slowly rose up, getting bigger and bigger until it seemed to fly away.

"You did that, didn't you?" said DS Kendrick accusingly.

"I didn't have any choice!" I said but even to my ears it sounded plaintive. "That was the only way anyone was going to get Telly out. If it hadn't been me, it would have been the firefighters."

Both the coppers looked annoyed. They knew nothing of 'ferromagnetic missile effects' and 'superconducting quenches' and it made them feel uncertain and vulnerable. And that made them angry.

Outside the window, the Clyde wended its way towards the Irish Sea. I could see the first hilly ripples of what would become the tsunamis of the Highlands. I was back in the Suffering General, this time on the sixth floor. And this time as a patient.

Between periods of gawping at the view, lying here in a hospital bed, my shoulder bandaged but still very sore, I'd managed to piece together what had happened; to make sense of the catalogue of horrors I'd seen in the magnet room. The sight of the black clad figure fleeing the building had provided the final missing piece of the jigsaw.

It was also the only reason I hadn't been arrested for murder.

The coppers wanted explanations and they wanted them now. The only thing that gave them pause was the medication I was under for my injury but consultation with the hospital staff seemed to reassure them I should be compos mentis. Whatever I'd been given must have been unimpressive because the cops started to look at me as though I were a wimp.

One thing they had been kind enough to tell me was that Telly was dead. A post mortem was under way even as we spoke. Not that I needed a skilled forensic pathologist to tell me how he'd died. I reckon I could have written the report myself.

"From the top," said Philban, "and I would remind you that you are under caution." As emphasis, he put a neat little recording device on my bedside table and intoned all the names of those present.

They still hadn't got round to using my proper title. Pricks.

I sighed. "I was showing Telly Lamarck around the MRI Unit..."

"Are you allowed to do that?" said Kendrick sharply.

"Well..." I couldn't think how to tell the truth and come up smelling of roses.

Hesitation must be like cat-nip to these guys. "So, you're in trouble with the university?"

I very nearly said 'No shit, Sherlock' but even I could tell that wouldn't be a smart move. I gave a one-shouldered shrug.

Kendrick looked even more annoyed. "I thought these places were supposed to be locked up when not in use."

They took me through every single detail of how I'd got in. In fact, we went through it three times until I couldn't help myself:

"For God's sake. This is so unimportant. Don't you want to know about the murder?"

"We decide what's important," said Philban. He said it quietly but, somehow, I sensed the hidden depths, full of cold and dark and monsters and all the other stuff he'd seen as a copper in Glasgow, and it shut me up. My future was very much on a 'shoogly peg' (*Scottish vernacular: an unstable hook barely holding up one's coat*).

"Telly... Lamarck insisted he wanted to see the magnet. It was part of some deal he'd made with my head of department. Then he insisted on lying in the magnet so he could meditate in the high magnetic field."

"Did that make any sense to you?"

"Not the slightest. But I was there to keep the nutters... sorry... the conference attendees happy. Lamarck was one of the organisers so I had to keep him sweet most of all."

"So, you... loaded I suppose is the word... you loaded him into the magnet."

"No, it all went wrong before then. He was on the couch but sitting upright and still just outside the magnet. Then he saw something, something behind me."

"What, exactly?"

"I don't know, I was facing Lamarck. Before I could turn round it hit me."

"What hit you?"

"The fire extinguisher that was chucked into the magnet room. The high magnetic field took it, accelerating it to absurd speeds in an instant. It must have caught me a glancing blow, otherwise the bones in my shoulder would be confetti. As it was, the trigger or the nozzle gouged a furrow across my back." The nurses had been kind enough to hold up two mirrors so I could see the damage when they changed my bandages. Red and deep and so arrow straight in my flesh it was like a machine had made it.

"OK, then what?"

"It must have caught Telly in his abdomen, driving him backwards into the magnet hole, doubling him over like a rag doll."

And smashing his insides and breaking his spine, though I could not bring myself to say that. "It would have been like being hit in the midriff by a cannon ball."

The two policemen exchanged glances. Even for blank-eyed Glasgow coppers this was a turn-up for the books.

"So, what did you do then?"

"There was a terrible hissing sound, really loud. I'm guessing the valve on the cylinder had been dislodged when it hit me or Telly, and the compressed gas inside escaped. I'm presuming it was carbon dioxide because it came out very cold. So, the CO_2 sort, right?"

They didn't react. Perhaps they weren't sure either but weren't going to admit it.

"I was pretty messed up by then, physically and mentally. Tried to get him out using the couch controls, but the cylinder, once it got to the centre of the field, stayed there, trapping Telly. The couch just slid out from beneath, leaving him still pinned inside the magnet."

Kendrick gave a slow blink. He'd probably dropped physics at school with a sigh of relief and yet here it was years later and snapping at his heels again.

Philban licked his lips. "And you couldn't just pull him out?"

I remembered the pillow; that had weighed bugger all but it had taken the two of us to get it out. I shook my head. "I'd have needed a winch or a team of horses to pull him out of the field."

"So that's why..." He pointed at the screen of the iPad.

"That's why I initiated a superconducting quench, as they call it. These extreme magnetic fields can only be produced by very large currents and the only way they can do that without melting the wires is by bathing the windings in liquid helium at minus 270 degrees Centigrade. Under superconducting conditions, the current would theoretically circulate for eternity unless..." I was having trouble remembering what I'd been told. Like Kendrick I thought I'd bid farewell to all that physics stuff when I was still at school.

"Unless?"

"I think the only way of turning the damn thing off is to heat it up a bit, turning the liquid helium into an awful lot of gas in an instant. Essentially, it's an explosive event. To stop the magnet blowing up like a grenade, a big pipe takes the gas and sends it out into the air above, hence the mushroom cloud. Helium is invisible but it's still very cold so what you see is a cloud of water vapour frozen out of the air."

Philban didn't seem quite as discomforted as Kendrick. "Judging by the size of the cloud that must have been a lot of helium."

"Thousands of litres, I believe."

"Is it expensive?"

"Very."

"So, you're not going to be flavour of the month with the university."

"I thought we'd already established that," I said and couldn't help sounding tetchy. "But, then again, it was the only way to get Telly out."

"Couldn't you have gone round the back of the magnet and pulled him out from the other side. The cylinder would just have been left behind."

Surprised, both Philban and I turned to look at Kendrick. I hadn't thought of it at the time, but he was right. Bastard!

Kendrick, tilted his head a little and I could have sworn I saw a hint of redness on his cheeks. "Not just a pretty face," he said gruffly. Although times were changing, coppering was still regarded as a working-class pursuit. Being clever was still probably frowned on.

"One way or the other that damned thing had to be turned off," said Philban. "It was a crime scene after all. I don't think we can do you for initiating a... whatever that was."

"And I'm also off the hook for killing Price, right?"

"Why?" Philban seemed genuinely puzzled.

"Because obviously the person who chucked the cylinder at us, the one who we saw scarpering out of the fire door, that was the person who killed Price."

"I don't know what it's like in the academic world, Mr Younge, but in the police we're not allowed to jump to conclusions at the drop of a hat. These incidents could be unrelated."

"Come on, DI Philban. Two attendees at the same conference are murdered in unrelated incidents? That's way too much of a coincidence."

"You could have been in conspiracy with someone else. Maybe you fell out or they saw you as a threat."

He said this with the full authority of a time-served policeman but something about the eyes wasn't going along with it. I may not have escaped it entirely but I'd fallen quite a bit further down their shit list.

The civilised thing at that point, after I'd supplied the information, would have been for them to leave me to recover. Instead Philban said: "There's something I'm not clear on."

That was nonsense. Despite all the physicsy fol-de-rol they'd gotten the drift. Nevertheless, they took me through the whole thing again and again.

And again.

And again.

CHAPTER THIRTEEN

Nobody can fall so low unless he has a great depth.
If such a thing can happen to a man, it challenges his best and highest on the other side; that is to say, this depth corresponds to a potential height, and the blackest darkness to a hidden light.
Carl Jung

Mo sauntered in as I was struggling into my shoes. The gouge in my shoulder was heavily bandaged but it still stung like buggery every time I moved. My shoulder didn't feel too happy either but they'd taken X-rays and assured me nothing was broken.

The medics had insisted on keeping me in overnight as I'd blacked out and they suspected a head injury, but in the end a CT had revealed the usual kilo and a half of undamaged neuro-porridge. A doctor had told me I was free to go.

Mo said nothing as he watched me struggle with my shoe laces. "Should I—"

"Fuck off!" I snapped. If he tied my shoelaces for me then I'd be hearing about it for years.

Eventually I got them fixed after a fashion and straightened up, no doubt red in the face with the effort. "Did you manage to park nearby?"

He shrugged. "A couple of hundred metres. Can you manage?"

"Of course I can manage." Even I could tell I was being quite the charmer.

He held the door open and I left my little room behind. One good point about this brand spanking new mega hospital was that patients, where possible, had their own private rooms. However, that didn't work for everyone. Following a series of single-room suicides, questions had been asked in the Scottish Parliament about this policy. Apparently, some people preferred communal wards; they found something reassuring about listening to strangers snoring and farting in their sleep.

I waved goodbye to the bed-headed male nurse on the ward reception desk and he gave me a distracted wave back. Leaving the ward behind, we found a lift and descended to the ground floor.

Not only did the hospital look like the Deathstar from outside, but it also managed to do so from within. All the wards and offices and what-have-you were clustered around an atrium at least twelve floors high. It was so wide that it was said you could have parked a 747 across it. However you cut it, the atrium was impressive. The place didn't look like a hospital at all.

Here on the ground floor were little coffee shops and kiosks. People chatted at tables like al fresco Neapolitan diners. There might be a lot of suffering and dying going on around them but it was well hidden.

I hadn't even been in here a whole day but I felt out of touch. There had been a TV screen on an arm I could position over my bed at any height or angle I wanted but it didn't matter because it wasn't working. I'd locked my metallic phone away in a locker at the MRI unit so I couldn't even use that to entertain myself. Getting it back to me had clearly not been a priority with the coppers. Maybe even now they were poking through its contents looking for evidence of a murderous conspiracy.

"How's all this been treated?" I asked as we made our way slowly towards the entrance. "Did it make the news?"

"Oh, that's a good one," Mo replied. "Check this out."

He led me over to something a bit like a corner shop as it sold a variety of food and drink, although it was as gleaming as everything else. I could easily see the newspaper rack beside the counter.

'Serial Killer Stalks West Scotia University' screamed the headlines of one local shit-rag.

'Psychics Slaughtered in University Bloodbath' intimated another.

With dismay I saw that even the UK national papers had picked it up. There'd been an air-crash in Madeira and many were feared dead and that was the main splash but our little story still made the front page, albeit in smaller type. The *Guardian* even had a snide 'Demon Haunted World of West Scotia University' item at the bottom of the page.

"I am so fucked," I said.

Mo didn't reply but his look of concern was not what I wanted to see. I'd have preferred him to laugh in my face.

"Do you really think they'll..." He couldn't finish.

"Sack me? Oh yes. I was borderline sackable to begin with. Then I broke their Health and Safety rules and someone died, not to mention the small matter of twenty grands' worth of helium going up in smoke. I could not be more fucked."

We both resumed our walk to the entrance, more slowly now. I could tell from the slightly tortured expressions crossing Mo's face that he was trying but failing to think of something reassuring to say.

"I'll take you for a drink," he said finally.

~~~

Late afternoon, before the office crowd surged in for therapy, the Bon was more or less deserted. Rather than prop up the bar we were spoiled for choice when it came to tables.

Mo bought me a Dalmore while he had settled for a Coke so he could legally run me back home in his battered old Ford afterwards.

No greater love has one man for another.

"So, I've been incommunicado. Give me a summary of what's happened since they carted me off to hospital."

Mo fingered the condensation on his glass. "Well, for a start, your precious parapsych convention is deader than the proverbial witch's tit. Unless they've got cast-iron alibis none of the attendees are being allowed to leave Glasgow. A few have been on TV denigrating the police. Apparently, some of the attendees reckon they've been called in by other police forces all over the world to find corpses and solve murders and what have you. Despite this, Strathclyde Police have refused their help, reckoning they can manage fine without them."

I held up my glass. "I'll drink to that."

We chinked glasses.

"Sally not been in touch?"

I shrugged, which was stupid as it made my shoulder burn. "She wouldn't even know what hospital I was in and, what with my phone being with the coppers, she wouldn't be able to contact me anyway. Besides which, there's the small matter of the two guys who were killed being her ex-lovers. That's something that won't have escaped Philban's and Kendrick's attention. Not only that but she was the only one I told about Telly and me going to the MRI unit."

"You know, if she really was some sort of Black Widow, that might explain why she kept trying to convince you that you were the murderer. You know, with all that Jungian stuff. She was setting you up to take the fall. Charming!"

"I think you're jumping to conclusions there, Hercule Poirot."

His eyebrows rose. "Really? Are you *so* sweet on her?"

That was a better question than I was ready to deal with. The silence stretched as I struggled to figure out an answer.

"No," I managed finally but neither he nor I seemed convinced.

~~~

We stopped on the way home at a little PC shop that, among overflowing racks of cables and jacks and assorted technocrap, also flogged cheap phones and sim cards. A dazed, otherworldly IT guy, ripped away from the comfort of his computer and unfamiliar with dealing with customers, saw to my needs with a complete absence of interest or enthusiasm. I'm not great with technology and asked him to put the sim card in for me. Diminished in the ways of men though he was, I marvelled at the ease with which he found and opened the slot, in one smooth movement breaking off the bits of the one-size-fits-all sim card and slotting it in.

A different breed altogether.

Mo dropped me at my door and, only when I reached in my pocket for the house keys, did I remember that as well as my old phone, I'd put them in the locker at the MRI Unit.

By now Mo had driven off and I was left alone on the sunny Glasgow street. I thought of phoning him but, of course, I couldn't remember his number. Who does remember nowadays, with phones doing all the remembering for them?

What the hell was I going to do now? I couldn't recall anybody's number. Then I remembered that I kept a spare set of keys locked away in my drawer at work. The key for the drawer was on my keyring so not accessible to me, but jemmying open the drawer shouldn't be a problem. I'd already hit the jackpot when it came to damaging university property, so a bust open drawer wouldn't be what ended my career.

I started to walk down the hill, taking it easy as I was still a little woozy. I was looking down as I put one foot in front of the other, lost in my own little world of discomfort when I heard a foreign-accented voice say: "Dai, my God you look like shit."

I looked up. My colleague, Lucas Grimsrud, the Pound Store Viking, had been coming up the hill and had stopped, a frown of concern on his face.

"I heard what happened at the MRI Unit. It sounds dreadful, Dai. Traumatic in fact."

I'm sure Lucas was well-meaning but I knew he was into CBT and other talking therapies and I just wasn't up for that. "Yeah, it was rough but I'll get over it."

I could tell he wanted to smile but was trying to hide it. "And you broke Donlevy's baby."

"I never pegged you as spiteful, Lucas."

"Fucker demoted me. Only way it could have been better if he and Rettner had been in the tube at the time."

"That's dark, Lucas. For what it's worth, though, I wish it had been her rather than the guy who was killed. I liked him."

"Only the good die young... oh, I'm sorry." His face reddened.

Somehow, I managed to laugh. "Don't worry about it, mate. My crappy name is the least of my problems right now. I hear Awang's done a runner."

He nodded. "Or at the bottom of the Clyde, poor guy. He's not built for what life can throw at him. Anyway, I've just been to the union and they're going to put a formal complaint to the university."

"On what grounds?"

"That Rettner and Donlevy are cunts, of course."

I laughed again. "Seriously, what's the position?"

Lucas shrugged. "There's various rights of appeal the Dreadful Duo neglected to mention. We probably won't be able to overturn things but the union reckons they can get us a better settlement."

He hesitated and licked his lips. "Maybe..."

I liked Lucas and decided to save him the embarrassment. "Yes, I reckon I need to talk to the union as well. I'm so fucked I've been turned completely inside out."

"In any event the union might like to speak to you as you were there at the meeting too. They reckon Rettner's explosive behaviour is right out of order."

"No kidding, but good luck with that." We exchanged numbers and I put his into my new phone. He also gave me the number of the union rep. He said he'd keep me informed of the case and we bid each other farewell.

Being reminded that other people had their troubles cheered me up just a little bit. It didn't actually put a spring in my step but at least the air seemed fresher and clearer.

The hill up to the Gothic university buildings was steeper than usual and I had to stop to catch my breath halfway up. Here, bodies of barely clothed office workers and postgraduates littered the grass, as if Kelvingrove had been the sight of a brutal battle. Sunshine wasn't quite as rare as reputed in Glasgow but the barest hint had people throwing off their clothes and splaying themselves on any patch of grass with hedonistic abandon. Even the red-haired ones.

"Twats," I thought to myself. It was unseemly for a man of my age but my eyes could not help straying to the female flesh on display.

I'm only human, after all.

It took a while for the copper guarding the door to let me in. He phoned Philban who said I could go to my office but under no circumstances was I allowed to go near the MRI unit, it being a crime scene.

I took it slowly up the stairs. It wasn't just my infirmity making my feet leaden, I was pretty sure nothing good would be waiting for me in my room.

Hutchison looked up in surprise as I entered. He didn't take vacations, or nothing long enough for anyone to notice.

In my absence his papers had spilled over from his own desk and were colonising mine.

"Good to see you're in one piece, Dr Younge, let me just clear this stuff off for you," he said hastily, getting up and sliding the papers off my desk into one big pile.

I plopped down into my chair. "Got a jemmy?" I asked.

"A jemmy?"

"To open one of these desk drawers."

He stood up and came round to stand beside me. "Which one?"

"The bottom one."

"Is the top one...?" But even as he asked, he was pulling out the top one which I never keep locked. He took it right out, revealing the exposed contents of the drawer below.

"I hadn't thought of that," I said peevishly, as if it was his fault. I could now reach in and fish out my spare set of keys.

"Lateral thinking," he said and went back to his desk. Smug bastard.

I pocketed the keys and looked at my rapidly blinking answerphone. It was full of messages and was desperately trying to catch my eye like a cow that needed milking.

"Oh, sorry," said Hutchison suddenly. "Must have swept this up by mistake." So saying he brought over a heavy, over-engineered envelope and laid it in front of me. Judging by the thickness of the paper this could only be bad news. I tore it open. There were two densely worded paragraphs but the jist was that I should come immediately to Donlevy's office and not Pass Go.

"Bad news?" asked Hutchison. "You look a little..."

I ignored him and pushed the button on the phone and listened to my messages. Donlevy's secretary had sent me over a dozen. Dryly professional at all times, her repeated summons to see Donlevy varied hardly at all, though my imagination freighted the subtext with an increasing number of expletives.

I looked across at Hutchison who was staring hard at some document, although his eyes were widening as the messages followed one after another, each the toll of a very big bell.

Somewhere in this litany a message from Sally came on. She sounded worried and wanted to know how I was. She'd had the sense to include her number.

The final call from was from Bill bleating on about getting the Union to take up the case of the four academics 'brutalised' by Rettner and Donlevy, as he put it. After what I'd seen in the MRI, I reckoned Bill didn't even know the meaning of that word.

The plight of the academics could wait. Instead, I got up and hobbled outside and called Sally. She answered on the third ring.

"Hello."

"It's me, Dai."

"Are you OK, I heard—"

"I'm fine. Smacked up my shoulder a bit. Where are you?"

"Shopping. Lots of nice stores in this city. Not much else to do now they've shut the conference down. I've been trying to take my mind off poor Telly. He didn't deserve that."

"Have the police talked to you?"

"They've done little else. I made the mistake of popping out for a bite to eat before my presentation and just before it kicked off in the MRI, so haven't got an alibi. The police are in the process of getting hold of CCTV footage along Byres Road to see if they can spot me. If they can't then I'm in trouble."

We both went silent, thinking about this. "At least you're off the hook," she said finally.

"Not according to Philban. I'm still at least notionally in the frame for killing Price."

She laughed but it sounded dry, unamused. "We're the new Bonnie and Clyde, at least in the coppers' eyes."

"What are they up to now? Did you get any idea?"

"They're interviewing all the attendees and that's pissing a lot of people off. The conference was due to end today and people were supposed to be flying off all over the place. Instead, they're stuck here for the foreseeable future. Look, there was something I was meaning to ask you..."

"Knock yourself out," I said, anything to delay my trip to Donlevy's Heart of Darkness.

"Well, as you can imagine, there's been a lot of talk amongst the attendees and quite a few seances as well. There's a story going round..."

I raised my eyes to the ceiling in anticipation.

"... that we awoke something at the swimming baths, something demonic. Or maybe Larry did summon a demon when he breached that tomb. That whatever it was put an axe through Larry's head then folded Telly double and shoved him into the MRI."

"I thought you didn't believe in all this, that you were into Jung."

"It's not incompatible. Perhaps what we did provoked someone's archetypes, the primal parts of us that live by drives and rules we don't understand."

"So, they're saying some Lovecraftian demon was made form and is going around with an axe and folding people up like a shirt?"

"The others are but I'm not. In Jungian terms it's just excited someone's archetypal behaviour, is making them do things they may not even be aware of themselves, or perhaps are somehow managing to explain away by some pseudo-rationalisation."

"Whose?" I couldn't keep the annoyance out of my voice because this was nonsense.

"I don't frigging know." Now *she* was annoyed.

I took a deep breath. "Let's both calm down. Look, why don't you come over to my place. Say around six. Maybe between us we can figure out what's going on here."

Hang on a minute, I thought. *She's now suspect Number One and I'm inviting her round to my flat.* Was I in so much need of sympathy?

"I could come earlier, if you like. I'm only in Sausageroll Street or whatever it's called."

"Sauchiehall Street is the name. But no, don't come now as I've got to see my boss. It may be lengthy or it may be quick but it's definitely going to be all bad."

"Ooh! Sorry to hear that."

"If I get out earlier, I'll let you know otherwise I'll see you at six. By the way, I've had to get a new phone. The number is..."

"It's OK, it's registered on mine. See you at six."

I went back into my office, thinking of Jungian axe murderers in a demon-haunted world.

Hutchison looked up again. "Everything alright?"

I peered at him and lifted up my hands, palms flat.

"Sorry, stupid question," he said. "I don't know if you're up for any more bad news."

Up until that point, I hadn't noticed what a punchable face he had.

He seemed to take my pregnant silence as encouragement. "It's Logan. He's very angry."

"Logan?" So much had happened my mind had gone blank at the name.

"Your student, the one who wanted you to mark his thesis, which he'd put in late."

It rang a vague bell.

"He's failed. He was here, in tears, wanting to see you. I'm glad you weren't here. Things might have got unpleasant."

"Fuck him. Any other news. Did my dog die?"

"I didn't know you had a dog," he said.

I went back out of the door and headed to my doom.

CHAPTER FOURTEEN

A man likes to believe that he is the master of his soul. But as long as he is unable to control his moods and emotions, or to be conscious of the myriad secret ways in which unconscious factors insinuate themselves into his arrangements and decisions, he is certainly not his own master.
Carl Jung

Even getting to Donlevy's office was a metaphor, remoteness being the watchword. Made from a row of tenement buildings, there were a number of possible entrances to the department. All had been blocked off except for the main entrance and the entrance to Donlevy's office. The latter was locked, with only Donlevy and his secretary having a key.

You could still get to his office from the main department, without having to go outside, but the connecting corridor was also locked and under the control of the formidable Ms Murdoch.

Donlevy's little enclave therefore gave him distance. He had probably been there for most of the conference, toiling away, leisurely summer breaks no longer available to hard-ridden heads of department.

After ringing the buzzer by the street entrance, and speaking into the intercom, I had been greeted by the frosty Ms Murdoch, whose distain was palpable. She barely spared me a glance as she went and knocked at Donlevy's door.

Without waiting for a response, she opened it and announced my presence. Only when an assent came from within did she move aside to let me through.

As I entered, Donlevy pointed at the seat in front of his desk. He was the sort of man who worked out and liked people to know it. He was wearing a blue jacket, the material so thin I could just about make out the muscles of his chest and torso. Underneath was a white roll neck jumper, again so thin it could have been a vest.

His cold blue eyes looked at me in wonder, then he shook his head slowly as though lost for words.

"Hello, Ted," I said to break the silence.

"Dai."

"You wanted to see me."

This seemed to confuse him for a second and I could see why. Both 'yes' and 'no' would be equally appropriate here. Instead, he wrong-footed me and said something that left me lost for words.

"I trusted you."

I found myself swallowing. Was the hurt in his tone for real? Donlevy wasn't a psychopath like Rettner, whose version of truth was malleable, to be fashioned into whatever weapon was appropriate for the moment. He wasn't known for telling lies, rather he was famed for his bluntness. He'd stitch you up, but it would be with facts and logic.

"Hey, none of this was my fault," I managed when I'd got over my surprise.

"You were in charge."

"I was the janitor."

"You were more than that, you were the representative of the university."

"I unlocked in the morning and locked away at night. I hung around in case they couldn't work the coffee machine, or whatever. That was the deal."

Donlevy put his hands on the desk, one over the other. He looked magisterial but for once there was something squirrelly about his eyes. "We needed a university representative and you seemed confident you could handle it."

Yup, distance. He was drawing up his skirts and stepping back, just like Rettner. I was being sketched into the frame for the whole damned mess.

"Not so fast! You made it clear my job was on the line if I didn't do this." I must have said this very loud because the continuous tapping of Ms Murdoch's keyboard, which up to now I hadn't even noticed, suddenly stopped.

"I don't recall anyone saying anything like that."

"Oh come on, Ted, you did this at the same meeting where you canned or clipped Bill, Awang and Lucas. The threat was implicit but crystal clear."

Donlevy wasn't one to argue the toss; it was beneath his dignity. If someone fought back, he switched. "You can't wiggle out of responsibility for what happened to..." he checked a sheet of paper on the desk, "...this poor chap Lamarck. What were you thinking taking him down into the MRI Unit?"

"Telly... Lamarck insisted I show him around before the demo tomorrow. He said it was part of the deal he made with *you*." OK, maybe that wasn't quite true but the only one who could support me on that was dead.

Sorry, Telly I thought.

"The demo the next day, supervised by qualified staff was the agreement. Nothing about a preview."

"He said it was a deal breaker. That he would complain. You told me to make sure things ran smoothly. I was using my initiative." I was getting loud again. Ms Murdoch still hadn't resumed typing.

Donlevy shook his head. "You're forcing me to spell this out, Dai. Against explicit Health and Safety protocols, you took someone into the high field environment and they died."

The jolt of pure guilt made me angry. "I didn't chuck that cylinder. I didn't kill him!" I really was shouting now. Fuck Murdoch and her typing!

"The fact is, if you hadn't let Lamarck in, he wouldn't have died." As I had gotten louder Donlevy had gotten quieter; the clever thing to do. I was surrounded by bastards.

He pressed on, into my guilty silence. "Aside from this terrible tragedy, there's all this." He reached down into his backpack or whatever he had behind the desk and brought out some newspapers which he dumped onto the desk. "The publicity has been awful; the university is a laughing stock because of your conference."

"*My* conference. *You* organised the damned thing. It's *your* mess." The red mist was really descending now (perhaps in a futile attempt to hide my own guilt).

Again, the switch. "Not to mention the £25,000 worth of cryogens that went up in the air."

"Money, that's all you care about." I knew it wasn't, but I was in full guilty teenager mode by now. "I'll pay that all back, don't you worry."

His barb about my responsibility for Telly's death had struck home and it was steadily working its way deeper into my gut. I stood up and slammed by palm flat on the desk. "You'll have the cheque by tomorrow."

I turned and stalked out.

"The money's not... come back, we haven't finished."

Roiling in anger, I ignored what he was saying. As I passed Murdoch's desk she gave me a look of utter contempt.

My head was so full of steam I didn't even know where I was going. By the time the red mist lifted and the pain in my shoulder subsided from all the gesticulating I'd been doing, I found myself approaching the Kelvingrove art gallery. I'd travelled almost two kilometres fuelled by anger and guilt. I turned and headed east and up the hill to Park Circus.

I lived in a long terrace of Georgian townhouses converted to flats. As usual the whole place looked deserted and I wondered once again what my neighbours actually did with their time. It wasn't as if all the apartments were residential. Some on the lower floors were offices for lawyers or the headquarters of smaller national bodies. One was an art gallery. All of them the sorts of places that benefitted from one big display room for effect, backed up by a few dinky offices in the back.

I made my way up the short flight of stairs to the main entrance with heavy, plonking feet. I loved my flat but I couldn't afford to keep living here if I didn't have a job. I began to wonder if my anger with Donlevy had been manufactured by my unconscious, an excuse to get out before he could fire me.

Jesus! Sally and her Jungian fixation was getting to me.

I let myself in with the spare keys from my drawer. Another heavy envelope lay on the mat, a copy of the missive from the university I'd found on my desk. There were also handwritten notes from Sally and Mo, wondering what had happened to me, which had been rendered redundant by subsequent events.

After all the angry striding around, the skin over my shoulder had started to burn and the bones had started to ache. I chugged back a couple of paracetamol and poured myself a generous whisky. I pulled an armchair over to the window, covered the firm back in some cushions then gingerly sat down.

That skeletal Gothic tower, the Victorian confection, now looked like a finger of judgement pointing up at the sky, telling me to make my peace with God.

Fat chance of that. Some time or other I had to go back to Donlevy. As with any modern public institution, even a Dean, never mind a department head like Donlevy, couldn't just sack people. There was a process and it could be long and messy, especially if you had a good lawyer or the union were keen to support you. Even so, if there was good enough evidence of your incompetence/ recklessness/ moral turpitude then sooner or later you'd had your chips.

I'd brought the university into disrepute but not deliberately. In a sense Donlevy and Rettner, the Gruesome Twosome, had done that themselves by being so desperate to take money from the parapsychs. That was a point I could wield like a weapon; maybe not enough to stop me losing my job but maybe enough to get some sort of settlement.

Letting Telly in to see the magnetic hippo was a clear breach of health and safety but was it a sackable offence? I couldn't say for sure but I had the feeling you could never be sacked for a one-off. You had to be given a warning first not to do whatever it was again. I had no intention of ever going near the hippo as long as I lived, so that wouldn't be a problem.

It was just possible I could get out of this. My reputation would be shot but that had hardly occupied the high ground to begin with.

Perhaps of more import was the matter of whether my life was in danger. I'd wanted some comfort, even just a cuddle, after my ordeal and that's why I'd suggested Sally come over at six. But suppose she was the murderer? The police were certainly interested and I could see their point of view. Price and Telly were her ex-lovers and that was a pretty strong link.

Perhaps she had been lying. Perhaps they'd both chucked her and she'd wanted revenge. I tried to remember what Telly had said about her. Did he give any indication that he'd been the one to end it? I racked my brains. He'd seemed well-disposed to her, which suggested that might be true.

Price's attitude to her had been more ambiguous. Although he desired her he hadn't seemed to like her, but, then again, he hadn't seemed to like anyone.

Did Sally have some kind of Black Widow deal going on? Did she hate men? Sex with her did seem more like hate-making than love-making.

But she *had* shown signs of affection; she seemed to be genuinely concerned about me. Was that a feint, something to lure me into a false sense of security?

I took another sip. Was there anyone else who might be in the frame?

Maude, maybe, as she seemed so set on making me a suspect. But then I remembered the video the cops had shown me, the one of the shadowy figure emerging from the back door of the magnet room. The CCTV camera had been a long way away and pretty crap to begin with so there was little in the way of detail. You couldn't even tell if it was a man or a woman, but could it have been the matronly figure of Maude? Hadn't it moved too quickly for that?

Without doubt the figure could have been Sally. For that matter it could have been Sam Murray or Andy Lister. Both clearly didn't like Price but I hadn't noticed any animosity to Telly at the vigil at the swimming baths. Assuming they'd turned off the motion sensors, any of the three could have pushed Price into the swimming baths.

Or had Telly done that, out of jealousy, and it had nothing to do with the killings?

Or was there more than one murderer? Had Price been killed by a random stranger while he was crossing the Park? In which case who had killed Telly?

But, except for Price, everyone seemed to like him. With Price already dead that left only the Black Widow theory.

By now my 'heid was burling' (*Scottish phrase: my head was spinning*). On balance, maybe I should phone Sally and call our meeting off rather than set myself up as victim number three.

~~~

But, of course, I didn't and I realised a kind of strange inversion had taken place. Sally had been attracted to me because she thought I might be a murderer. I'd found this perverse but had been happy to let her continue under this delusion. Not many single men would turn down an attractive woman throwing themselves at them. Not many married ones either.

Now she was the suspect, at least in my book. If she was killing her ex-lovers then I was well and truly in the firing line. I should double lock and bolt the door, turn off the lights and hunker down behind the sofa as if nobody was home.

Instead, I washed and shaved and put on some cologne. Although it was a painful process, I dressed in my loosest fitting clothes and put on my outdoor shoes (no man is ever going to look attractive if he greets a woman at his door while he's wearing carpet slippers).

I kept telling myself that I didn't think she'd done it but deep down inside I wasn't so sure. I thought of hiding a knife somewhere in the lounge or bedroom, just in case, but that was too weak and paranoid even for me.

Nevertheless, I jumped when the doorbell rang. All aflutter like a Victorian maiden, I went to open it.

She was dressed in a white raincoat over a bright red shirt and blue skirt. She had a bottle of wine in one hand and a bunch of flowers in the other. A line from an old Meatloaf song came back to me: *Would you offer your throat to the wolf with the red roses?*

"For me, you shouldn't have."

"Flowers for an invalid; it's the done thing." She gave me a quick look up and down. "But you don't look too ailing to me."

I stood aside to let her in. "What were you expecting?"

"When you said your shoulder was a 'bit banged up' I assumed that was heroic understatement. I thought you'd be in plaster and bandages."

"Bruised and cut, and there are bandages too."

She took a seat on the sofa and I sat by her. "So why did they keep you in hospital?"

"I passed out and they thought it might be a head injury."

"You fainted?"

I didn't much like that. Men don't faint. I opened my mouth to argue but remembered something about how real men never apologised, never explained. I managed to change it to: "Do you want a drink?"

She stood up. "I'll get it. Whisky or wine?"

"What wine did you bring?"

"A fortifying red, which is just what you need. Don't want you fainting on me." And with that she was gone, by now aware where my tiny kitchen was and where she could find a corkscrew.

Soon we were drinking a wine so full-bodied I was tempted to take a knife and fork to it. I relaxed back into the pillows of the sofa and let her interrogate me. Unlike with the cops, I only had to go through the story once.

I ended it with the superconducting quench. She'd been sitting forward, intent on my every word. "Christ, that's surreal."

And, if you didn't know about these things, it was. Her surprise seemed genuine.

Her lips, red with lipstick, curled as she thought it all through. "How come the cylinder hit you?"

"I was in the way."

"You're assuming the target was Telly."

"Well, yeah, second conference attendee in three days. It's obvious, isn't it?"

"Is it? Do you have any enemies?"

The cops had worried away at this a little and I gave the same answer. "I can't claim to be well-liked but nobody wants me dead." Even as I said this I thought of Logan. He'd flunked out of his degree because of me, no matter how much in the right I'd been. Even so, he was such a drippy little wanker I couldn't see him doing anything about it, except maybe letting it all out in a green-coloured diatribe posted anonymously on the web.

Now that I'd set out on this train of thought, memories of other students came back to me. I'd pissed off quite a few over the years but, if they didn't get their degree, or didn't get as good a one as they'd wished, that was always down to them and the work they did or didn't do. Obviously, students, like people generally, often blame others for their faults but if revenge for that was at all common, then the streets would run red with the blood of academics.

Then again, Logan had access to the department. The MRI had been going for nearly a decade and generations of workers had lost their keys and fobs. Even if Logan hadn't managed to get hold of any of these, he could have jemmied his way in. The coppers hadn't mentioned the door being forced but then they seemed under no compunction to tell me a damned thing they didn't have to.

Mind you, if a door had been jemmied, that might explain why they had only half-heartedly considered me a suspect. Come to think of it, how had the fire brigade got in after I'd passed out? Firefighters in my experience aren't shy and retiring chaps. If they had to get somewhere in an emergency, they just banged in any locked doors that got in the way.

"You've gone quiet," Sally said.

"Er... yeah. Just thinking. But no, Price getting killed as well, it has to be a serial killer picking off the nu... other attendees. Haven't the police even considered that someone like you might be a target rather than a suspect?"

"A bit, but without much conviction. I mean it's not like they could protect all the nutters, as you keep trying hard not to call them. That would take too many coppers. Would they field such manpower to protect a group of people on the fringes? It's not like we're kids or pregnant women or twinkly old-age pensioners. The police basically just told me to take care."

"Then what are you doing here with me?"

"We've been through this before. Anyway, I'm going off the idea that you're guilty, despite what your dreams keep telling you."

"Despite what *you* say my dreams keep telling me."

"Whatever." She put her wine down. "Now let's take a look at your poor likkle shoulder."

"My bandages need changing anyway; the hospital gave me plenty to take home with me. I can't reach so maybe you could do the necessary."

"Oh, absolutely. Can't get enough of that sort of thing."

Judging by the eager look on her face she wasn't kidding. I struggled out of my shirt and turned so she could get a good view of my back. She gently pulled off the tape that held the bandage in place and then I felt her lean in and her breath played across my back.

"Not bad! The metal staples they've put in are a nice contrast to the black and purple of the bruise."

"Fuck off!"

"You don't mean that. One...two..." She counted off my metal stitches, coming to a total of twelve. "You know, the wound looks a bit weepy. You'd be best to keep it open to the air, overnight at least. Mmmm, that presents a problem."

"What's that?"

"How are we going to have sex?"

I almost, almost, demurred but, of course, in the end I didn't. Instead, my infirmity ensured we had to take a different position so at least she couldn't ride me like the Pony Express.

It was almost like making love.

CHAPTER FIFTEEN

Madness is a special form of the spirit and clings to all teachings and philosophies, but even more to daily life, since life itself is full of craziness and at bottom utterly illogical. Man strives toward reason only so that he can make rules for himself. Life itself has no rules. That is its mystery and its unknown law. What you call knowledge is an attempt to impose something comprehensible on life.
Carl Jung

The blindfold is tugged from my eyes. The figure is large, shadowy and hulking over me like an oak tree over a fawn. It holds a hand like a spade out to me. Nestling in the palm is a bar of chocolate.

I've been fooled before but I'm only six years old. Concentration is still only wisp-like, easily dispelled. Before I know it, I've taken a bite and am enjoying the taste. By the time I've finished the first square, and have eyes for anything other than the chocolate, I find he's gone. I spin round but all I can see is hedge and grass and sky.

What a hedge, though. It towers over me like a canyon, its sides so densely packed with leaves it's just as impenetrable. Green is everywhere except the narrow strip of blue above.

I know for a fact he won't come back. I feel the wetness of tears on my cheek and my breath catches so I can't draw breath. But then my lungs suddenly find purchase on the air and I suck it greedily in before I scream in despair.

My little legs start moving. I'm at a dead end so have only one way to go. I quickly cover the short distance to the other end where there are two choices. I stumble, wailing down the left-hand turn.

Turning after turning presents itself and I choose my path without rhyme or reason.

A flicker of movement catches my eye. A crow hovers above me looking down. I can hardly make out its black eyes in the darkness of its feathers.

"Hasn't got a clue," it says.

It dives at me, trying to peck at my eye but I cover my face with my arms. I feel its beating wings like breath on my skin.

I veer around another corner and the crow is lost to view. I keep looking for it, scanning the sky, swiftly, jerkily, almost like a bird myself.

There is nothing to help me judge my direction, not that it matters. This maze is full of endless turns and no fixed point will help me.

I come to a dead end. Is it the same one? I'm breathless from my wailing and I feel like falling to my knees.

If I wait, will they come for me, a weak little part of me wants to know.

Of course they won't. They've demonstrated their indifference, heartlessly, time after time.

No longer wailing, just sniffling, I wipe my eyes then walk over to the hedge. I grasp handfuls of leaves and stems and pull as hard as I can with my little muscles. My hands slip before the twigs break and I'm left with just a few leaves and with palms and fingers covered in green.

I lose my temper, clawing and pulling at the hedge, feeling the hard wooden stems cutting my skin.

"Cathartic temper tantrum. How typical!"

I look up and now a thrush is hovering above me. It's more feminine than the crow but no less hateful.

I take a deep breath. This time I deal with the hedge one twig at a time, twisting each back and forth until it parts. It's work that hurts my cut hands, and it takes me a long time but finally I have a pile of leaves and twigs. Now I'll know if I'm coming back to the same place.

"Aha," says the thrush. "System at last. Heuristic. Transcendence of anxiety and dysphoria."

I'm off again. Without a guide all I can do is try to sense which of the endless turns is the right way. I come to many dead ends but none have the pile of leaves.

"Persistence." The crow is back. I dart down the next turn to the right and the crow is gone again.

Dimly, a dreadful thought creeps into my mind. Throughout I'd assumed there was a way out. I'd felt it with such certainty, but that's gone now, leaving only an abyss. I feel like the roadrunner just after he's run off a cliff. I look down stupidly and see only void.

I shit myself.

"Has he given up?" The thrush is back above me.

I pull down my trousers, reach in for the hard little turd and hurl it at the bird. It strikes its wing and the bird comes fluttering down in a messy spiral. It hits the ground on its back.

"Simian, atavistic," it cries as I bring my foot smashing down on its skull.

~~~

"And did they really leave you in a maze?" asks Sally wonderingly. Her cold hand on my brow had brought me back from nightmare. In my stamping and kicking I'd sent all the bedsheets to the floor, leaving our nakedness exposed.

I'd told her about the dream. Although I hadn't talked about them before, to her credit she'd immediately realised that the birds were my parents.

"No, the maze is just a metaphor. Rat in a maze. Something to be experimented on."

She frowned. "Darkling thrush is straight out of Thomas Hardy. And the crow as well, both symbolising death, darkness and winter. I'm appalled but also impressed by the texture of your dream symbolism. So, what kind of stuff *did* they do to you?"

I pulled up a blanket from the floor and spread it over us. If I had to talk about this, then we should both be warm.

"Well, they were committed researchers in their way, but as far as I can tell they didn't have an original thought in their heads. They just seemed to want to replicate the experiments of others. Harmful ones only. You wouldn't believe what psychologists used to put kids through before all the ethics busybodies got involved."

"Like what?"

"Stuff like Albert and the rat, performed originally by good old John Watson a hundred years ago. The guy is buried in Connecticut, apparently. I have a pipe dream of flying to the States, loading up on a really high fibre breakfast and then taking a monumental dump on his grave."

"Not that you're bitter."

I shook my head. "Oh, I'm bitter. And you're not going to feel too happy about the Johnster either when I tell you what he got up to. He took a trusting little toddler called Albert who, being young, had no fear of rats. Watson would show him a live rat and then made a deafening noise so the kid was startled and shocked. Kept doing it until the kid associated the fear with the rat and became completely phobic about them. Not only that, but the conditioning extended to anything white and fluffy. Fucked the kid up across a much wider spectrum. When the kid saw Father Christmas with his big white beard, he literally shat his pants."

"OK, I see your point, this Watson guy isn't winning me over. What happened to little Albert?"

"The kid died."

Sally's hands came up to her mouth. "Oh, my God!"

"In fairness, it was hydrocephalus, an undiagnosed build-up of water in the ventricles of his brain, that did for little Albert when the tyke was only six."

"And did anything useful come out of the kid's suffering? Trying to look on the bright side here."

"No, for a start hydrocephalus in the young can be associated with mental retardation so that might have affected the results. Maybe a more *compos mentis* kid might have been smart enough not to make the association between the noise and the rat. Not to mention that Watson's extensive study had a sample size of only one, namely poor little Albert. That wouldn't cut much ice nowadays."

"What happened to Watson? I suppose it's too much to hope he was bitten by a rabid rat and died in agony."

"You're confusing this world with Disneyland. Watson's still thought of as a pioneer of psychology in the sense that he considered psychology to be scientifically observable, which gave carte blanche to my psychopathic parents."

"OK, but your parents didn't do the rat thing with you?"

"Nope, they did it with milk."

We'd both been lying there looking up at the ceiling but now she turned her head to look at me and out of the corner of my eye I could see a faint smile. "You don't have a phobia, do you?" I asked.

"Well, I'm not great on heights."

"Can you walk up a flight of stairs without clinging to the handrail?"

"Not if the stairs were on the side of a cliff."

"That sounds more like a sensible fear of heights. A rational fear if you like. A phobia on the other hand is an irrational fear. It's visceral. I suppose from your Jungian point of view, the actions of my parents excited an archetype, something primitive and fearful, something responsible for flight rather than fight."

"So, like, milk gives you an upset stomach?"

I breathed out, more angrily than I had intended. "I'm not lactose intolerant. I can eat cheese because it doesn't look or taste or smell like milk. I can eat custard even though it's almost all milk."

"So, it really is purely psychological? You're a psychologist so you know that, you understand that. Doesn't that make the problem... I don't know..."

"Go away?" I prompted.

"Yeah. Why doesn't it go away?"

"Wow, your grasp of Jung is just skin deep, isn't it?"

She sat up. "Calm down, sunshine!" The blanket had slipped down to almost-but-not-quite reveal a breast but even this couldn't divert me.

"For fuck's sake, Sally, you're always going on about unconscious influences not subject to rational control. My parents did their shitty little milk experiments when I was only three years old, just when connections are being make, when neural pathways are being laid down like crazy in the infant brain. They literally hard-wired a hatred of milk into me." I found I'd sat up and was pointing a finger angrily in her face.

"Okay, okay." She batted my finger aside. "I get it. I do. But... milk. I mean it's sort of innocuous after all."

I knew from long experience that people just didn't understand. How to explain the joy when opaque paper cartons replaced glass milk bottles. In the old days it had been a nightmare, milk bottles at every door proudly displaying their filthy contents as I made my way to school. It was like walking through an art gallery displaying only specimens of fresh shit.

And even when I got to school, being herded into a room at break to drink our free bottle of milk (I may have many reservations about 'Margaret Thatcher—milk snatcher' as the tabloids called her, but at least she did away with that obscene practice). Other kids soon worked out I had a problem as I had to stand there, pretending to drink, my eyes firmly shut. Naturally they'd grab me, prise my eyes open and force me to watch the milk being drunk, then let go and dash out of range of my uncontrollable vomiting.

No point telling Sally. People take milk for granted, not really noticing it until it's not there when they want it. So:

"They didn't just do it with milk."

"What else?"

"Snakes."

"Well, that's a common fear. Anyway, you live in Glasgow. Not many black mambas around here."

Sure, I thought, but that's a rational response. Despite all her talk, Sally really didn't understand the power of the unconscious.

"Yeah, I'm making a fuss over nothing." I lay back down and turned away from her.

There were a few seconds of silence then: "Are you sulking?"

I said nothing.

"You wretch!"

"Fuck off!" I shouted.

And she did.

CHAPTER SIXTEEN

The pendulum of the mind oscillates between sense and nonsense, not between right and wrong.
Carl Jung

My shoulder was still hurting like hell the next morning and the flesh not covered by the bandage had turned an even deeper shade of purple, as the mirror revealed. I'd seen bruises before but not covering a whole shoulder blade. It was as if I was wearing a lurid scarf casually draped over one shoulder.

Even more alarming, I found I'd run out of coffee. Sally had used it for the final two cups last night but hadn't thought to tell me we'd run out.

Yes, she was definitely unsuitable. Never mind dismissing my phobias, never mind the perversity of her attraction to someone she thought was a murderer, but the coffee business clinched the deal.

I dressed as best I could and got ready to set off down to the nearest corner shop. I was closing the main door when I heard someone on the steps below me. I turned slowly as twisting my torso didn't help my shoulder. What I saw made me do a double-take and my heart jumped in my chest.

Before me was a giant bat with two sets of wings. The lower set extended to the ground and were jet black. Above them a second smaller set as purple as my bruise were coming out of the sides of the creature's head.

"Murderer!" the being shrieked.

I staggered back, banging the back of my head against my own front door.

Still struggling to make this damned thing out, I realised that instead of slit eyes, it had big hemispheres standing proud of its face. Below this was a little piggy nose and below that a thick expanse of skin broken only by a deep furrow under the nostrils. This led to lips as thick as sausages.

And all of it was black.

"Foul fiend, from hell's dark veil I spit at thee," roared the creature but its big lips didn't move.

I was looking at a mask!

I leaned forward to get a closer look. The lower wings were just a voluminous black cape draped over two outstretched arms. The upper wings I now saw were a bit wobbly and I realised they were plastic, sprouting out of the mask.

The figure took a step upward but I held my ground.

"May thy soul turn putrid and may maggots consume thy genitals. May thee never again know a single moment of peace."

The voice, though hard and strident, was a woman's and it was vaguely familiar.

"May thy hatred and shamelessness consume thee and may thy bowels be riven by the bloody flux."

"Maude," I said, "is that you?"

"Begone foul demon! Go back inside thy lair and never re-emerge."

"Is everything... what the fuck?" said a voice.

I looked up. Tariq, darkly handsome with a perfectly sculpted beard, my neighbour upstairs, was leaning out of his window. He looked as alarmed as I felt.

"It's OK, Tariq," I called up. "Everything's under control. This whole care in the community thing—it just isn't working."

Tariq seemed lost for words and who can blame him. Then again, it served the bastard right for all the wild parties he had. Parties he never invited me to.

"I'll call the police," he said like it was a threat.

"Knock yourself out, Tariq."

I turned back to the bat which, now my fear was residing, was starting to look more sad than scary. "I'd bugger off if I were you, Maude. You're making a fool of yourself."

For a second the bulbous eyes regarded me; for long enough that I could make out that the irises were actually holes so the wearer could see out.

Maude reached up and ripped off the mask. Now she really did look scary.

She took another step up towards me. There was nothing grand or reserved about her now. I wasn't psychic but I could feel the hatred radiating from her. "You murdering bastard," she said. "You'll pay for this, you filth-ridden vermin."

"Calm down for Christ's sake! I didn't kill anybody."

"I *saw* you."

"Oh, I'm definitely calling the police," I heard Tariq say above me. For a second, I contemplated arguing about the definition of *saw* and how, in Maude's case, it was more fluid than Tariq understood.

I was about to plead my innocence when Grand Old Maude brought her head right back, made a godawful hawking sound and then spat straight at me. Perhaps too ladylike to have ever learned to spit properly, it all went wrong, most of it dribbling down her front and over an expensive looking amulet hanging from her neck.

With that she turned imperiously, her arms still outstretched, strode down the steps and over to the entrance of the park.

"What was that all about?" Tariq was still there but I saw now that he had a phone in his hand, although he wasn't yet doing anything with it.

"I don't know where to start so, to be honest, I can't be bothered. But to summarise: Maude's a nutter. End of."

"She said you were a murderer."

"I refer to my previous answer. Tell me, Tariq, have you read any local papers or seen any local news on the TV recently?"

He looked up to scan the horizon in a lofty way. "Got my mind on more global issues, Dai."

"Yeah, well check some out. It's all there. You'll see I wasn't the murderer, but rather the victim of collateral damage."

"What are you talking about?"

"Tariq, I just can't be arsed to go into all this right now. Call the cops if you must but I'm off to buy some coffee."

~~~

Not only did I buy a jar of coffee but I also went to a coffee bar that overlooked the River Kelvin for something a bit fresher. Trying to shut out the sound of steam frothing up milk (puke!), I took my cup to a table as far from any of the other customers as possible and settled down for a good old brood.

What in God's name was I going to do now?

First up were job prospects. Clearly, I should be taking a charter flight to my union representative but the trouble was, the first thing they'd ask was if I'd actually been sacked and the truth was I didn't know. I'd stormed out of Donlevy's office before anything definitive had been said and before anything substantive could happen.

OK, so that meant I had to see Donlevy again but I just didn't feel up to it right now.

The next big problem was my personal life. The fact was I liked Sally and usually felt comfortable around her. She was funny and intelligent and had a certain direct charm which was disarming enough to stop people getting upset when she challenged them. Even the parapsychs seemed to tolerate her, indeed even respect her, although she was basically saying that all the spooky stuff was the product of their imaginations.

So, she had a lot going for her and yet I'd pushed her away.

On the other hand, she believed I was a murderer and this stimulated her sexually. Hardly a healthy basis for a relationship.

On the other, other hand did that make her any different from some of my previous girlfriends? From Imogen who believed that the government and royalty were lizard people, or Alice who was so OCD that even stepping on a crack on the pavement would make her double up with anxiety.

Looking back with the benefit of hindsight, when all the sexual furore had died down, I'd come to realise that part of their attraction for me had been their perverse psychology. In the case of poor Imogen, I'd come to realise that she'd been seduced in the same way that perhaps the parapsychs had: that they thought they had discovered a secret that nobody else knew about and that made them feel special. For people who usually felt insecure and innately inferior this could be a heady brew and not to be discarded lightly. If they did, they would just be ...normal.

Alice on the other hand had got her OCD when, as a young child on a bike, she had strayed out of her traffic lane and had been whacked by oncoming traffic. Traumatised, she'd spent the rest of her life staying in her metaphorical lane.

Perhaps I went for damaged women because they were the only ones who would put up with me.

Finally, to add my list of woes, there was the small matter of the double murders. Like most punters, at least those who didn't watch crime shows on TV and had been deluded into thinking they would make great detectives, I had no pretensions of discovering who the murderer was. That's what the police were for, after all. Though Philban and Kendrick were difficult to read, they seemed reasonably competent. When they'd taken me through the events with the magnetic hippo again and again (and again), trying to catch me out, it had soon become obvious they'd been listening closely, pouncing on any uncertainties or ambiguities like tigers on a tethered goat.

So I should leave it up to them to sort out, right?

Except I'd nearly been killed myself. Not only that but I'd got too close to Sally who was, if not quite the prime suspect, a person of interest who might be killing her ex-lovers.

And I was probably an ex-lover now as well. And I had done the rejecting.

What it all came down to was that perhaps I shouldn't just leave it up to the cops. I needed to carefully think this all through, if only for my own self-protection.

It had all really kicked off at the swimming baths. If we were to make the tentative assumption that it wasn't a demon from hell that had pushed Price head first into an empty pool, then who could it have been? Poor old Telly would be a suspect, jealous ex-lover that he might have been, but of course he'd been the second victim. The only other people who had been there were me, Sally, Maude, Loris, Sam Murray and Andy Lister.

Whoever had shoved Price had known enough to disable the motion sensors and whatever else the parapsychs had in their bag of tricks. Murray and Lister had seemed to know their stuff so it could have been one of them but what might their motive have been? Professional jealousy, perhaps?

Sally might have been smart enough, but she'd been on the same side of the pool with me and I'd have known if she'd moved.

Did Maude know how to work the equipment? Somehow it didn't sound likely.

As for poor old Loris, could a depressive who ineffectually flapped about kill a robust man like Price? Would she have been smart enough to figure out how to kill Telly using magnetism?

Both Sally and Maude had pretty much accused me of being the murderer. Leaving aside Sally's crap-for-brains notion that I was being worked like a puppet by my unconscious, this could be classic diversionary tactics, a red herring to send the sniffer dogs of Strathclyde police on a wild goose chase.

Which brought us to who killed Telly. Professional jealousy might be a motive for the first killing but I didn't get the sense that Telly had been such a big wheel in the parapsych roadshow.

The only one who might have a motive was Black Widow Sally. Yup, I could see why the cops were interested in her.

Not only did that resolve the third problem but it sorted out my second problem with personal relationships as well. I had to avoid her like the plague.

That only left my first problem. Did I still have a job?

I got my new phone out and went to dial Donlevy, bracing myself for his secretary's icy response when she realised it was me who was calling.

But instead, somehow, I dialled Mo's number and we agreed to meet in the Bon.

After all, I needed to impress him with my sleuthing skills.

CHAPTER SEVENTEEN

The difference between a good life and a bad life is how well you walk through the fire.
Carl Jung

I emerged smoothly and easily from sleep. That seemed odd. It had been days since I awoke naturally, neither scared out of sleep by nightmare, nor pulled out by Sally shaking my shoulder.

It was almost blissful, but for the pain and stiffness which seemed even worse than yesterday.

I lay there, just managing to keep away the darker thoughts. I always buy high-quality Egyptian cotton sheets and today their smoothness and comfort were balm to my weary, battered body and soul.

But, with the full return of consciousness the dark clouds came rolling in. One way or another, I needed to confront Donlevy and receive either a verbal kicking or my P45. Obviously, I needed to talk to my union rep as well.

The faint mental calls for a reviving coffee became more insistent and I pulled the sheets off and levered myself out of bed. The hospital had given me painkillers and they'd worked well. Only twice had I been brought awake by the discomfort in my shoulder. The extinguisher had only struck me a glancing blow but the bruising and swelling would take weeks to subside and I'd be left with a scar.

Not having any female company, I was back in my jammies. I pulled the slippers from where I'd surreptitiously kicked them under the bed when Sally and I had staggered in here the first time, clawing at each other.

Jammies and slippers: hardly redolent of Don Juan but it was nice to be back to adult comforts. After all that had happened in the last week, a quiet life of bachelorhood didn't seem quite so bad after all.

The slippers didn't have a back so I slapped my way into the kitchen and fired up the kettle. I grabbed a bowl and tipped out some muesli. I got a smoothie from the fridge (instead of milk, obviously) and poured it onto the cereal. As always, studded as it was with raisins, the stuff looked like cat litter sprinkled with rabbit droppings.

I checked the smoothie's contents. Guava, starfruit, kumquat and tamarind, ferfuxake! Where did this relentless search for novelty come from? And wouldn't the tamarind make it bitter?

I got a spoon from the cutlery draw and took an experimental taste. It was OK to begin with, smooth and ...er... fruity but then the bitterness came in as an aftertaste like the bill at the end of a wonderful meal. Then again, like said bill, the tamarind gave some context to the foregoing sweetness.

Standing there in my kitchen, a breakfast bowl in my hand and with only trivial thoughts to occupy my mind, I came as close to being as happy as I had in weeks.

By now the coffee was ready and I took it and the bowl of cereal into my stately lounge. I put them down on the coffee table next to the sofa. Then I hauled open the long curtains to let in the light of another Glasgow day. I went back to the sofa and sat down.

The first sip of coffee was like one of those flashbulbs in an old camera, searing an image of the blood vessels onto my retina.

I took a long slow blink and welcomed the world. Out of my window only a few clouds hung over the city. I could hear the birds chirping away in the park.

I felt the bottom of my pyjama trousers brush against the bare skin of my ankle. It felt weird and I reflected that, thanks to Sally, I hadn't worn my jammies in days.

I took another reviving sip of coffee and wondered what Sally was doing now. Should I give her a ring?

Don't be silly, another part of me warned.

Again, the pyjama bottom rubbed at my ankle. The skin seemed overly sensitive. Had I scraped it when I'd been knocked down next to the MRI?

It happened again and this time it didn't feel so much like a brush of cloth but rather a definite scrape. I lifted my foot and shook it then put it down.

My foot came down on what felt like a piece of rope. It writhed.

Then something bit me.

My lower leg shot up, as if a doctor had hit my knee with a reflex hammer. But it wasn't just my foot that came up. Something was hanging from beneath it.

I tried to focus on what seemed to be strip of greenish cloth. Was there a needle in it that had poked me?

Then the strip of cloth wriggled and I realised it was a snake.

A hundred-pound weight fell on my chest, kicking all the air from my lungs. The whole world telescoped away while the snake zoomed closer.

Time lost all meaning. I will never know how long I sat there, my foot in the air, the birds still twittering, the serpent with its fangs in my ankle. I had time to appreciate the zig-zag pattern down its grey-brown back.

Wasn't that a bad sign? some still semi-sentient part of me asked itself. Didn't that mean the snake was poisonous? Wasn't it nature's way of warning other creatures?

Who knows how long this nature debate might have gone on had I not realised the snake's jaws were moving, pulsing, trying to pump even more venom into my ankle.

It had taken a long time coming but now it was here, full-out panic hitting me like a freight train. In a frenzy I shook my leg, the long body of the snake whipping back and forth. I felt my first few mouthfuls of breakfast rising to once again meet the day.

I needed to get the snake off but I couldn't bring myself to touch it. I grabbed up my cereal bowl, its contents splattering across the room. I ran the rim of the bowl down my leg and against the serpent's jaws. I pushed hard but it held fast. I pushed again, this time putting all my strength into it. I felt my skin tear and the snake flopped down, making hardly a sound as it hit the carpet.

I jerked up my other leg so the snake couldn't get at it. Unbalancing, I flopped sideways onto the sofa, the impact sending a little cushion bouncing onto the floor.

Under it had been another snake. Suddenly revealed, it uncoiled like an obscene spring. Its evil little head opened to show its fangs.

I got my feet under me, pushing myself upright so I could step up onto the armrest. I launched myself as far out into the room as I could. I landed in a heap but scrabbled quickly up, spinning round, scanning for the snake that had bit me.

Blackness was edging in. After the breath had exploded out of my chest, I hadn't replaced it. Now I did in a long juddering inhalation.

Taking high absurd steps like a comic character in a cartoon stepping through a minefield, I got to the lounge doorway. To my left was a couple of metres of corridor leading to the door that would get me out of here. I took a step towards it then froze.

Coiled up in the corridor like turds from a healthy gut, lay two more snakes.

Once more my breath fled. The world started to spin and I grabbed the lounge doorknob to keep myself upright. Across from the lounge was a table with a bowl of potpourri and another for keys.

I grabbed the potpourri bowl and hurled it at the far snake. It missed but both snakes uncurled like magic and slithered away into the lounge.

The coast suddenly clear, I raced to the door, fumbling at the key, sure all the snakes were right behind me, aching to bury their fangs into my bare ankles.

I felt the key turn and I ripped open the flat door, staggered down the little communal corridor, and barged my way through the main door. Already out of balance, I lost my footing on the doorstep and tumbled down the stone steps.

The stone pavement at the bottom broke my fall. Winded, I lay on my back looking up at a spinning sky.

Tariq's face span into view. He was peering down at me.

"For fuck's sake, stop screaming!" he yelled.

Until then, I had no idea I had been.

CHAPTER EIGHTEEN

Man is the only creature with the power to control instinct by his own will, but he is also able to suppress, distort, and wound it... Supressed instincts can gain control of man; they can even destroy him.
Carl Jung

Philban and Kendrick did not look amused.

This time, I'd been put on a lower floor of the Death Star. The view wasn't so impressive. Not that the coppers paid much attention to that anyway. For them, interviewing patients in hospitals must have been as regular as taking a piss in the morning.

"A push into a swimming pool, two murders, an attack with...uh... snakes, a disturbed woman laying down a curse, and only one common denominator," Philban said.

Having established that anti-venom and antibiotics would not affect my rationality, and so they could question me to their hearts content, they weren't holding back. Apparently having all rationality flee from your horror-ravaged brain because of being bitten by a snake didn't count as a reason not to interview me. Nor did they seem put off by me checking for serpents under my hospital bed at crazily short intervals.

The educator in me was pleased that Philban even knew what a common denominator was, though I didn't appreciate it being applied to me. "How can you possibly put all this at my door? I'm a victim twice over."

"Yes, you've been attacked twice. But why? What have you done?"

"Nothing!"

"You're at the centre of this web, Younge. How can we stop this happening again if we don't know why someone's doing it?"

This made me feel suddenly faint. Could this sort of thing really happen again? It didn't bear thinking about. It would be the straw that broke the camel's psyche.

The person responsible for this last outrage couldn't have hit me harder. Snakes, my biggest fear.

Finally, I put two and two together.

"Sally," I said.

"Sally Vale?"

"Yes, I saw her the night before last and I told her I have a thing about snakes."

"A thing?"

"A phobia; a horror about the damned things."

"So, you think *she* did it?"

"Well, it would be a hell of a coincidence otherwise."

"Really?"

"You don't sound surprised. I mean surely you had her in the frame for the two murders. She's killing off her ex-lovers, and I'm one of those so she tried to murder me too"

Philban's brow creased and I realised that for the first time he was hesitating, not sure what to say. Behind him Kendrick had a definite smirk on his face.

"You see," Philban began, "what happened to you would be difficult to class as attempted murder. Not really. Actual Bodily Harm for sure but murder... not so much."

"Excuse me. Venomous snakes are dumped through my flat's letterbox and that's not attempted murder?"

"Adders," said Kendrick.

"That's right, venomous snakes."

"Yes," Philban said but there was reluctance in this agreement. "Except nobody's died from an adder bite in Scotland in over thirty-five years. It can be nasty, with bruising, sickness and a bit of diarrhoea, but otherwise..."

"But people *have* died from adder bites."

Philban held up his hand, palm flat, and wiggled it from side to side. "We talked to the doctors about that. Some medics take the view that those who die do so from anaphylactic shock, which is like an allergic reaction. Now, if someone knew you had an allergy to adder venom and they'd used snakes on you then we'd have them bang to rights. But you're not allergic are you, or you wouldn't be here and breathing. I mean, you look... fine."

"I don't feel *fine*."

"You do look it, apart from that bandage around your ankle. As murder attempts go, it was pretty shit, if you'll excuse my French."

I must have looked at them with such vast incomprehension that they both glanced away in embarrassment. Not that that lasted long; these were Glasgow hard men.

Philban looked back with his best unblinking stare. "In fact, even Grievous Bodily Harm is probably shooting a bit high. I mean, a bruise and a bit of diarrhoea? Actual Bodily Harm, yeah, but GBH, no."

"What's the penalty for that?"

"Three years maximum, usually quite a bit less."

"For what I'd been put through? Being disembowelled and made to eat their own intestines would be the only fit punishment for whoever did this. Look, officers, this has screwed up my whole life. You do realise I can never go back to my flat?"

"Why not? We've had the zoo people in. They've collected them all up."

"How many?"

Philban looked at Kendrick who furrowed his brow in concentration. "It was three, right?"

"Four, there were at least four of them. And those were only the ones I saw. Fuck knows how many more were coiled up elsewhere."

"The zoo people have been through your place with a fine-tooth comb."

"Oh, for Christ's sake!" I held my arms up in exasperation. "You know what those old flats are like. Holes everywhere. Did they look under the floorboards? Did they check out all the wall cavities?"

Philban just shrugged.

I couldn't believe I would never be able to set foot in my flat again.

Not that these plods had a hope of understanding how I felt.

"You're obviously very upset," said Philban, showing his complete mastery of the blindingly fucking obvious. "Maybe we should come back later."

"For what?" I shouted. Even Kendrick looked startled. "I don't know what's going on here. All that I know is that my life has turned to shit and I haven't done a damned thing to deserve it."

"You must have annoyed someone."

"I annoy everyone sooner or later, but nobody's ever tried to kill me before."

For a second Philban looked as if he was going to correct me but decided against it. "Think carefully, Mr Younge. Has anyone got it in for you?"

Life was too short to answer that one and, anyway, we'd wandered off the subject. "Never mind that, what about Sally Vale? Are you at least going to interview her?"

"Of course we're going to do that and, by the way, thanks for telling us how to do our job."

Not so long ago I might have been intimidated by his tone. "And that Maude woman. The one who put the curse on me, she's got to be in the frame too. Maybe she uses snakes in her weird ceremonies."

"Again, your advice is invaluable but, since you raise the subject, why did she put a curse on you?"

"She thought I'd killed Price. She and all the women seemed to have the hots for him."

"So she had feelings for him. Did he have feelings back?"

"Look, Detective Inspector, I don't know these people. Until a week ago I'd never met any of them. I mean, for what it's worth, Maude seems a bit matronly for the likes of Price who could have his pick. Sally would be more his speed, but then I have no idea about Price's preferences. Maybe he liked older women, maybe he wasn't fussy, maybe she enraptured him with a love philtre."

Philban's eyebrows rose in surprise.

"That was a joke, for God's sake," I said wearily.

~~~

After we'd spent another hour endlessly going over the same ground again and again like an OCD hamster on a treadmill, the cops left. I promised them that once the medics let me out, I'd inform them where they could find me. I told them I'd rent somewhere for now, there being plenty of spare flats as the students had gone home for the summer.

But before I started phoning up letting agencies I considered my position. One thing was becoming clear: I'd given the police more credit than they deserved. Nearly a week had gone by since Price had broken his bonds with Earth but they seemed nowhere nearer working out who'd done him in. Were they ever likely to solve any of this?

Mo came to visit me in the evening. He tried mightily to be solicitous but I could tell that deep down he found it all a little bit funny even though he knew how I felt about snakes.

That annoyed me, so I decided to mess with him a little. "Obviously I can't go back to my place, so I'll need you to pick some stuff up for me."

"Er... what are you talking about?"

"I can't ever go back home, but there's stuff there I still need. Clothes, laptop, mail that sort of thing."

"Just a second, white man. Why don't you just go back and stay in your own house, you big girl's blouse?"

"I've suffered a wrenching trauma. I mean I keep checking under this bed every ten minutes to make sure there are no snakes. I'm fucked up big time. Isn't this the sort of thing friends are for?"

"The reason you don't want to go back is because you're afraid they're still there, maybe coiled up in your smalls. And you want me to go rummaging through them instead?"

"You're not afraid of snakes."

Mo put his hands over his chest. "Yes, but I don't fucking like them."

"Anyway, the zoo people took a good look and reckon they're all gone."

"The zoo people? Who the fuck are they? Are they fully getting-adders-out-of-houses certified?"

Good questions.

"Look," he said, "why not get the pest controllers in? They could... I dunno... fumigate the place."

I shook my head. I'd already looked into this on my phone. "Believe it or not, adders are a protected species. Nobody is allowed to kill them."

I watched him think this through until he smiled grimly. "Sorry to say this, sunshine, but you sound well and truly fucked."

"Oh come on! Get one of those stick things with a claw at the end. The sort you can close with a trigger in the grip, like the ones they use for picking up litter. You could pluck out my clothes with that, at a distance."

"Out of striking distance, you mean? Meanwhile one of them has slithered up behind me and bit me in the arse. Come on, being bit by an adder, would you recommend it?" He pointed at my bandaged foot.

Truth to tell, my ankle hurt hardly at all now. As soon as the cops and ambulance people had turned up, one of the police had seen a snake and recognised it immediately as an adder. By the time I'd got to A&E, they'd had the anti-venom ready. Bite to remedy had been less than half an hour. The medics were keeping me in overnight for observation, but it seemed only a matter of form.

"Please," I said.

"Get... to... fuck!"

"Pretty please."

The sides of his mouth turned down and he put his hands on his hips, the picture of put-upon annoyance. "And where would I get one of those sticky things with a claw at the end?"

"Litter pickers, they're called and you can get them from Amazon for under a tenner." I'd already checked this. "Oh, and wear a stout pair of boots just in case."

He looked as if he wanted to hit me. "Stout boots don't go up to the thigh. They barely cover the ankle."

"Christ, adders aren't like cobras, they don't rear up before they strike." I said this with all the certainty I could muster though I actually had no idea if this was entirely true. The one on the couch had reared up a little bit.

Philban had brought my house keys. I picked them up and offered them to Mo. He called me all the names under the sun but took them.

There was a knock at the door. As soon as I saw who it was my scrotum tightened like it was in a vice. "Get her out of here!" I yelled.

"Don't be such a pussy!" said Sally, striding in. She had a posy of flowers that she thrust in my face.

I screamed like a banshee. Sally stepped back in alarm and I could hear rapid footsteps approaching down the corridor. A flustered nurse appeared.

"Snakes!" I screamed pointing a shaking finger at the flowers.

"Oh, come on!" said Sally, ripping away the flimsy wrapping paper and twisting the posy through all angles so we could see it was just flowers.

"Check her handbag!"

"For God's sake." Before I could stop her, she flicked open the catch of her handbag with one hand and tipped the contents onto the blanket over my lap. The vice cupping my genitals grasped even tighter.

Tissues, keys, lipstick, a purse, a phone and a little book tumbled onto the blanket.

But no snakes.

The nurse, a little out of breath from her running, looked at me quizzically. "Is everything all right here?"

"Yes, but…" I pointed a finger at Mo. "Don't you dare leave!"

He shrugged and the nurse, vaguely satisfied, disappeared.

"The cops cleared me," said Sally. "So calm down."

"Cleared you?"

"I had an alibi. CCTV in the corridor of my hotel showed I never left my room all night."

"You could have climbed out the window."

"I'm not on the ground floor and I'm not Tarzan. You need to take a deep breath, Dai. You're getting completely paranoid."

I pointed at my bandaged foot and my damaged shoulder, both of which spoke more eloquently than I could.

Sally grimaced, my point taken. "I didn't do it."

Ten out of ten for earnestness, but could I believe her?

"I mean, I know it looks bad. You tell me about your snake issue and next day... this. But then again, I bet you've told lots of other people.

"He's told me at least five times," said Mo. "Once he gets a drink in him and starts feeling sorry for himself."

"Besides which, look at the practicalities. I'm a stranger in Glasgow. How would I get hold of a bunch of snakes at such short notice?"

Mo nodded. "I've lived here all my life and I wouldn't know how to get them either. Can you get them from pet shops?"

I'd checked this and as far as I could tell from my manky little phone's access to the internet, you couldn't. Perhaps it had something to do with them being a protected species.

"Maybe you brought them up with you from England."

Sally snorted. "Oh, piss off!"

"Then who would do it?"

"It wasn't Maude either," said Sally. "She was so surprised when she heard what happened. Either that or she's a really good actor."

"Of course, she's a bleeding actor. She's a fucking medium who holds seances. That seance where she accused me of murder—that was Olivier level."

"That wasn't an act. She still thinks you're the killer."

"Isn't me in hospital with a snakebite hard evidence to the contrary?"

She shrugged. "Maybe you set the snakes on yourself."

Disgusted by the very thought, I looked away from them both and out the window. I wondered if the cops had the same suspicions. Surely my reaction, so redolent of a frightened little girl, would have been convincing?

Everything had spiralled out of control and I found myself in a world where I couldn't trust anyone and apparently nobody could trust me.

"Had any more dreams?" she asked, all innocence.

It could have gone either way, the toss of an emotional coin. I might have started shouting but instead I laughed, which rather surprised Mo. He looked from me to her.

"Dreams?" he asked.

Sally shrugged. "I've been winding him up a bit. He's been having some revealing dreams and I've been saying it shows he's the one who killed Larry."

"You weren't just winding me up, you really believed it."

"Maybe. Now you've been hit by a missile and bitten by a snake I've sort of abandoned that hypothesis. Look, I came here to make amends. You don't seem that ill so I guess you'll be out soon. I could come back to your place and look after you."

"My place is out, for now at least."

"He's worried they might not have found all the snakes," said Mo.

"Well, I'm in a big double room in a nice hotel and I've got it for another week because the police told me not to leave town. Come back and stay with me until you're better."

The less rational part of me had already noticed how nice she looked and the sweetness of her perfume. My rational mind was playing catch-up and figuring that if the police really thought she was a suspect, for the snake thing at least, they wouldn't have let her go so quickly.

Jung was right, in this instance at least. Some part of me, more archetypal, more primal, wanted to be with her. My intelligence was playing along, already trying to construct a rationale for a decision already taken at a more visceral level.

And so I agreed to stay with her when the hospital let me out.

However, before that happened, I still had to get the all-clear from the medics. After Mo and Sally had gone and while

I was waiting, to my considerable surprise Bill Steadman, the academic forced into early retirement by our esteemed Dean Rettner, rocked up. Though I had had little to hide from Mo and Sally, the same was not true of Bill. Being seen in hospital-issue jammies is never a good look and I pulled the bedsheets over me like an unwell elderly spinster being visited by the vicar.

"What are you doing here for God's sake?" I asked.

With the sallow skin of the heavy smoker, it was Bill who looked as if he should be in a hospital bed. He held a hand up in acknowledgement of the strangeness of this visit. "Sorry, Dai," he said, wafting a bunch of folders in his other hand, "this is business. Have to say, though, when I found out what happened to you, I did want to visit. More out of curiosity, to be honest." At this he looked a bit bashful, but I respected his honesty.

"And how did you find out? How did you even know I was here?"

Bill shrugged. "I went to your flat, or rather I got as close as the circus would allow and…"

"Circus?"

"Police, environmental health, even a big van from some zoo. Your whole block was cordoned off and your neighbours had all been turfed out into the street. You're not flavour of the month, by the way."

Apart from Tariq, I had only nodding acquaintances with my other neighbours in my converted townhouse. Their disapprobation wouldn't be the worst thing that had happened to me, but I didn't wish them ill. Could snakes climb stairs? It seemed unlikely.

Then I remembered the young guy called Simmons in the basement flat and felt bad for him. For an instant I had a vision of a multitude of snakes, roiling around each other like the strands of a rope, as they tumbled down the basement stairs.

I felt queasy. I also felt guilty and had to remind myself this wasn't my fault and, anyway, I had a lot more on my plate to worry about than the feelings of near-strangers.

"So, you talked to…?"

"A guy called Tariq," said Bill. "He told me what had happened. Again, he's not a fan of yours. Anyway, I asked a copper and he told me they'd brought you here. How are you, by the way?"

"Swell," I replied. "So, what's this business you want to talk to me about?"

He hesitated, perhaps trying to work out whether I was displaying heroism or sarcasm. "It's our case against the university. The union need our signatures before they'll proceed." With this he placed the papers gently on the bed.

I leafed through them listlessly. Wading through legalese was the last thing I felt like doing. "Can't this wait?"

Bill shook his head apologetically. "Our rep's going on leave, it's the summer after all. Says we need to set the wheels in motion now for getting union approval, so it's all teed up for when he comes back."

"Have Lucas and Awang signed?" I asked peevishly, looking for an excuse not to do anything.

Bill shrugged. "I'm seeing Lucas later and he's agreed to sign. Awang has disappeared off the face of the earth. Doesn't answer his phone and nobody at his flat is answering the door."

Another reminder I wasn't the only one with troubles. "Do you think he might have…?" I couldn't bring myself to say it.

Bill was made of sterner stuff. "Topped himself? Maybe. We'd have Rettner then." He must have realised how harsh that had sounded because he held up both hands. "Sorry," he said, "got carried away with my dislike of her and Donlevy. No, Awang's a nice chap but he strikes me as quite ineffectual. Can't seeing him managing to…"

He didn't finish, but he didn't need to.

The hell with it! "Got a pen?" I asked.

"Don't you want to read through it all first? I can wait." But even as he said this, he was getting a pen out of his jacket pocket.

"Where?" I asked and he pointed out where I was to put my moniker. I scrawled it out and gave him the pen back.

Bill still looked unhappy. "Look, I'm sorry about…"

What he was sorry for I was never to find out because just then a nurse and a doctor arrived and ushered him out. He gave me a wave and was gone.

CHAPTER NINETEEN

Knowing your own darkness is the best method for dealing with the darknesses of other people.
Carl Jung

Mo came back later to pick me up after the doctors had given me the all-clear.

Leaving the Death Star revealed an unwelcome slice of life. The hospital's maternity wards were near the back entrance to the hospital estate. Within the grounds of the hospital smoking was prohibited so, rain or shine, heavily pregnant women would waddle out through the gates in their dressing gowns, and light up to their heart's content. Mo and I regarded them bleakly as we drove past.

We headed north, diving down into the Clyde Tunnel, its green-tiled walls making it look like a giant's urinal. Emerging, we climbed up to the arc of an overpass in a broad sweep and headed towards the university on the Clydeside Expressway. To my right the Science Centre looked like a giant robotic mussel emerging from the sand, its titanium cladding glinting in the sun. Titanium was a big feature in this part of town. Ahead, the two conference halls, one shaped like an armadillo, the other a flying saucer, all added to the futuristic look of the place. The Transport Museum, its large metal roof folded into spiky peaks and troughs like an electrocardiogram just added to the sense of temporal dislocation.

"Are you sure about this?" asked Mo.

"Why not?"

"Because not so long ago you reckoned she was the killer. And now you're going to bed down with her!"

"You think she did the snakes thing?"

Mo was a conscientious driver and he kept his eyes on the road. "No, that does seem unlikely, but have you thought that maybe the snakes and the murders are two entirely different things, done by different people?"

"Some coincidence, don't you think? I mean, two people having it in for me at once."

"I don't think you should underestimate the number of people who might have it in for you. Sometimes I think you have no idea of how annoying you can be. Anyway, weren't you just collateral damage with your magnetic hippo? That Telly chap was the target. Sally's still a suspect for that and for the Price killing."

"Thanks for that, I mean about how unloved I am. But also, do you really buy this Black Widow theory? Doesn't that only make sense if the widow is driven by bitterness. Does Sally strike you as bitter? Isn't she more the love-'em-and-leave-'em sort?"

"Maybe Price and Lamarck treated her badly and she's just getting her own back."

"I wouldn't put anything by that Price prick, but Telly seemed pretty decent."

"Seemed? You only met those people a few days ago. For a cynic you can be awfully naive. You don't know anything about any of them."

"Whatever! *I* haven't treated her badly."

"You kicked her out of your flat. That must have hurt."

But I didn't believe it, at least the bit about her having it in for me. The jury was still out about Price and Telly. Even if it was true, I realised I still liked her. For me, a martyr to chronic emotional constipation, that's saying a lot.

We pulled up by a large Scottish baronial mansion on Great Western Road. Once this might have belonged to a wealthy merchant who'd made a fortune out of tobacco and slaves but now it was a hotel. It stood on a grassy rise above the road, with a circular drive that led up to the grand front door.

I got out of the car. My snake-bit foot had gone to sleep on the short drive and I had to wiggle it a bit before it could take my weight. Hanging onto the side of the door I leaned back in so Mo couldn't avoid my eyes.

"Clothes, laptop, toiletries, remember!"

Mo shook his head. "Order new ones from Amazon!"

"Come on!"

Mo groaned in exasperation. "I'll order a litter picker or whatever that thing is. And I'll wait for a very bright day so I can see what I'm doing, then, and only then, I might go fishing in your flat. In the meantime, order new clothes online. Believe me, your charm isn't robust enough to last without a decent change of clothes every day."

I watched his car pull away and circle down to the busy road. Follow that and it took you out of the city and to Loch Lomond. Normally the thought of its bonny banks might lift my heart but now they were just grass and undergrowth hiding legions of serpents.

Whoever had done the thing with the adders had messed me up, perhaps for life. The coppers had better find whoever did it, because if I got to them first then I really might become a murderer.

And that's when, for the first time, I contemplated trying to beat the cops to the punch. To exact a little punishment of my own before the justice system got its toothless grip on the criminal.

Through the main door, I found myself in a massive oak-panelled hall. To my left a dark wood and rather grand staircase curved up to the first floor. From the outside the house looked big but only now could I appreciate its scale. The hall was large enough to hold a formal ball and I could imagine the tobacco barons waltzing away into the small hours while families, ten to a single room in Gorbals tenements, coughed and shat themselves to death from TB and cholera.

That Scotland had never had a revolution was still a wonder to me.

I hobbled up to the reception desk where a receptionist in white shirt and tartan skirt was already beaming at me. The Americans must love this place when they came back looking for their Lowland roots.

"Dr Younge to see Ms Vale," I said.

"Of course." She picked up a phone and poked out a number. She was young and pretty with red hair; it was no hardship waiting while she made the call.

"Hello, it's Morag at reception." Her soft Highland tones were rather fetching. "There's a Dr Younge to see you." She waited as Sally said something on the other end of the line. "Would you like me to show him up? Are you sure?"

She put the phone down and looked up at me. "She'll be right down."

"Thanks." I turned and wandered over to a large armchair covered, inevitably, in tastefully subdued tartan material. Around the walls were the equally inevitable pictures of mountains and lochs and stags. It could all have come across as way too ersatz and cheesy but everything looked as though it had been on the planet at least twice as long as me. The effect was classy but just this side of fusty.

It must have cost Sally a pretty penny.

She appeared at the top of the stairs. She'd changed her clothes since the hospital and was wearing a cream shirt and dark trousers that fitted her well. She took the stairs as if she'd been up and down them every day of her life.

She stopped at the desk. "Spare key please, Morag. Dr Younge will be staying with me."

Morag's little smile lasted just long enough to show a couple of dimples in her cheeks. Sally too had the remnants of a complicit smile as she turned to me and watched me fill in the registration form.

When I finished, she took my hand and without a word we mounted the stairs.

"How's the foot?"

"A bit swollen but hardly sore at all. Must be the painkillers."

"And the shoulder?"

"Still achy and I won't be sleeping on that side for a while, but mustn't grumble."

"Really? I thought that was all you did."

"Making fun of the infirm. Should have seen that coming."

By now we had gone down a short corridor, the carpet made of yet more subdued tartan. We came to a large oak door and she waved her key card across an almost hidden plate.

The door clicked and we were in a bedroom fit for a tobacco baron.

"Best room in the house?" I asked.

"Dunno, haven't been in the others. Bit of all right though."

And it was. The bed was big enough for a rugby team and their wives. You could have built a castle with all the pillows arrayed across it.

Sally must have seen what I was looking at. "I don't know why they do that in flash hotels," she said. "The cleaning staff must spend all their time arranging all those pillows on the bed, only for me to spend all my time pulling them off."

"Opulence, thy name is cushion."

"The bathroom, which is more like a cavern, is through that door. You could drown a heifer in the bath and you could stock a market stall with all the towels."

Before I could stop myself, I pulled her round to face me.

"So, we're OK?"

She stepped back slightly, as though to get a better overall view. "'OK' might be shooting a little high. 'Reached an accommodation' is closer."

"I was panicked, angry. Said some things I shouldn't."

She shook her head smiling. "If you think this sudden admission of fault is going to melt my heart then you can go whistle, sunshine."

"But seriously, you don't think I'm a killer, do you?"

She tilted her head from side to side, considering. "It's looking less likely."

"Does that mean you find me less attractive?"

She flicked a couple of fingers across the tip of my nose. Not gently either.

"Vulnerability and neediness don't work with me, mate. No more of that sort of stuff!"

"Fair enough," and I sat down on the wonderfully yielding bed. "So, are we going to fuck, or what?"

~~~

With my injuries it turned out to be more 'or what?' but we both got there in the end. Afterwards, lying beside her, my good arm under her neck, it felt nice.

So nice, I could have stayed there forever. Mind you, this was only after I'd had a sneaky peak in the wardrobe when she'd gone to the bathroom. I made sure there was no viperarium there or under the bed.

"Tell me, what's in your stars, Professor Dai?"

"Very droll. Who's good on astrology in your lot?"

"Well, Loris is pretty much the only one who holds to the old astrological ways *in my lot*, as you put it. Astrology is something that has fallen out of favour even among those who study the paranormal."

"Why?"

"I'm not sure. Everything has a fashion. I suppose that now people realise that the constellations aren't made up of clumps of stars in proximity to each other. It just looks from our viewpoint that they're close together even though some may be tens of thousands of light years further away than others. It makes it hard to believe that such a scattered bunch of stars in, say, Sagittarius sends out some strange beam of energy which makes people born 'under' it, want to travel. Or that people born under Taurus have quiet resolve."

"So, there is some sense *in your lot* after all? That's reassuring."

"I'll ignore that. Anyway, were you deflecting? You still haven't answered my question."

"No, I'll tell you what I'm going to do. I'm going to come off the bench. I'd kind of assumed the coppers knew what they were doing but, as far as I can tell, they've got nowhere, so it's time I did their job for them. I mean, there were only eight of us at the swimming pool and the first murder attempt. And two of them have since been killed. Plus, I've seen attacked twice so I must be off their suspect list. That leaves Loris, Maude, Murray, Lister and you, no disrespect."

"Some taken. Remember I had as alibi for your last 'attack' so I'm not as interesting to the cops as I was."

I held up a warning finger. "Word to the wise: don't go dissing what happened with the serpents. I'm not in the mood. Anyway, if you're in the clear, that leaves only four. It's gotta be Maude, after that display she put on outside my front door. Barking!"

"Not that you're jumping to conclusions. I mean, if you're going to be an ersatz copper, there's the whole boring business of means, motive and opportunity."

"For Maude? Professional jealousy must be a possibility, as far as Price is concerned. Plus, maybe sexual. Did she have 'things' with Telly and Price?"

"Doubt it. She's a bit old and not in their league when it comes to looks. Just like the difference between you and me. Anyway, why would she attack you so savagely?"

I turned my head on the pillow and caught her quick smile. "Seriously, I have a complete sense of humour failure when it comes to the snakes."

"Sorry!" She pecked me on the cheek like that would make it all better. "I can see why she might denounce you at the seance and outside your flat, to throw suspicion on you and away from her. But why shove snakes through your letterbox? Doesn't that seem like the actions of someone who really believed you were the murderer?"

"What about Loris then?"

"Well, the same sort of things apply. Also, I'd bet my bottom dollar neither Telly nor Larry had flings with her."

"Maybe she wanted them to. Unrequited love, that sort of thing."

"Wouldn't she have been more likely to go for me, out of jealousy? I'd gone where she wanted to."

I put my hand on her shoulder. "You need to watch out for yourself as well. Maybe you're next."

She didn't look convinced.

"Then there's Murray and Lister to consider. Professional jealousy the motive."

She shook her head. "And again, why would they come after you? Fine, I can see how you were collateral damage with the MRI. You were literally in the way. But putting snakes through your letterbox took deliberation and effort. It doesn't make sense."

I remembered what Mo had said. "I'm beginning to think the two aren't related. At least not directly. Either Loris or Murray or Lister are the ones who offed Price. Maude jumps to the conclusion I did it because we had a bust-up, and she tries to get revenge on me with the snakes."

"Hold on! You're forgetting Telly in all this. He wasn't a big success with books and TV programmes. Why would anyone want to kill him?"

I tried to keep my face impassive but something of what I was thinking must have showed.

Sally levered herself up on one elbow so she could look me full in the eyes as a I lay there. "You bastard!" she said.

"What?"

"You're thinking that I'm the only one with the motive to kill him. This whole ridiculous Black Widow thing. Then Maude assumes it's you and does her bit with the snakes. It all makes sense to you, doesn't it. It explains everything."

"Not everything. Maude didn't know I hated snakes so it's a big coincidence that she'd use them."

Sally leaned in so I felt her breath on my face. "Maybe I told her."

I found myself pulling the sheet up, like a spinster who's just seen a ghost. "You didn't, though, did you?"

"That's for you to decide. Either piss off or stay here and risk waking up with your throat cut."

And with that, she turned away, pulled the blankets up over her and soon gave every appearance and sound of falling sleep.

I'd only been a detective for a few minutes but I was already finding it hard going.

I pulled up my side of the blankets and tried to follow her into the Land of Nod.

~~~

It was only after a nice breakfast the next day that I detected the first signs of a thaw.

Well, by that I mean Sally stopped looking as if she wanted to strangle me.

Once this had been a fair-sized dining room, large for a modern house but small by restaurant standards. There couldn't have been more than five or six bedrooms in the place so it didn't run to an extensive buffet but rather cooked breakfasts from an array of ingredients. By the time I'd eliminated the more grossly carnivorous stuff—the clotted blood of the black pudding, the sheep's intestine and chopped up liver of the haggis, and the anus and eyelids of the sausages—I was left with hash browns, beans, smashed avocado with poached egg on toast and a few slices of bacon.

Sally, ogre-like, was consuming the lot. She pointed a yoke-stained knife at my plate. "Seriously?"

"You know what the Germans called a plate of assorted meats—a slaughter plate."

"Your point being?"

"Is there no part of an animal you won't eat?"

"You can be really quite prissy sometimes, Dai. This is costing £30 a head. You're an idiot not to make the most of it."

Not surprisingly I finished my food before she did and sat there watching, drinking my coffee, as she ravaged her food like a Georgian trencherman, or at least someone from an age where dyspepsia and liverishness were king. How did she stay so slim? How did she keep it all down?

"So, what are you up to today?" I asked.

She poked at her second egg with her knife, opening its big yellow eyeball so all the fluid leaked out. "*You* tell me! This is your city. The police have told me not to leave Glasgow so I can't even visit Loch Lomond. It's only been a couple of days but it's already doing my head in. What about you?"

"I've got a busy day ahead. I need to get my phone and departmental key card back from the police. There's also stuff I need to look up. Then I need to arrange to see my boss, Donlevy, and find out where I stand."

"What stuff do you need to look up?"

"Oh, detective stuff. Nothing to worry your pretty little head about."

"Fuck you!"

"Like I said last night, time for me to come off the back foot."

"So, what 'detective work'? Give me a laugh!"

"Did Holmes always keep Watson in his confidence? Did Poirot blurt everything out to Hastings?"

Sally tapped her knife against her plate. "Are you seriously putting me in the subordinate role here?"

"As you point out, this is my city and I walk its streets. Glasgow—no mean city. I must go where angels fear to tread."

"Either that snake bite or the sedatives have gone to your head if you think I'm going to be Robin to your Batman, Passepartout to your Phineas Fogg."

"So, you're coming sleuthing with me?"

I could see she found this tempting. Constraining someone like Sally, even if it was to a whole city, would be like trying to put a hurricane in a tin can.

"And the first place we'd be going is somewhere very picturesque."

~~~

East Glasgow, generally speaking, will never win prizes for its looks. It begins, more or less, at the Necropolis, a hill covered in Victorian tombs of weeping angels and cloth-draped vases representing the veil between life and death. Reached by the Bridge of Sighs, it looks down on the cupolas of an old Victorian hospital called the Royal Infirmary. For two centuries its patients must have looked up at the Necropolis and experienced a whole panoply of emotions.

Five hundred metres down from the Necropolis is an area called the Barras and that's where I took Sally.

"This," she said, "is the complete opposite of picturesque."

"I'm a fan of irony."

"No kidding."

We were only at the entrance but already we could see that the Barras looked like an explosion in a junk yard. It was a market that seemed never to have made up its mind whether it was open air or not. Markets around the world can pull off the open-air thing because of the weather but in Glasgow even makeshift market buildings had to be just a bit more substantial to keep out the rain. Transparent corrugated roofs kept most of it off the trestle tables, which held everything from cuddly toys to the latest pirated software. Ebony carved figurines from the darkest nightmare of an African Shaman jostled for the punters' attention with ragged rubber trees and bloody, plastic wrapped joints of meat.

Here and there little food stalls plied their carnivorous trade, the only vegetables offered being chips. We were passing one stall and Sally stopped to marvel at a pan of boiling mussels the size of human hands.

"Where do those come from? Mars?"

"They're called Clappy-doos."

"It looks like they've been boiling for hours. I mean look at all that yellowy foam."

"Only way to soften them up. Some say the really big ones can only be found in the cooling water outlet from Hunterston nuclear power station on the West Coast."

We dodged around tables of bric-a-brac: magazines, books, records, discontinued lines of everything from clothes to hairdryers. One stall seemed to specialise in vehicles, from illegal electric scooters to used wheelchairs.

"Everyone looks so... furtive," said Sally in wonder.

And it was true. Although it wasn't raining and wasn't cold, everyone seemed to have their hands in their pockets and shoulders hunched up as if they were warding off inclement weather. Nobody was meeting anyone else's eyes.

Sally frowned. "Christ, what the hell are you here to buy—a stolen thermonuclear device?"

"Well, you're right in one regard, the provenance of a lot of this stuff is dodgy to say the least. The result of house clearances, with or without the owners' permission."

"In the latter case I take it you mean burglaries."

By now we had come to an actual building with semi retracted shutters that looked like it could withstand a tank shell at point blank range. From the entrance we could see the place was crammed with old furniture and cabinets full of ornaments. I was no expert but to me the wares seemed to inherit that grey area between antique and utter crap, with a heavy weighting towards the latter.

"So, what are you going to buy here? A blunderbuss?"

All the furniture was out of the rain but Glasgow could be damp and everything smelled of mildew. We made our way through the jumble of rotting sofas and chairs where a million plonked-down bottoms had literally knocked the stuffing out of them. I was following the smell of tobacco smoke and, sure enough, rounding a stuffed bear, I saw the proprietor puffing on a roll-up fag.

The man raised his eyebrows by way of greeting. A sleeveless denim jacket revealed tattooed arms the size of hams. Black hair, short but thick, framed his face from the top of his head to his chin.

Any sign of effusiveness in the Barras was equated with being a target for a con so I kept it laconic.

"Walking sticks," I said gruffly.

He nodded and turned and we followed him past rocking chairs and cribs, hatstands and lights with plasticky lamp shades. We passed along a large dark wood display case containing glass domes under which stuffed birds nailed to twigs failed to sing. Beside them, smaller stuffed animals filled the shelves. One poor ferret had a look on its face as if it'd been stuffed while alive.

The man pointed at a faux elephant leg containing a number of walking sticks. Some had cute little ivory handles carved like the heads of snakes (no thanks!), others had curved tops like shepherds' crooks. A single aluminium crutch with socket for an arm looked anachronistic among the canes. Some had dogs and cat's heads and didn't look like they were comfortable to hold.

None of these were what I was looking for (and the snake head ones made me gulp) but I saw just the thing immediately. The cane itself was gnarled and twisted and made of dark wood and, nestling at the top, was a ball of ebony that would make a good handful.

I grabbed it out of the elephant's leg and, grasping it halfway down the cane, swung it so the ball smacked into my palm.

A proprietor in a real antique shop might have recoiled at such a display of violence but we were in the Barras. I could have smashed in someone's skull right before the man's eyes and he wouldn't have blinked. With the punters he'd get in here, showing fear wasn't an option.

"The Speckled Band! You're kidding me!" I'd forgotten Sally was there and both the proprietor and I turned to look at her.

She was on the money but I wasn't going to admit it. "Don't know what you mean."

"Sherlock Holmes and the Speckled Band which was a snake that he whacked with his walking stick."

Before I could answer, the proprietor held up a finger to quiet us, then bent and reached into the stand and pulled out a metal tube about the length of my forearm. He gave it a flick and it extended like magic.

"That's a police baton," said Sally wonderingly. "Is that even legal for members of the public to have one?"

The man shrugged. He'd kept quiet for so long it would have been wrong for him to say anything now.

I waved the ball-headed cane. "How much?"

"Twenty." He seemed annoyed he'd had to use his voice.

"Ten."

"Fifteen."

He nodded reluctantly, as if I'd shafted him. If he'd paid more than a couple of quid for it then I had most certainly come up the Clyde on the proverbial banana boat.

"Do you take a card?" I asked.

Both Sally and the man snorted.

After I'd paid in greasy notes, we left the shop, me experimenting with walking with a stick, Sally tutting like an old maid after the vicar had farted.

"Look, Sherlock, if all you know about crime comes from the Victorian pen of Arthur Conan Doyle then I don't give much for your chances."

"Humour me, Watson! Having a stout stick in my hand makes me feel better already."

"But you look like such a dick."

And in the Barras I certainly did. This was a hooky world of drugs and guns and stolen gear, not of some guy walking affectedly with a cane.

Apart from a few puzzled looks, we made it unmolested back onto the road and took a taxi to police headquarters. An earlier phone call had secured the release of my property that the police had taken after the MRI incident. It was clear that returning my phone, wallet and departmental key card weren't high on the desk officer's priorities. An old red-haired beefy chap, he seemed more diverted by my swish new cane, though more in a 'who's this twat with the cane and can I class it as an offensive weapon?' way rather than with admiration. He made us wait with a sad old woman who'd lost her cat.

After an hour of the desk officer not appreciably doing anything, another officer appeared with my stuff. I checked it all and signed the release.

United with my old phone I felt whole again. I flicked dreamily through my contacts, once again plugged into the world.

"You've paid less attention to my breasts," said Sally.

"Oh, they give me great pleasure, but this... this gives me everything." I cradled my little friend in my arms.

I was joking but I could see from her look that this and the cane weren't increasing her admiration. I resolved to make all this up to her, somehow.

Another taxi took us back to the department, which seemed deserted, although I imagined specialist technicians would have been called in by the MRI manufacturer to get it back up and running. Refilling the helium for a start.

"What are we doing here?" she asked as I fobbed us through the main door.

"Detecting."

"This I've got to see."

But all she saw was me rifling through the filing cabinets in the file room behind reception. "What are you after?"

"This." I showed her a file.

She looked blankly at the photo attached.

"Is that supposed to mean something?"

I tapped my finger on the address next to the photo. "All will be revealed. But first we must summon another hansom cab."

~~~

No horse-drawn vehicles were available so instead we got an Uber. We took it south of the river to a district that had seen its fortunes come and go. Once Govan had been the ultimate shipyard, its docks and others on the river supplying half the warships, ocean liners and cargo ships for the whole world.

Wages for the welders and riveters may not have been good but they had been steady. Even after the money had gone its working-class culture had bequeathed Govan a vibrancy which outsiders found bracing.

After the war, the building of the bigger ships had moved to Japan then South Korea. Margaret Thatcher then denationalised and broke up the shipyards. Without government support, one by one they closed and became empty rusting memorials to better days. The district's fortunes had reversed yet again, albeit temporarily, as it became the site of the 1988 Garden Festival. Derelict docklands came to bloom and the locals were fooled into believing they had entered a one-way street to a glorious future.

But the blooms disappeared just as quickly and the garden site reverted to abandoned docks once again. Sporadic initiatives followed but the financial crash of 2008 marked the end of those and Govan spiralled down, becoming a sin bin for disruptive families and cheap accommodation for refugees from Sudan and all points south and east.

The Uber stopped on a street overshadowed by tenements. I paid the driver and got out. I realised he was giving us an appraising look before he pulled quickly away.

"Maybe I should have asked him to wait," I said.

"Somehow I don't think he would have," said Sally. "What is this place anyway? Stalingrad? And, if so, who's laying siege?"

Dark men in raggedy old clothes stood in the doorless entrances to each tenement close, puffing on cigarettes and watching us warily. Little kids ran riot in the streets. Perhaps fresh from sub-Saharan climes, they weren't used to heavy traffic.

Then I realised how few cars there were. The tenements were five storeys high and must contain ten families each, yet

I saw only three parked cars. Tenements were common in districts near the city centre and parking was usually a huge problem.

Cheap rents meant that quite a few students lived here even though the universities weren't exactly on the doorstep. You had to go over the Clyde on the pedestrian bridges then up through Finnieston to the dreaming spires, only a mile but a whole world away.

"You owe me an explanation. Why have you brought me to this shithole?"

"All will be revealed." I scanned the little numbers above the close entrances.

Number 10 looked like all the others. The men loitering did not look surprised at my approach, a stout stick for smacking snakes no doubt a standard accoutrement where they came from. They shuffled aside to let Sally and me through, their eyes never leaving us.

I don't much like the smell of stewing mutton and this was leavened only a little by the liberal use of spices. Above the mutton smell wafted the tang of urine. The closes being open, dogs and returning pub goers could call in if caught short.

Over a hundred years old and little maintained, the tiles on the upper half of the walls were cracked or missing. Once upon a time people took turns to clean the stairs in closes and woe-betide a wifey who didn't do her bit. This ethic had long since gone and the stairs were filthy and junk of every description had been left on the landings. Sally and I picked our way through rubbish sacks, wheel-less bicycles and broken pushchairs until we got to the second floor.

I checked the note I'd made. It said 2/R so the flat I was looking for was the one on the right. Meanwhile Sally was looking back down the stairs, no doubt checking that the men weren't following us up.

"Start revealing," she hissed, "or so help me I'll do you."

I was tempted to rap on the door with my cane, as Holmes would no doubt have done, but instead I pushed the door bell, stepping aside so I couldn't be seen through the fish-eye spyhole. Only Sally would be in view and I hoped that would be enough to pique the interest of the inhabitant.

I heard bolts being pulled. The door came open and a head appeared, looking at Sally. It took a few seconds before the person realised I was standing to the side. That was long enough for me to see the bandaged hand.

As the head swivelled around, and without a single conscious thought in my head, I punched Logan hard in the nose.

Fucking Jung!

~~~

"You're a menace," Sally said, slouching in her chair, arms crossed over her chest. "Why am I here, officer?" She looked up at the copper who stood beside us. "I didn't do anything wrong."

"You're a witness, Ms."

"I seem to spend my life in police stations nowadays." She turned to glare at me. "And it's all thanks to you."

I kept on looking straight ahead. "Just this once, maybe. You were in the frame for what happened to Price and Telly. Those times were nothing to do with me."

"You fingered me for the snakes, remember. Three hours they had me under interrogation."

She had a fair point. "They'll be charging you any minute," she said and it sounded as if that would suit her just fine.

"No, they won't."

"What the hell do you know, Sherlock?"

"The police don't want everyone knowing I had to do their job for them. This'll go away, trust me." I tried to make that sound like it was written in stone, but my confidence was paper-thin.

"Even if that were true, this Logan guy'll insist on bringing charges. I mean, I didn't get more than a second to get acquainted with his nose, but it looked OK before you flattened it."

I shook my head. "Up here, it's the Procurator Fiscal who brings charges and he's not going to do that as I can't see Logan agreeing to testify. If he testifies against me then I'll testify against him. Besides he's lucky I just punched him and didn't crack his skull like an eggshell with my stick."

"Small mercies."

Perhaps I shouldn't have been surprised that the refugees had phones. Logan's wailing had had them all dialling within seconds and the first police car had arrived within minutes. Logan, if he'd had any sense, would have denied everything but it turned out his snake bite had gone septic. He'd been too afraid to go to hospital as he was sure the police would be alerted. He actually seemed relieved it was all out in the open so he could get treatment. An ambulance had carted him off to the nearby Death Star, a copper in attendance.

Putting snakes through letterboxes without getting bitten himself had shown yet again that much lay beyond Logan's expertise.

I was relishing the thought of fangs sinking into his hand and it must have showed.

Sally snorted. "You smug bastard. By the way, how did you know it was this Logan guy?"

"Because he was one of the few people who knew about my fear of snakes. Normally I don't spill my guts about my private life to students, but he was doing a dissertation on conditioning. Having been a victim of conditioning by my parents, I'm something of an expert. Logan's descriptions were desert dry and I thought that by telling him about my induced aversions to snakes and milk, it might gee him up. Might put some life into his stuff. Instead, he stored the information away then used it to hurt me, mentally and physically." I rubbed my bandaged ankle. "Bastard succeeded in both."

"Imagine: a phobia about milk," she said in wonder. "You pussy!"

I waved this away, too tired to go down that road. "Also, when I was looking up his address in the file, I noticed something he'd never mentioned to me. In his application to the University, under 'Hobbies' was 'Herpetology'".

"Do what?"

"Herpetology. The study of reptiles. What a giveaway! And then when I saw the bandage on his hand, everything fitted perfectly like a key into a lock."

She frowned. "Did it? Did it really?"

I didn't answer. That's the trouble with non-detectives, they underestimate the role of intuition when it comes to sleuthing.

Me, Sally and the copper were all in a bare walled interview room. Sally and I had been arguing incessantly since we'd been dragged back to Helen Street Police Station—with which we were becoming all too familiar. Perhaps the coppers had thought we'd start fighting; hence the policeman in attendance.

The door opened and in walked Philban and McKendrick. As usual they didn't look happy.

Sally had long since passed the need for niceties. "Why am I here?" she asked without preamble.

Philban didn't miss a beat. "You were brought here under suspicion of aiding and abetting an assault."

Sally leapt to her feet. "Oh, please. I didn't even know this Logan guy existed, had never heard of him and I had no idea this idiot was going to punch him." She didn't point but we all knew who she was talking about.

"Sit down, Ms. Vale, and let's try to sort this all out. As for you Mr Younge, we have good news." Though the expression on his face was saying the opposite.

"Can't wait."

"Mr Logan seems to have had a dark night of the soul. He has repented."

That was such an archaic expression from a Glasgow copper I must have smiled.

Philban's eyes narrowed and he seemed to have to force himself to continue. "Mr Logan has decided not to testify against you, Mr Younge. That being the case, and no crime therefore being committed, you are no longer under suspicion. So, Ms Vale, there will be no need for you to supply a witness statement. In fact, you're both free to go."

I sat forward. "But you're charged him with attempted murder, right?"

"Attempted murder by adder was never going to fly. He's admitted to Actual Bodily Harm and the Fiscal seems happy with that."

"Whoa! Adders do kill people, you know."

"So do bees. If someone had put couple of bees through someone's letterbox, how's that ever going to be attempted murder."

I pulled up my trouser leg to show the bandage. "Does that look like a bee sting to you."

McKendrick piped up. "Bee stings can be nasty too. My niece nearly died from one. Some people are allergic to them. Then there's the whole anaphylactic shock thing."

"That's just not good enough! Maybe adder bites aren't as big a deal as people think, but I bet he believed he was trying to kill me. I insist an attempted murder charge is brought against him."

"If the Procurator Fiscal thought we could get away with it then we would. Between you and me, the Fiscal doesn't want all the nonsense that would go with it if it went to trial.

OK, maybe an adder bite is worse than a bee sting but on a wider scale it's far closer to that than to a bite from something like a puff adder or Gaboon viper. Now, those are serious snakes."

"So, the Fiscal's dodging this out of a fear of embarrassment?"

Now Philban leaned forward. "Word to the wise, Mr Younge. If you kick up a fuss and try to get a more serious charge against Mr Logan, then he's going to want us to charge *you* with Actual Bodily Harm. Now you wouldn't want that now, would you?"

So, my guess that the law was keen for this all to go away had been correct. The Fiscal didn't want a circus, and the cops didn't want the press to know I'd done their detecting for them. They'd got an admission of ABH and that seemed to be enough for them. Move on, nothing more to see here.

In the silence that followed Sally butted in. "What about the murders of Larry Price and Telly Lamarck? How's that going?"

"We're still following various lines of enquiry," said Philban with a smile as bland as his words.

"Can I go back home, back to England, back to civilisation?"

"Not yet."

"You can't keep me here for ever. I have work to go to."

"When *are* you due back at work, Ms Vale?"

Sally hesitated and I suspected she was contemplating lying but, in the end, decided against it. "Well, Wednesday."

"This is only Sunday. According to the hotel you were due to stay in Glasgow until today anyway. We're not inconveniencing you yet."

"I had plans, things I had to do back home before Wednesday."

"I'm sorry, Ms Vale, but we've had a double murder. It's all been very inconvenient, not least to the two victims who were, at some point, your friends."

That shut Sally up. Philban turned to me. "One last thing, Mr Younge. Please talk to us before you go around taking the law into your own hands. In fact, I'm instructing you to leave it to the professionals altogether."

It didn't matter what he said, or with how much conviction, we both knew the cops had messed up. They'd assumed the same person who did the killings had tried to adder me as well.

What other false assumptions were they labouring under, I wondered.

Though I had plenty of ammunition for a sarcastic retort, for once I decided to keep my powder dry.

~~~

Back outside Helen Street Police Station, and having phoned for a cab, I tried to work out where I stood with Sally.

"You're annoyed. Should I find somewhere else to stay?"

She considered this for a few seconds. "Being with you is like being in a war. Long periods of boredom interposed with brief moments of intense action."

"The periods of boredom being..."

She put her thumb over her shoulder, pointing back at the cop shop. "Waiting in interview rooms."

"And the periods of intense action?"

She looked away.

"Well?"

She shrugged. "When you punched that guy, so out of the blue."

"You sort of liked that, eh?"

She shrugged again.

"And what about the intense periods of action in bed?"

She held her hand out flat and wiggled it from side to side.

We stood there waiting for the taxi. Hidden from sight in a cutting below us, traffic droned by on the M8. Behind us was the hill in Bellahouston Park, once the sight of the Empire Exhibition in 1938 to show the wealth of the British Empire. A huge glass tower had been one exhibit that soared nearly two hundred metres into the air. All the countries in the Empire had had their own sleek pavilions. Restaurants dotted the large site. Visitors were bussed around on a dedicated network. There were open air concerts, film theatres, displays by the armed forces, as well as numerous side-shows and games.

A glimpse into the future, it too, like the Garden Festival, had been plucked away as quickly as it had appeared. Buildings were dismantled and shipped to places like San Francisco to be reconstructed to make cinemas and factories and even canteens. One more toy bounteously bequeathed to then snatched away from Glasgow.

The taxi pulled up. "Back to your place?" I asked, not sure what the answer would be.

"For now," she replied.

CHAPTER TWENTY

I must also have a dark side if I am to be whole.
Carl Jung

On the phone, Donlevy did not sound pleased to hear from me.

"Look, Dai, this is out of my hands now. There's to be a formal tribunal with the whole shebang—HR, union reps, you name it. I'll just be a witness; they'll be the ones who decide what happens to you. Talk to your union rep and wait for the tribunal to contact you."

Sally's room looked out on Great Western Road. Across the four lanes of traffic, stately sandstone mansions, the product of bygone wealth, basked in bright summer sun.

Meanwhile Sally seemed to be following my phone conversation with particular interest. That should have put me on my guard.

"There's been a development," I said to Donlevy. "Everything's changed."

"Like I say, Dai, this is out of my hands."

"You can still stop this whole thing, Ted. Muzzle the dogs, shove them back in their kennels."

"And why would I do that?" Donlevy sounded weary. Sacking someone, even someone as manifestly dangerous as me, was always going to be long-winded and painful. Like many public institutions, the university had a Medusa's hair of procedures designed to tangle and retard any change, no matter how justified.

"Because one of your student's tried to kill me."

"One of *my* students?" Donlevy sounded mystified and with good reason. Senior academics were supposed to keep on *some* teaching and have their own postgraduate students but, in his meteoric rise, Donlevy had managed to leave them all behind, farming them out for supervision to other members of staff.

"As Head of Department, you have the little matter of duty of care to your students and staff. I mean, think of the publicity."

He sighed. "Who is this student?"

"Saul Logan."

I heard Donlevy clicking away as he brought Logan's details up on his workstation.

"He's only an undergraduate! I can't be held responsible for all of them. There's hundreds of the little bas..."

I cut him off. "It's OK, I'm fine."

"What do you mean?"

"I mean I survived the murder attempt, though I was badly injured. Thanks for asking."

This shut him up for a second so I continued. "And you know what really annoys me? I confided in him, confided in my fear of snakes and how it was psychologically conditioned into me. Because that's what his final year project was about—conditioning. I tried to help him, teacher to student, and he betrayed me. By trying to murder me with snakes."

It's strange the stuff that comes out of your mouth sometimes. I hadn't been aware that I even felt betrayed but clearly it had been bothering my unconscious.

Fucking Jung!

"Snakes?" he said, clearly surprised. "Looks, let's start again. What exactly..."

"No, Ted, I want to talk about this face to face, not over the phone."

"As I say, it's out of my hands. Let me—"

"No. This puts a whole new complexion on everything that's happened. The murder attempt on the MRI machine, for example."

"Attempt? That chap Lamarck *was* killed."

"But was he the target? It seems likely this was Logan trying to kill me, and poor Telly Lamarck was collateral damage. In other words, Logan used *your* MRI machine to try to kill *me*. And in response you try to get me sacked. Looking messy, Ted."

"Is Logan still at large?"

"Nope, cops have arrested him."

"So, you're in no immediate danger?"

This made me hesitate. That hadn't been a by-the-books chilly managerial query. Hard to believe, but maybe there was still a hint of humanity left in old Ted.

"We have a lot to talk about, Ted, and I want to do it eye to eye."

"Fine. I'm away at the Scottish Office this afternoon but I've got to come back here before I go home. My secretary will have left so you won't be able to get in by the street door. Phone me when you're outside and I'll let you in. Seven o'clock."

"See you then."

"Hang on a minute!" said Sally loudly and snatched the phone away from. "Professor Donlevy, this is Sally Vale. I need to talk to you."

She listened and I guessed Donlevy, blindsided, was struggling to work out who she was. What she said next confirmed this.

"Then let me help you out, Professor. I am one of the organisers of the conference, or perhaps I should say one of the *surviving* organisers of the conference. Because, you know, one of the organisers was slaughtered on *your* MRI machine, in *your* department in *your* university... don't interrupt me, Professor!" Her face was getting red and her voice was rising, as was my alarm. "Not only that but the whole conference had to be abandoned. A total failure and all down to your shambolic management. And to think that we paid good money for the privilege. Well, let me tell you something, mate—we are going to sue your fucking arse off and we're going to haul your precious university over the coals… no, save your breath, I'm not interested in your apologies. Too little, too late…" By now I was trying to wrestle the phone away from her but she was having none of it. "We'll have you, sunshine, we'll have you!"

I jerked the phone jack out of its socket. From the look on her face, I was pretty sure she wanted to plant the handset deep between my eyes. I held my hands up, partly in submission, partly to protect myself.

"Whoa, whoa! Take a deep breath! Christ, where did that come from?"

"Back the fuck away from me if you value your life!"

So that's what I did.

~~~

It took several hours for her to calm down, long enough for me to realise how self-absorbed I'd been. I hadn't been thinking of things from her point of view as an organiser of a conference that had tanked so spectacularly. I had no idea how she'd financed it. Had she gotten a loan or perhaps even used her own money? What sort of financial position might she be in now that all the attendees would be demanding at least some of their money back? Might she in turn be sued? More than a few of the attendees could truthfully claim to have been traumatised.

When I gently tried to enquire, she brushed me off and, still tetchy, she had a go at me and the phone conversation with Donlevy that she had hijacked.

"Do you always lie so fluently? Can anyone trust a word you say?"

"What are you talking about?"

One cheek inflated as she blew out a breath from the side of her mouth. "The bollocks you said to Donlevy. I mean, let me see. For a start nobody except you seems to think Logan tried to murder you with snakes. Causing you pain and trauma yes, murder no.

"Secondly, calling a sore ankle a bad injury is pushing the envelope of believability. But thirdly, and most importantly, where did this bit about Logan trying to kill you on the magnetic hippo come from?"

"It's possible."

"But what about Larry Price? Why would Logan kill him as well? Also, there's the matter of who pushed poor Larry into the empty swimming bath. Are you saying Logan sneaked his way in? Why would he do that to him, why wouldn't he have pushed you in instead if he had the chance?"

"Maybe he mistook me for Larry."

"So, you're saying he was mistaken at both the swimming baths and when Larry was walking through the Park? You know, when Logan is supposed to have planted an axe between his eyes. Doesn't sound likely."

"Maybe not, but I bet the cops are gagging to charge Logan with everything. I mean they don't seem closer to arresting anyone else for Price's murder. If they can, they'll do Logan for it. Anyway, it all helps to muddy the waters with Donlevy. If I stir up enough muck, then maybe he'll back off."

She took a sip of coffee she'd made using an upmarket machine that came with the room. "It doesn't sound like the most coherent strategy but it might work. The university is in this up to the eyeballs and I can see how your man Donlevy will be keen to minimise the stink. I suppose if you went to the press with this you could paint quite a picture. I'm very seriously thinking about doing that myself."

"*Student Serial Slayer and the Dopey Don*—I'd pay good money to read that."

She shook her head. "Don't get too carried away, Pinocchio. Do you really believe Logan did it all?"

"Maybe the thing on the MRI but, no, I can't see why he would kill Price. I doubt Logan even knew that he existed."

"So, we both agree there is still a murderer out there?"

"Yeah, but at least there's one upside."

"What's that?"

"That whoever it is, they're probably not after me."

"There's no justice in this world," said Sally.

CHAPTER TWENTY-ONE

The most important question anyone can ask is: What myth am I living?
Carl Jung

Sally had wanted to come along to see Donlevy but that had to be the worst idea imaginable. A serious adult conversation leading to an amicable resolution really wasn't on the cards. A knock-down drag-out fight was far more likely. So I insisted she stay behind and headed out alone and was at the university well before seven.

It was evening but Glasgow was still warm from the cloudless day. Mo had very, very grudgingly brought me some clothes from my house. So grudgingly I'd got a stick and shaken them all out once he'd left, just in case he left in a snake or two out of spite.

Finally convinced they were snake-free, I was now wearing a T-shirt and jeans with no jacket but I still felt overdressed in the remaining heat of the day.

How was I going to play this? Being careless in the lair of the magnetic hippo, and letting Telly talk me into putting him in the magnet, had been unforgiveable and the university would need to be faced with a shitload of toxic publicity if they were going to let that slide.

I'd been injured and that helped a little. Logan having tried to top me would also give the university pause, but would it be enough? The university had a duty of care not to let people get killed on their premises and to stop students slaughtering their lecturers, no matter how much they'd asked for it.

If the press got its teeth into the notion of an administration out of control and rocked by scandal that would very much hurt Donlevy.

Dismissal, demotion or a severe ticking off just about summed up his options as far as I was concerned. If I promised not to kick up a stink as a double victim of this mess, maybe I'd get the last one.

But, if he was hard-nosed about this, I would settle for the middle option. Living on a lower income would be tough, the whisky I drank would have to be less smooth, the holidays less sub-tropical and lavish, but I could handle it. And I definitely wasn't going back to my expensive flat. No siree!

I tried the door to Donlevy's offices and, sure enough, it was locked. I chapped the door just in case he was near enough to hear but, at the same time, I was getting out my phone.

Nobody answered the door and my call to his office landline went to voice mail. Maybe he'd gone to the bog.

Donlevy had never entrusted me with his mobile number so I had no choice but to wait. I gave him a few minutes to finish whatever he was doing and tried the door and the phone again.

Still nothing and we were already ten minutes later than scheduled. Donlevy was too professional to be late for anything and, even if it couldn't be avoided, he'd have made sure I knew he would be late. He had everyone else's number though few had his.

I distrust technology, mainly because I don't understand it. Had his landline gone down? Was he in their cursing me because I was pissing him about by keeping him waiting.

There was a way round this, though. I fobbed myself into the main department next door. I found the key to the key cupboard and quickly fished out the one that opened the internal door to Donlevy's domain.

I hurried down the little corridor and came to another locked door but I'd picked up the key for that as well. There was a sign saying entry was strictly by permission only. I sort of had that so I turned the key and pushed my way in shouting—"Ted, it's me, Dai."

As expected, his secretary wasn't there and her desk was as clear as a nun's conscience. She probably scoured it down with her dragon's breath every night before she left.

"Ted!" I called again as I approached his door. I gave a couple of raps on the wood but still there was no response.

I waited for a few seconds, calming myself and pulling down my T-shirt to smooth out any wrinkles. I took a deep breath then opened the door.

I needn't have worried for there was Donlevy, arms wide open to welcome me.

Except... except...

I shook my head, trying to understand. Was it Donlevy? It was the same Nehru jacket but I couldn't see the man's face as his head was down. Was it some weird art exhibit, a man turning into a bird? Or was it actually a painting sitting behind his desk? I looked around the room to see if Donlevy was lurking in a corner, enjoying my confusion.

That's when I nearly wet myself.

The wall to the right normally held a large canvas of modern art, circles and lines screwing each other, or something. It was Donlevy's property rather than the university's and he was proud of it.

But now it lay discarded on the floor. The wall behind was covered in a scrawl of letters, the red paint dripping down like it was melting.

HERETIC—BURN IN THE FIERY DEPTHS OF HELL! it intimated.

I knew I couldn't keep staring at the message. I knew that sooner or later I had to turn my eyes back to Donlevy's desk and the abomination hanging behind it.

I gulped hard and slowly swivelled round. By now I kind of knew what to expect but my eyes and brain still weren't doing their jobs.

I stepped forward slowly, carefully. I bent down so I was looking up at the face under the lowered head.

It was Ted alright. My eyes travelled along one outstretched arm to the hand. A big black nail went through his wrist into the wall, blood dripping down like the paint from the message.

"Ted," I whispered. Gingerly I eased myself around the desk and placed my finger against his throat just below and to the side of his ear. He wasn't entirely cold and, just for an instant, I thought I felt something pulse, though very faintly. I pushed a little harder and then realised that all I was feeling was the frightened blood pulsing through the tiny vessels of my own fingertips.

I edged out backwards and tried to take in the tableau. Whoever had crucified Ted hadn't been able to lift him up. He was hanging by his hands, but his legs were splayed out under his desk.

If his legs were free, wouldn't he have kicked out at his assailant, or at least stood up to take the pressure off? That meant...

A bright red stain was running down from the centre of his chest to his legs where it took a bifurcated path around his thighs. I realised the carpet below the desk was no longer grey. Wonderingly, I raised up my foot and turned it so I could see the underside of my shoe. Bright red!

The carpet behind the desk was sopping with Ted's blood. If I hadn't been focusing on his head, I would have felt the squelch as I put my feet down.

Stupidly, and way later than I should have done, I checked around to see if the killer was still there. The sheer weight of the silence made me sure they were long gone, but

I went out to reception and checked under and behind the secretary's desk.

I went back into Ted's office. It occurred to me to do a runner. Me finding the body was never going to look good to the coppers but I'd openly walked here. There'd be plenty of CCTV coverage. Not only that but I was leaving a bunch of bloody footprints.

This last thought made me take a closer look. There were other footprints on the floor. Some led to a chair in reception. They approached then turned, as the person had sat down. There were no footprints leading away. The murderer had changed their shoes here, so as not to leave a blood trail. That showed forethought.

Which was more than I could be accused of.

Sighing, I took out my phone and tapped in the three nines.

~~~#

I hate lawyers. My parents had named their lawyer as their executor and it had taken a hammer and a chisel to weaken his grip on their estate. In the end I'd had to take him to court and he still got away with a greedy amount in jacked-up fees.

So, I wasn't keen on hiring a lawyer but the cops had lost what little laissez faire they could muster. Just talking this out like civilised people wasn't an option, if it ever had been. Coppers are focused on securing a conviction and, for some of them, whether their suspect is innocent or guilty is less of a concern.

As soon as the cops arrived, the twin enticements of motive and opportunity had them arresting me on the spot.

Of course, I dobbed in Elsie and her Christian Fundamentalist band who deplored Donlevy the Soul Hunter. The ones who protested out front every day of term. The message written in blood was *so* them.

But that wasn't anywhere near enough to stop the police carting me off to the cop shop. Once there, for two hours nothing happened. I had time to inspect the bare, easily washed down cell walls on which, I had no doubt, bodily contents had been smeared by flipped out junkies and against which the more emotional had been banging their heads. Despite the smell of bleach, there was that sadly human scent of unhappy people who hadn't had a wash as recently as they might.

On one side a metal grill shielded a window which, judging by the sounds of motors starting and stopping, looked out on the car park of the police station.

In the next cell a lunatic was bawling and slapping the walls, while in another the inmate was shouting, "Shut up, shut up, shut up."

It's only when your freedom is taken away that you realise how much you've taken it for granted. There wasn't even a pot to piss in so I had to ask for permission to be taken to the bog like an infant in school.

I'd had plenty of interactions with police over the last week or so but when one of them came to take me from my cell to the interview room, I noticed something different.

He was a young chap, tall and lean but with a round face which would one day run to fat. If coppers are working on reception in a police station, or leading you from one place to another, or even loading you into an ambulance while you're writhing in horror from a snake bite, then you're kind of not there. You're just one more member of that indistinguishable mass called the public. Basically, you're just making their life difficult.

But this copper was looking at me with something in the proximity of respect. It had taken committing murder by crucifixion to bring me into focus, coalescing me in front of his eyes into an honest-to-God individual.

And that was when, even before he snapped some cuffs on me, I realised I really did need a lawyer.

Even more scary was when I was shown into the interview room to find Philban and McKendrick already waiting. Usually, whenever they'd talked to me, I'd been made to sit alone in the interview room until their lordly appearance.

And when I saw they were looking at me like the young copper, with a mixture of revulsion and respect, that's when I knew my goose was well and truly cooked.

"I didn't kill Donlevy," I said before I'd even sat down.

For an instant Philban looked disappointed in me. Perhaps he was expecting a verbal fencing session with an intelligent but manipulative psycho. Instead of Hannibal Lector he was getting any old Glasgow Ned (*Scottish noun: Non-educated Delinquent, hooligan*).

Philban waved the young copper away but rather than snapping on the recording device and describing for its sake who was in the room, he just sat back, arms crossed, looking at me.

Finally: "Crucifixion and snakes. I mean, for fuck's sakes. What is it with you?"

"I want a lawyer."

"Yes, and I'm reliably informed the sky is blue and the grass is green. So what?"

"So don't go turning that thing on. No point."

Philban unfolded his arms, palms out in an expansive, agreeing gesture. "No problem, but come on, just between us and these four walls, what in God's name did you think you were doing? We're genuinely gobsmacked here."

"I'm glad you view this as some form of entertainment. I hate to burst your bubble but, as you well know, I was the victim of the snakes, not the one who shoved them through the letterbox. You've got a snake-bitten student called Logan for that."

"Victim or perpetrator, it's all so... gothic."

"And I didn't crucify anyone. Do I look strong enough to single-handedly crucify a grown man, especially a well-fed six-footer like Donlevy?"

Philban shook his head. "You're being too modest, Dai." Since when had we become on first name terms? Again, with the weirdly mis-placed respect. "A clever man like you would find it easy enough to figure out the bit with the chair."

"Chair? What are you talking about?"

"The chair. The one Donlevy was sitting in when you stabbed him. Once he'd bled out you rolled it back against the wall, nailed his arms up, then just took away the chair. Straightforward, really."

Kendrick sat forward, almost eagerly. "Bit half-arsed though. Not proper crucifixion, really, not when the victim's feet are touching the floor."

"You're criticising my crucifixion technique?"

"Just saying. Looks awful, sure enough, but in your true crucifixion your victim's still alive and all the weight is taken on his arms. Donlevy's bum was only a couple of feet above the floor. He could have gotten his legs under him and taken his whole weight on his feet. It would have still been sore, what with the nails through his wrists, but he wouldn't have died. The weight's got to be taken on the arms, weakening the chest muscles and causing death from asphyxiation. But, of course, you knew that, being an educated man."

"What the hell do you think I studied at university? A Masters in Murder, a Bachelors in Brutality? And anyway, why go to the trouble of crucifying him?"

"Spite," said Philban. "To show your spite because he was going to sack you."

"Oh, for God's sake. I want to see a lawyer."

He shrugged. "Means, motive and opportunity. The full set. Come on, just get it off your chest."

"But what about Lamarck? You know I didn't kill him. You had the CCTV of the killer leaving the building. Surely they're the one who killed Price and Donlevy as well."

"Why, what would be the motive?"

I could feel my brow furrowing as I tried to get my head round this. "So, you're saying there's two different murderers at work here."

"Why not?"

"It's a bit of a coincidence."

Philban shook his head. "Someone was killing the paranormal people, maybe something to do with sex or internal politics or jealousy. You may not have done it, but you saw an opportunity, as cover for when you settled your own personal score with your boss. You figured we'd blame it all on whoever killed Price and Lamarck."

"Lawyer, please."

~~~

Not that the lawyer helped much. His presence was in the end totemic. He did tell me how long they could hold me before charging me: twenty-four hours. In the end the cops applied for an extension and I was there for three whole days.

They were keen not to give much away but a picture began to emerge from the questions they asked and also from the questions they stopped asking.

For a start, they must have got the estimate of the time of death from a pathologist. Donlevy definitely felt a lot colder than he should have been when I touched his neck. They stopped assuming I'd killed him and then immediately phoned the police. Instead, they tried to get me to admit to killing him earlier, then rushing home, perhaps to fetch my crucifying tools, then sauntering back across the park.

They'd have dragged up all the CCTV that might have covered my approach, departure then approach again. I could tell they weren't happy and it sounded as if I would have had to be invisible and to have moved like lightening to avoid all the cameras and to get it all done in the timeframe required.

They also had me stripped down and inspected for wounds by a police surgeon who reeked of booze. They took swabs. I got the impression old Donlevy might have put up a fight before he bled out and maybe little bits of his killer remained on Donlevy's hands or under his nails or whatever.

As one day turned into another, and then another, I could tell Philban and McKendrick were starting to harbour doubts (doubts they could secure a conviction, rather than about my guilt). Apart from where the cylinder had gouged my back, and where the serpent had sunk its fangs into my ankle, I was unmarked apart from a couple of bruises. When I asked about what the DNA swabs had shown they ignored me.

So, I wasn't too surprised that when the ninety-six hour make-or-break point under Scottish law was imminent, they released me. I found myself on the pavement in front of Helen Street Police station with just my returned phone for company.

I phoned Mo. "I need a drink," I said.

Then I did exactly the same thing with Sally.

~~~

The Bon, well used though it had been by generations of drinkers, never looked better.

And the whisky never tasted finer.

"A triple murderer," said Mo thoughtfully. "Don't think I've ever drunk with one of those before."

Some comments just aren't worthy of response. I turned to Sally. "Cops been bothering you?"

She was on the Dalmore again. "Same old, same old. Me, Loris and Maude and a couple of others who don't have clear alibis. We've been in this damned city getting on for two weeks now and we're all getting fed up. We have jobs to go back to, family to see."

Mo held up a warning finger. "Only *we* can diss this city, the people who live here."

"Oh, I do beg your pardon."

"You could at least sound like you mean it." Mo was on an Ardbeg, a whisky made by wafting alcohol at a mound of peat. Personally, I thought it was like drinking liquid dirt. Dirt that had cut its leg then been daubed with a paint brush dripping with iodine.

"Not only that, but I think your coppers are crap." Sally pointed a finger at me. "The only crime solved so far was cracked by Sherlock here. And he's an idiot."

Bit, hit and traumatised, I expected better from my supposed friends so I turned away. It was early evening and the pub would soon be 'stowed oot' (*Scottish vernacular: full*). I wasn't intending to stay much longer as I needed my bed.

Then I remembered I couldn't go back to my own bed and it would have to be Sally's instead.

I turned back to them, trying to smile.

"You're right about the cops. I'd kind of assumed they knew what they were doing, Philban especially, but they've gone down in my estimation."

"They're lower than whale shit in mine," said Sally.

"So, what are you going to do, Dai?" asked Mo.

"I guess I need to go sleuthing again. I don't think they're serious about me killing Price, and even they don't believe I killed Telly. But they *do* like me for what happened to Donlevy and they have a point. Means, motive and opportunity. Opportunity is the only one they're a bit shaky on, as they know he died before I arrived. I bet even now they've got fit young coppers sprinting back and forth between my place and the department but missing all the CCTV. You know, to show I could have done it in the time.

"Basically, I don't think I can sit around until they find some way I might have done it and the hammer comes down."

"So, what *are* you going to do?"

"Sitting in that shitty little cell between interrogations gave me time to think. I know exactly what to do."

I let that hang.

"And?" said Sally finally and in exasperation.

I held up a finger. "Hode yer wheest, Watson!"

"Do what?"

"Let me translate, Sally," said Mo. "Hode, or hold, yer or your, and wheest means quiet. Our Tartan Sherlock here is fobbing you off."

"He must like sleeping rough."

I shook my head. "I have an idea, that's all. I need to work on it. As soon as I'm sure, you'll be the first to know."

"He probably thinks you're the killer," said Mo unhelpfully.

"Or you, Mo."

"And he might be onto something there. Getting him into trouble is the work of my lifetime."

"And you're doing a pretty good job," said Sally holding up her drink.

Mo did the same and they chinked glasses.

CHAPTER TWENTY-TWO

Show me a sane man and I will cure him for you.
Carl Jung

That last morning in the jail cell, I'd woken up and known with great certainty who had done the killings.

Trouble was, I hated the way I knew, I didn't believe the way I knew, I didn't trust the way I knew. It was all way too parapsych, way too crazy old Jung.

It couldn't be true, it mustn't be true and by God I would prove it!

And so, I would set out determined to prove that the person I thought was the killer, wasn't. And in doing so, I might be able to prove it was someone else. Then everything would be roses.

That all meant I had to be a detective again. Trouble was I didn't read crime novels. I didn't watch crime dramas on TV. In order to become a detective, I had to rely on my native intellect.

I was screwed.

Nevertheless, I had no choice but to soldier on.

And that's why, a couple of days later I was here in Hyndland. Even though I had been detecting in earnest for just three hours, I had already learned a very important lesson that no amount of crime fiction could have brought home with quite such force. The lesson was as follows:

Stake-outs are really, really boring.

Crushingly so, in fact. For a start the opportunities for entertainment are limited. Sitting in my car watching the tenement where my suspect (hark at him and his detecting terminology) was living meant no TV or books. The radio was great for about thirty minutes followed by ten minutes of channel hopping trying to find something not designed to rot my brain. I don't listen to much radio and I'd forgotten how annoying the DJs were. You went from the vapid and moronic on the pop stations to emollient and oleaginous on the classical ones. Either gibbering or soporific but one note all the way.

I ate all the food I'd brought within an hour, chewing disconsolately on my cheese sandwiches and watching a world in which very little happened.

Hyndland was a district of sandstone tenement canyons west of Glasgow University. Not that these were the usual Glasgow tenements, although they looked so from the outside. I'd once had a fling with a woman who lived in one of these and had seen an entrance hall big enough to land an aircraft. Off this vast expanse, an array of doors led to many other rooms. Not so much a flat, more like a small village.

My suspect wasn't wealthy enough to afford anything like that so it must be a multi-tenancy deal.

With nothing else to think about, my mind dwelt on the probable futility of what I was doing. Some people stayed in their houses for days at a time. I'd only spent three hours waiting for my target to come out so I could follow him, but already I was out of my skull with boredom.

Plus, there were still other suspects. If this one turned out to be a bust then I'd have to do it all over again.

I inspected the facades of the buildings closely, trying to find an interest in guttering spilling over with weeds that had taken a hold, at holes where mortar had cracked and dropped out from between the sandstone blocks. The sandstone itself helped me pass fifteen minutes. All red at first sight, I became aware of subtle variations that made the tenement cladding quite subtly but beautifully parti-coloured.

Young mothers with buggies were the predominant pedestrians. Either cooing down at the ensconced infant or ignoring it, their ears pressed against mobile phones.

Everyone here seemed to have cars so there was nowhere to park, both sides of each street lined with expensive metal. The myriad delivery drivers had to stop in the middle of the road. Luckily it was a working day for most so these side streets didn't have much traffic.

But then it all kicked off when a delivery driver was away too long and a bin-lorry coming the other way couldn't squeeze past. Traffic began to build up on either side and horns came honking to life. One chap in a big Beamer even got out and stood there, hands on his hips and looking around angrily as if that might achieve something.

It was all getting very exciting when the delivery driver appeared out of a close entrance, a penitent hang-dog expression on his face as he scurried to his cab.

He drove off and all too soon the traffic cleared and I was left back where I started. A traffic hold-up had been the high point of my day.

And that's all it took to make me snap. Before I knew it, I was out of the car and striding up to the close entry. Beside the locked door was an array of buzzers with names under little plastic visors. Some had been there so long they had faded away, but I found what I was looking for easily. One little visor had five names squeezed in under the plastic.

I rang its buzzer and waited.

"Yeah," said a grumpy voice.

"I'm here to see Awang."

"Who?"

"Awang Che. He's a lecturer at the university. He lives here."

"No, he doesn't."

"Are you sure? Nice chap, well built..."

"The Filipino guy?"

"Indonesian."

"Whatever. Yeah, come to think of it, name rings a bell. Nah, he's gone back to the Philip–, I mean to Indonesia."

"When was this?"

"Er..." The owner of the voice was clearly in need of a coffee. "Well it was a week or two ago."

"So at least five days ago."

"Yeah."

"Did he say why he left?" I don't know why I asked this. Donlevy and Rettner had effectively sacked him so going home had been his only option. Unlike me, who was on a permanent contract, Awang had lived from year to year on grants and his last one had been just about up. Donlevy would need to jump through all sorts of HR loops to get rid of me and Bill but Awang had been much easier.

"Who is this?" said the voice, its patience now run out.

"Thanks for your help," I said and walked back to my car.

So, the direct approach had worked where the covert one had failed. Should I use this with the remaining suspects?

I was quite disheartened as he was my prime alternative suspect (assuming the person I knew had done it actually hadn't). I'd figured it might have been an academic with a grudge who'd done for Donlevy and Awang had the biggest grudge of all. He'd made going back to Indonesia sound like a death sentence.

That said, the Christian objectors were still in the frame but I didn't know where they lived, whereas it had been easy to filch my suspect's addresses from the department files. Hopefully the cops were looking into Christian zealots, now they had released me. If they found they were responsible then all well and good. If they didn't, then I should try to be one step ahead of them, again.

Donlevy must have 'let go' a lot of academics in his time, to use that pusillanimous phrase. But if he'd canned them long ago, presumably anyone aggrieved enough would have done him in a long time ago.

It was more likely it was someone he'd messed with recently. The only ones I could think of were the four at the meeting with Rettner: me, Awang, Bill Steadman and Lucas Grimsrud. Awang had been suspect number one as he'd lost his job. Number two was Lucas who had been demoted. Bill was the outlier. He was passed pension age anyway, so it wouldn't have been so traumatic for him.

The big problem I had with all of them was that I didn't see any of them as a crucifying killer, and perhaps even a serial murderer to boot.

Coupled with that, Awang's return to Indonesia meant he wasn't even in the frame for doing Donlevy. When I'd learned this the wind had been taken out of my investigative sails.

I almost gave up then and there but instead started the car and drove over towards the Botanic Gardens. I parked in another side street which at least would provide me with a different view while I tried to sort this out.

Maybe I should just leave it up to the professionals. Then again, if they couldn't find anyone else to take the rap, maybe they'd go for me by default and leave it up to the courts to sort it all out. The trouble with that was how little faith I had in the Scottish legal system, or any legal system for that matter. In every country in the world people who could afford it splashed out for good lawyers for a reason. To some degree your chances of getting off were a function of their abilities.

Not only that, but in Scotland as well as 'Innocent' and 'Guilty' we have a third result, some call it the bastard verdict, namely 'Not Proven'. The implication of this last was that you were probably guilty but the police just hadn't made a good enough case.

Imagine going through life with a verdict like that hanging invisibly over your head.

I don't mind people thinking of me as a grumpy, dour bugger because that's what I am. However, being considered guilty of murder, either explicitly or by a nudge and a wink, did not sit well with me.

So, yes, right now I had to bring the full weight of my relentless sleuthing to bear on Lucas Grimsrud, the next most likely suspect. Grimsrud lived in a leafy suburb called Clarkston, five or six miles south of the river Clyde. A place where bungalows and houses were more spread out, where lurking in a car surveilling someone would easily be noticed and the friendly neighbourhood coppers summoned. And, unlike in some no-go parts of Glasgow, they'd come. Maybe not right away but eventually.

Perhaps there was no other choice than the direct approach. Lucas was big but faded and I quite fancied my chances if it all kicked off.

Plus, of course, I had my stick.

~~~

The union was still considering whether to take up the case we four academics were bringing against the university. A decision was not expected for quite a while, so Lucas had sounded a little surprised when I'd phoned him out of the blue. The occasional coffee we took together in a cafe during the working lunchtime had never evolved into doing anything together in the evening. He'd always come across as a little bit stiff and, no doubt, he felt I was a little too louche.

Even so, he agreed to meet at a pub near where he lived. When I arrived, I found a converted old bank with a few decent real ales to choose from. Since my traumatic experience with the serpents, I found I was drinking more. In fact, I was gulping more than drinking and, if you did that on whisky, you were on a charter flight to a pile-driving headache. It seemed prudent to go for bigger but much weaker drinks.

I was halfway through a pint of Timothy Taylor Landlord when Lucas rocked up. The first thing I always checked was the state of his eczematous skin as it correlated unsurprisingly with his mood. Today only one cheek showed a patch of redness and I hoped it was emblematic of the rest of his body.

I'd sometimes wondered if his reserve when we talked was more to do with his mental tussle not to scratch whatever bit of him was itching. He always sat upright and still, making as few movements as possible.

He waved to me, made the tilting glass sign of asking if I needed another drink, and I responded by covering the top of my glass with my hand.

When it came to communication—so far so good. From now on it might get a little trickier.

Having got his drink, he came over and sat down. Summer vacation or not he still sat upright, not even leaning against the chair back. "Cheers," he said and we chinked glasses. He took a swallow of ale and then looked me directly in the eye.

"So, what's this all about?"

Grimsrud was from a town in the south of Norway called Christiansand. He'd been lured here by the prospect of using our high-tech equipment to solve all sorts of psychological conundrums. Eventually he'd fallen out of love with the technology but had somehow never had the energy to leave. That and the fact he'd married a Scottish woman who'd given him two sons and who didn't want to move anywhere else. He still had some good research ideas and had been pretty successful.

Academics may sometimes be unworldly but they're never stupid. He was a psychologist like me, so I had no illusions that this made him a better lie detector than the man off the Govan omnibus, but he would be acutely aware of the importance of motivation.

This was going to be a tricky conversation so I took a strategic decision and started with a lie.

"I wondered how you were doing. I mean after we all got a kicking from Donlevy and Rettner."

"Speaking of which…" and he held up his glass, "… to Donlevy, may he rest in peace."

I chinked his glass again, not sure if he was being genuine or ironic.

Like I say, psychologists are as useless at this as anyone else.

"You don't have any hard feelings? I mean about Donlevy and what he did?"

He looked at me, eyes narrowing as though suffering a twinge of discomfort, perhaps from his eczema. "The guy's dead. That trumps the twenty or thirty grand my demotion will cost me."

"That's magnanimous of you. Not sure I'd have been so noble hearted if I were in your shoes. Not sure I wouldn't go and crap on his grave."

"Huh!" he snorted, evidently amused. "That's so you, Dai. But, as you brought it up, why aren't you crapping on his grave? Wasn't he out to sack you for what happened on the MRI?"

"But I may have an out." I told him about the snakes, laying it on thick about attempted murder by a student.

"Fucking hell! You've been through the wars. But surely little Logan wouldn't say boo to a goose? What did you do to him? Massacre his family?"

That stung. Trying to keep my dignity I explained about refusing work that was late.

"Couldn't you have bent the rules just a little? You ought to lighten up a bit!"

This was rich coming from a poker-up-the-arse type like Grimsrud. I tried to tamp down my anger. "Christ, it wasn't like the first time he'd been tardy. We've got to set some standards."

Lucas' eyes slowly travelled up the length of my body that he could see above the table. "If you say so," he said.

That really did set me off. "He put serpents through my letterbox! He tried to kill me. Don't give me this butter wouldn't melt in his mouth crap and lay all the blame on me."

Amused and shaking his head slightly, Lucas held up his hand, palm towards me. "Sorry, you're right. Whatever you did to him, you didn't deserve that. Anyway, let's change the subject. So, who killed Donlevy?"

A pint of good beer in my guts and anger still buzzing around my skull like bees, I blurted it out.

"You did."

His eyebrows rose and he sat back in his chair. "Did I fuck as like." He looked more closely at me. "My God, you're serious." Maybe he was a little better at this psychology thing than I am.

"Motive, means and opportunity."

This detective business wasn't so new to me as it was to him so he took a bit of time.

"Motive, OK, but means, opportunity?"

"We all have key-cards to get us into the department. From there you could have got to Donlevy."

"What about means? How did he die? That's something the media doesn't seem to have established, or at least they're not reporting it."

"He was crucified."

"You're fucking joking!" If he was lying this was Oscar-winning stuff. The colour even drained a little from his face.

He went quiet for a second. "Doesn't it take a lot of people to crucify someone? Are you saying I'm working with someone else?"

"No." I explained the nature of the crucifixion and how it could have been done by a single person. I ended with, "Like I say: means, motive and opportunity."

"From what you say, everyone in the department who had a fob had the opportunity. Also, you had means, motive and... oh, I get it. You reckon it was one of us at that meeting. Well, don't forget, Awang and Bill were there as well. What about them?"

"Awang's gone back to Indonesia and B..."

"How do you know that?"

Thinking about it, I realised this information had come from a disembodied and unrecognised voice on the other end of a tenement entry phone. Lucas didn't need to know that. "It's kosher but I can't reveal my sources."

"Can't reveal your sources? Who do you think you are?"

This was getting uncomfortable so I forged on. "And Bill's too old for all that."

"Bill Steadman? He used to run marathons, did you know that? And that's despite being a heavy smoker. Guy could drop you and not break a fingernail." That was exactly not what I wanted to hear.

As well as surprise, Lucas was beginning to muster a pretty fair simulacrum of genuine outrage. "Also, this must be tied in with those dead psychics. What the fuck do I know or care about psychics? Awang and Bill as well. The only one who's had dealings with them and Donlevy is *you*. Why haven't the cops arrested you already?"

He stopped a second, then nodded his head slowly. "Or have they?"

I wasn't on the ball enough to come up with a good reply fast enough. He pointed a finger at me.

"You're under suspicion, aren't you. And this is your way of trying to get that finger pointed elsewhere."

"But I didn't do it." Even to my ears I sounded peevish.

"You want to get off the hook by putting me on it. You bastard!"

When he put it that way, it did sound kind of bad. Some people are natural liars but I just couldn't put Lucas in that category. He'd got into trouble with the university because he couldn't help telling the truth, at least the truth as he saw it.

By now he'd stood up. "I've a good mind to tell the police about this."

"Why, is it a crime to buy someone a pint."

"You didn't buy me a pint."

"Well, I was going to," I said but again it sounded peevish. I wasn't coming out of this well.

"But do they know about *your* motive, about how they'd demoted you to a menial job?"

"Don't worry about that. They know all about it. And they still let me go. Being made to be a janitor for a few days is weaker than water when it comes to motive."

"But you're so spiteful."

"No, I'm not!"

Maybe I said this with conviction because he hesitated. He stood looking down on me for a while then suddenly sat down again.

"Maybe not. You're a miserable git but I don't think you care enough about anything to be actively vengeful."

He was shooting more than a little high there but I wasn't going to correct him.

"Look." I leaned forward earnestly. "I'm in a jam here. The coppers are useless but I'm the only common factor in the three killings. I had a barny with the first victim, was there when the second was killed and I found the body of the third. As far as the cops are concerned, if they can't find someone better, I'm the default setting. The go-to suspect."

"But, and you've got to understand it's a big but, if what you say is true then surely it won't hold up in court, not if they don't have any real evidence against you."

I sat back and folded my hands. "Do you have much faith in the justice system? Are you confident that's true?"

He shrugged. "Don't really know much about it."

"Me neither. Would you bet your freedom on it?"

He didn't answer. Instead, he tapped the table a few times with his forefinger. "I really didn't do any of this, Dai."

"Yeah, that's the impression I get. You don't strike me as a natural liar, nor someone who bears a grudge to that sort of psychopathic degree. But if it's not you and not Awang and not the psychics, then all I'm left with is Bill Steadman who's an old pussycat and wouldn't hurt a fly. And who's passed pension age anyway."

I'd tried to say this with confidence because, of course, I'd finally realised that Bill was the old man in my dreams. The one who'd tried to kill me. The one I knew, with far more conviction than the notion deserved, was the triple killer. The dreams had distorted him, as through a glass darkly, but finally, belatedly, I'd realised who it was.

What really messed me up was that Bill had appeared in my dreams before any of the killing. If it was true then crazy old Jung and his archetypes and his all-knowing collective unconscious were correct. Either that or I had been able to foretell the future and the nutty parapsychs were correct.

Either way it sent my world view crashing down onto the rocks.

I'd hoped Lucas would shrug in agreement and shut up but, no. "Well…" He narrowed his eyes. "I wouldn't get too teary-eyed about old Bill. He's no pussycat."

"Why do you say that?"

"Because he screwed me over once. And all over a rinky-dink little bursary."

"When was this?"

"Just a year or so ago. There was some left-over money from a big grant of Donlevy's and Bill and I applied for it. I had an idea for a sweet little project and got the money. Bill, who'd cobbled together some bullshit idea, didn't. You see old Bill had a post-grad student he had a bit of a thing for. Can't remember his name—fey little chap with a buzzcut. The bursary would have kept him in Bill's clutches for another year. As it was, the bird had to get a job elsewhere and flew the coop."

"Bill's gay?"

Lucas shook his head sadly. "As an observer of human nature, you're pretty obtuse, Dai. Of course he's gay."

I'd worked with Bill for years, albeit peripherally, but there'd been enough departmental meetings and faculty parties for us to get acquainted. Had there been any indication he was gay? I mean, I knew he wasn't married but then neither was I.

Once more, I wondered whether my degrees in psychology had been a waste of time.

"OK, so you put his nose out of joint. What did he do then?"

Lucas shrugged. "Who do you think turned the woke police onto me for, you know, having the temerity to suggest that men and women were different? That they're literally hardwired to think differently; that because I'm saying they think differently, that I'm dissing women. Which I'm not."

"But what makes you think it was Bill who was responsible? It could have been any of your students."

"For the simple reason that Bill wanted me to know what he'd done. No point in taking revenge if the victim doesn't know about it. Came to my office, told me to my face, seemed almost begging me to take a swing at him."

"And did you?"

"Like I say, bastard may be old and smokes like a chimney but he's tougher and stronger than you'd think. So, no, I didn't take a swing at him. I figured that if I had done, he'd either have cleaned the floor with me or, even worse, he'd have fallen down screaming. People would have rushed in and seen forty-year-old Lucas Grimsrud standing over the beaten pension-age Bill Steadman. That's never going to be a good look. And, believe me, he'd have done that just to make sure I was sacked."

"I had no idea he was such a bastard. Come to think of it, there's the whole matter of why he never made full professor."

"Well... not every academic does," said Lucas.

"Yes, but remember, Bill was suckered into this whole searching for the soul thing of Donlevy's. When that proved a bust, Bill was left high and dry in a research dead end. In the meantime, all that grant money Donlevy raised made him a shoo-in for head of department when Sorenson retired. Donlevy soared to higher things leaving poor old Bill behind in the shit."

I still didn't want to go there but, once I'd started, I couldn't stop. "And now Donlevy gives him the push, without a by-your-leave. Makes sense and, coupled with the spite you reckon he showed you, then maybe he really is in the frame."

"Yeah, but enough to do all this? Really?" Lucas didn't sound convinced.

"Still waters." It still didn't explain Price doing a header into the empty swimming pool. Bill Steadman would need to be a crack cat-burglar to break into the baths and move around undetected. I doubted his abilities stretched that far.

"You don't happen to know if he has a criminal record, do you? Breaking and entering, that sort of thing."

"How would I know? Doesn't sound likely, though."

He hesitated a moment. "You're going after him, aren't you? If there's anything I can do to help, then let me know. Just no rough stuff. Like I say, don't underestimate him on that front. Are you going to tell the police about your suspicions?"

"It's not like we've got any evidence."

"So, what *are* you going to do?"

"Good question."

CHAPTER TWENTY-THREE

You always become the thing you fight the most
Carl Jung

"Let me come with you." Sally and I were again on her bed, which was only tastefully disarrayed. My wounds still meant our love-making was more circumspect than an outright battle. Fine for me but I sensed a hint of disappointment from her.

I shook my head. "I can look after myself."

"We could keep each other company."

That sounded sweet but I wasn't sure it would last. Sally wasn't the patient type. Shut up in a car waiting for hours, sooner or later we'd get into an argument. Besides which, I was worried about her. No matter how much I hated the notion, Bill was now my primary suspect for killing Donlevy. It was even possible he'd done for Price and Telly as well, though the motive there was less clear.

At the very least Bill could get nasty, according to Lucas. Who knew what he was capable of?

Annoyed by my refusal she nevertheless checked my war injuries. The swelling on my ankle was almost gone and the gouge in my shoulder was healing nicely though it was still sore. Getting my shirt on was still wince-inducing but I could do it all by myself.

"What am I going to do all day while you're sleuthing?" She'd put on one of the hotel's bathrobes, mischievously leaving it only loosely tied so I glimpsed her breasts every time she bent over.

"You were supposed to be back at work by now. You've got your laptop. Up here in Scotland we've got hot and cold running water and wi-fi and everything. I'm sure there's plenty you can be doing on-line."

She came over and put her arms around my neck, the front of her robe opened and I automatically reached out and cupped her breasts.

"Wouldn't you rather stay with me?" she asked in a throaty murmur.

Enticing though this was, somehow, I managed to leave. I left Sally with the nearest thing to a pout that she could muster.

And, somehow, I kept this iron resolve up for the next three days. I gave up her beautiful breasts plus other delectable accessories for skull-crushingly boring stake outs.

I deserved a medal.

I don't know how the cops and private investigators do it. Listening to podcasts did help, as did audio books. My previous short exposure to surveillance had put me off the radio for life. What I was going through wasn't much different than what we all go through on plane flights; we're constrained to a seat and have to try and keep ourselves amused.

But there was one important difference. Once you're on the plane you have no choice, you can't leave. The problem with surveillance is you always have a choice; you can up-sticks and bugger off to the pub or whatever.

What made it worse is that I wasn't even confident in what I was doing. Sally and Mo were convinced I was wasting my time. Neither was shy of articulating this belief. As the three days wore on, Sally grew more irritable at my absences until I had had enough of her sniping. Today was my last day, I had promised.

It was late afternoon and traffic was picking up on the Great Western Road as people started heading home. Sally's hotel was at a high point and, to the west, I could see the Campsie Fells paralleling the Clyde. Behind them, nestling within the rising ground of the Highlands would be Loch Lomond, only ten miles away as the crow flies.

Bill lived about a mile from where Sally was staying, in the West End and within walking distance of the university. He lived just to the west of the Botanic Gardens. The Gardens housed a series of glass houses that had given generations of Glaswegians their only taste of the tropics. The biggest of these was the Kibble Palace; long, with curved sides, it looked like a transparent dirigible that had come down and was subsiding gently into the earth. A central cupola over its long body gave space for the taller tropical palms to flourish.

On the other side of the gardens was Kirklee Circus. This was not so much circular as vagina-shaped and in the centre nestled a little well-kept island of green. The houses that surrounded it were terraced blond sandstone affairs with high ceilings and tall narrow windows. Some had little gardens with chairs and flowerpots and no fencing between them and the street. This was a surprise for the West End was the heart of student land where high-spirited and drunken youngsters distracted themselves with littering and mindless acts of vandalism.

But the Circus, not being a through road, was like a little oasis of calm and refined living. Tides of rampaging students would surge back and forth along the main road but this was a backwater, a city haven for academics and the respectable middle classes.

That Bill Steadman lived here had come as a surprise. He had no partner or kids, as far as I was aware, so what was he doing living in one of these big and very expensive houses? This suggested he didn't need the money and being made to retire early wouldn't have been the end of his financial world. That was good, as it meant less of a motive for killing Donlevy. I would be quite happy if I was wasting my time on these stakeouts.

With only one way in and out, the Circus was easy to monitor. As usual, I parked the car on the main road, just down from where the Circle touched it. I'd loaded my phone up with all sorts of podcasts I hadn't listened to before and settled down to wait.

My plans were basic and ill-defined. They all depended on Bill leaving the house. Unfortunately, the Billster had stayed put and for the last two days all I'd ever seen of him had been periods when he stood at a window, looking out and rubbing his chin in a pensive way. Something was bothering him because he'd stand there for minutes at a time.

I couldn't help jumping to the conclusion that he was planning something and trying to judge whether the moment was right.

If and when he did finally leave, I could follow him by car or by foot, although I wasn't sure what I'd find out if I did. Alternatively, I could take the opportunity of his absence to break into his house. I'd even brought a ski-mask along for the sake of any lurking CCTV.

I was kidding myself, of course. Things may be looking dire but I just couldn't see myself as a house-breaker. After a lifetime of more or less keeping to the law, you can't just veer off the straight and narrow so easily. Besides which, the only way to break in that I could think of involved smashing a window. This was a place not used to disturbing sounds like that. At the first tinkling of glass, a multitude of hands would be reaching for phones.

So, following him was just about all that was available to me, though to what end wasn't clear.

By the time the sun had gone down and Glasgow was in full gloaming mode, Bill finally left his house and came walking around the Circus, his long white hair catching my eye. I ducked down a little in the seat. Just as well because when I peeked over the dashboard, he was taking a definite look around, checking the road either way. Apparently satisfied, he set off to the right and away from me.

I hesitated for a second or two. Quaint though the Circus was, everyone had cars and they filled the kerb all the way around. Perhaps Bill hadn't been able to find a parking space there and had parked further away. If I followed on foot he might get into a car and zoom off before I could get back to mine.

Following someone, which had sounded easy, was already throwing up conundrums. I hesitated for a second, then got out of the car. I quickly crossed the road so a line of cars was between him and me. I kept hunched over and low. A passing woman in an expensive looking suit gave me a withering look.

Bill came to a curving right turn opposite a primary school with its gatepost proudly displaying a large motto in Greek (so West-End!). The curve meant I could cross the road and make up some of the distance between us without him seeing me.

Leaning out from the curve, I saw him following the road as it dived down towards the river Kelvin.

My peering around corners was getting more looks, this time from a woman pushing a pram and an older lady with finely sculpted grey hair. It didn't help that I was carrying my stout stick like a weapon rather than leaning on it like I should.

The longer I remained like this, the more suspicious I became. I glanced back at Bill who had got to the bottom of the steep slope and had obligingly turned left on the path along the river and out of view.

I hurried after him.

Over the eons the river Kelvin has cut a deep but narrow gorge through the heart of Glasgow. Trees grow up its steep sides and, along the top and on either side, red sandstone tenements and villas soar high above, making the river valley seem ever deeper. Down by the river the sounds of the city are muted and you find yourself in a different world.

And it's a strange world, one where the infrastructure remains from an older civilisation are revealed as though excavated by archaeologists. Abandoned railway bridges, supported by beautiful soaring marble columns partly span the gorge but peter away on either side into broken-down pilings. Vast sandstone alcoves, deeper than a man and taller than ten, buttress the slopes. Behind these, deep under the ground on which the prosperous villas stand, long-abandoned railway tunnels snake under Glasgow.

Here and there flying buttresses hold the hillside back, stopping it collapsing and sending the heavy villas above down into the black waters of the Kelvin below. Walls made of sandstone blocks have been hammered into the sides to support trees, erosion having exposed their roots.

Thus, I found myself, in the fading light, like Sherlock Holmes following Moriarty through the traces of Victorian civilisation. Only sulphurous fog curling creepily under the pillars of the bridges was missing.

Down by the river it was even darker and it was difficult to make out Bill as he followed the riverside path, crossing over on a footbridge to the other side of the river when the path gave out. Still part of the Botanic Gardens, I could just make out signs put up beside significant trees. Behind one I saw the red dots of cigarettes and smelled the herby fumes from joints and could just make out a small party of youths sitting on the grass. There was a pop and hiss as someone opened a can of booze.

Without having thought it through beforehand, I had on my usual black leather jacket and trousers and even dragged out a cap from the depths of my wardrobe. Some of the pasty high-latitude white of my face might still be visible but by this time in the evening I'd be difficult to spot if Bill did turn and look behind him.

So, I picked up the pace a little, crossing over the little bridge then following the path as it led up to city level. Bill was striding ahead athletically, as though he still had a long way to go. I realised he was heading towards a less salubrious part of the city. I remembered Lucas' assertion that Bill was gay and I wondered if he was off for an assignation with some Maryhill rent-boy.

If so, this was going to be another wasted day.

And now blocks of flats, grey and twenty-odd storeys in height, loomed like tombstones. However, what seemed like a down-market trajectory suddenly altered when Bill turned onto a bridge which crossed back across the river into Kelvinside and its sandstone villas.

And the villas got bigger, going from simply prosperous to sprawling Scottish Baronial and up towards veritable castles. You'd have to buy an awful lot slaves and get them to pick a mountain of tobacco to build one of these fortresses. Three storeys high, plus lower floors deep in a depression to look like a moat, they were topped by a myriad of fancy chimneys and cupolas festooning the roofs. You could have quartered an army in each, although they had in their time been occupied by a single, very wealthy family.

It was dark by now and there was even less chance I'd be spotted. In any case old Bill seemed focused on whatever he was doing for he had not looked back once.

And that's what nearly caught me out. We had come to another prosperous-looking villa, not big enough to quarter an army but which could certainly accommodate a large platoon if they were all very friendly. Suddenly and exaggeratedly, like a pantomime villain, he whirled to survey the road behind him. Luckily, I'd been passing under a large untrimmed tree hanging over the path and this shaded me from the yellow streetlights.

His gaze swept over me without a trace of hesitation as he scanned the whole street. He hadn't seen me!

Or maybe he was just very good at this cloak and dagger stuff; perhaps he had seen me but pretended he hadn't and was going to waylay me further down the road.

Somehow, I didn't think so but I grasped my knob-headed stick tighter. Recent events had served to build an image in my mind of the killer as a determined, Machiavellian monster. A Glaswegian Moriarty indeed. But now it occurred to me for the first time that Bill, if he was indeed the killer, was as amateurish and as out of his depth as I was.

After his sweep of the road, instead of resuming his steady athletic pace he slipped quickly into the driveway of the mid-range plutocratic villa, keeping to the side where trees and bushes screened him from the house next door.

There was something unquestionably furtive about the way he moved and for the first time I began to wonder if my half-arsed theory might be correct. Maybe Bill was about to do something killerish, or he was reconnoitring for a future crime.

Who would live in a place like this, I wondered. Well off, obviously, but not extremely so…

And that's when I got it. Had I had half a brain, or if I'd been a crime story afficionado, maybe I'd have got there ages ago. In that instant of revelation, my rational mind reluctantly caught up with what my unconscious had been trying to tell me and I knew for sure he had killed Price and Telly and Donlevy. It didn't explain who pushed Price head first into an empty swimming pool, but now I could make a damned good guess.

Keeping the parked cars between myself and the driveway, and ducking below their rooflines, I got to the low sandstone wall that separated the grounds from the footpath and road and crouched beside it. I peered over.

To the side was an easily hurdled wall that formed the boundary between the two adjacent properties. Rather than slip into the victim's driveway, and perhaps get clobbered by a waiting Bill who'd twigged he was being followed, I entered the next-door driveway and made my way along the dividing wall. Luckily the driveway was mono-block and not gravel because otherwise it would have made quite a noise. Some damned bushes were all along the wall so I could only get glimpses of the front of the other house.

I'd lost sight of Bill and began to think he'd gone all the way round the back when, through a gap in the bushes, I made out a darker shade leaning against the villa's side wall. I froze and watched as the figure reached up and pulled something all the way over its head.

I was still pondering this just as the figure stepped away from the side and a security light flared, smashing the figure's shadow back across the wall. As he made for the front door, I could see that he'd donned a face-covering balaclava. In his hand was a wickedly long knife.

I moved quickly back along the next-door drive so I could see the front door, but the damned bushes were getting in the way again. I gently eased the bushes apart, trying not to make a noise, until my view of the door was more or less unobstructed. There was a wash of light as the door opened.

Bill surged forward, the arm without the knife outstretched, like a rugby player storming for the touchline, palm open and facing out to fend off opposing players. Before he disappeared from view, he kicked the door shut.

I scrambled over the bushes and ran along the drive to the back of the house. Another security light flared, revealing a large garden. I passed a hulking, darkly coloured Audi. This drive was gravel so there was more noise but I doubted it mattered now. All the lights in the back of the house were on and I saw a substantial kitchen, its stainless-steel units anachronistic against the high ceilings and cornices and arched wooden doors.

The kitchen was empty. I kept going, passed the back door and then to the windows of another room of a similarly ridiculous size. This seemed to be the lounge with a television the size of a cinema screen.

Just as I got there, I saw a figure come reeling through the door. It was a small woman and she was staggering backwards. The back of a sofa stopped her and she almost tipped over it, her hands held up to protect her face.

And then Balaclava Bill was there too, grasping her hair in one hand, knife held against her throat with the other.

I froze again, unbelieving. Was Bill really going to slit Dean Rettner's throat?

Was the look in her eyes fear?

Not a chance. Rettner was made of sterner stuff. All I could see was anger and I saw her lips move as she spat words at Bill. If it had been an ancient gypsy curse, I wouldn't have been surprised.

Instead of cutting her throat, Bill let go of her hair, reaching up to pull off his balaclava.

When she saw who it was, Rettner didn't seemed surprised. Instead, I saw her lips move faster and could only imagine the stream of vitriol directed at Bill.

Lines suddenly appeared in his face as though gouged by the talons of a witch. Now he really did look like the old man of my dreams and I marvelled I had not recognised him earlier.

Clearly, Bill didn't like what he was hearing.

Instead of shutting the fuck up, and perhaps gaining a few more seconds of life, Rettner kept up her barrage, her face twisted with the ugliness of whatever she was saying.

She may not be willing to try to save her own life, but I was. Without really thinking about it, I brought the ball of my stick down on the glass.

The single pane shattered like a grenade. Hard enough that fragments of glass showered them both. They flinched, but Rettner recovered more quickly. With both hands she shoved Bill in the chest and he tottered back. In an instant she had raced around him and was making for the door.

Quickly, I turned and retraced my steps, thinking she would try to get out the kitchen door but, when I came to the kitchen windows, I saw the room was empty. Through one of the open doors, I saw a long hallway leading to the front of the house. A small shadowy figure was running down it, but then a larger figured appeared and raced after her.

Now I was running hard, the gravel of Rettner's driveway sliding away under my feet. The security light had gone out but my movement made it flare again, blinding me.

I whirled around the corner at the front of the house just as I heard the front door being unlocked. As I reached it, it was jerked open. I got there just in time to see Bill, one hand around Rettner's neck and dragging her back, the other with the knife trying to push the door closed again.

I hit the door hard, shoulder first, batting Bill's knife-hand away. At the same time, Rettner twisted round, grabbed his head in her hands, yanked it down and sank her teeth into his nose.

Bill roared in pain and disbelief. The arm holding the knife swung round, it's point heading for her back. I just managed to block it with my stick.

Rettner had gone primal, so angry she didn't care if she got stabbed or not. She spat out a large chunk of Bill's nose, then twisted round to his side, grabbed his long hair and yanked it back.

"Now!" she screamed.

I had long since yielded all conscious control but whatever demon was working me knew just what to do. The ebony ball on the end of my stick followed a perfect arc before crunching down onto Bill's exposed forehead.

He hit the stripped pine floor with all the animation of a bag of spuds.

Rettner was looking at me. Her mouth opened in a ghoulish smile, her teeth and mouth red with Bill's blood.

"I knew you had to be useful for something," she said.

CHAPTER TWENTY-FOUR

The most terrifying thing is to accept oneself completely.
Carl Jung

"So, what's new?" asked Mo.

God knows, I like dourly comic understatement as much as the next man but, after three days of interrogation by the dour Philban and McKendrick, my sense of humour was missing in action.

"Fuck you!"

"The papers have been saying..."

I held up a warning hand. "I don't want to know."

Mo's brow creased. "You're obviously distraught. Here, let me buy you a drink. Half a pint of shandy?"

Try as I might to resist it, I felt my po-face break into a reluctant smile, although in the bar-room mirror it looked more like a grimace.

"Dalmore eighteen-year-old. And better make it a double!" he called to the nearest barman.

You can never fault the service in the Bon and a glass of the amber reviver was nestling in my paw within seconds.

"Tell your Uncle Mo all about it."

I looked around the Bon, which had disconcertingly remained the same as ever while my life had staggered from one cataclysm to another. Slightly used-looking punters, none of them spring chickens, sucked on their drinks in resignation at a life perhaps not fully lived. It was still only four in the afternoon, before the more rambunctious and up-for-it office crowd thundered in.

Not only had the world continued to roll on unaffected by my problems but I realised that barely a couple of weeks had gone by since I met my first parapsych and my life had gone into a tailspin.

"Well, believe it or not, but the cops didn't seem entirely delighted that I'd solved their case for them."

Mo nodded. "Typical copperish ingratitude. But come on, what actually happened?"

I told him but it cost him another double. For once, he seemed eager to pay.

By the time I'd finished his eyes were almost poking out on stalks. "Are you winding me up?" he said.

"God's honest truth."

"So, you *did* actually kill this guy Steadman."

"Cracked his skull like an eggshell. Never underestimate a stout stick!"

He nodded his head slowly. "I guess not."

I let the silence last. He had a lot to process.

Such had been his focus that his glass was still full but mine was empty. I tipped it over so it was lying on its side.

"Jesus!" he said and ordered another.

He took a substantial swig of his own. "So, Steadman kills all three men. Why and, especially, why those two parapsychos?"

I took another sip, already glowing inside from the water of life. "We'll never know for sure, him being dead and all, but I'm guessing he wanted to humiliate Donlevy and Rettner. They must have represented the malign influence that has altered academic life beyond all recognition."

"Well..." Mo tapped my arm gently, "...just to play devil's advocate here, rather than malign, perhaps some might call it the modernising influence. You know, dragging academia kicking and screaming into the twenty-first century."

I was in too mellow a mood to rise to this. "Whatever. As far as old Bill was concerned, a very agreeable job turned inexorably into the hardscrabble of modern academia. No more respectful students, no more freedom to research topics at a whim, no more sinecure. Instead, he's constantly having to justify his existence and please everyone like a circus pony while being hag-rid by brutes like Rettner. I'm a lot younger than Bill, and came too late to experience the halcyon days of academe, but even I hate the dog-eat-dog world the university has become. We all do.

"Anyway, getting back to your original question, allowing the parapsychs to have their conference at the university was iffy to say the least, no matter how tight the finances. The theory is that Bill figured that killing a high-profile figure like Price would bring it all out into the open, to Rettner's and Donlevy's vast discomfort. Unfortunately, it wasn't enough. The conference went on and the press didn't link Price with the university. Sinking an axe into Price's head had been a waste of Bill's time. The Gruesome Twosome were still not on the hook."

"So that's why he killed that other guy..."

"Telly."

"Yeah, and on university premises, in the department itself. Even the press couldn't miss that. But why did he try to kill you as well?"

"I don't think he did. I just got in the way a bit. Those magnetic fields around the hippo are a little weird. They're kind of rugby ball shaped so ferromagnetic missiles don't necessarily travel in straight lines. Telly was actually covering the bore of the magnet and the cylinder was going to end up there whatever happened. It's trajectory before that was less certain. Maybe Bill tried to miss me but..."

"You'll never know."

Not that I cared. My shoulder still hurt and I'd bear a scar for the rest of my life. If that didn't deserve pulverised frontal lobes, then I didn't know what did.

That's when I realised this whole business had changed me and not necessarily for the better.

"So, this Bill chap had embarrassed, even disgraced, Donlevy and Rettner. Why go on to kill them?"

"Maybe, at the end of the day, he felt it just wasn't enough. For Bill, those two personified all that had gone wrong with academia in the last forty years. He'd built up a lifetime of spite and it had to go somewhere."

"But it seems so disproportionate."

"No kidding. Steadman was way more of a whack job than I'd thought. And yes, before you say it, chalk up one more failure to my grasp of psychology."

Mo finished his drink and signalled for another. I raised my eyebrows and turned my eyes to my half empty glass.

He shook his head. "You need to do some more singing for your supper. You're sure it was this Logan student who gave you the vapours with his snakes, and not Steadman?"

"Bill had nothing against me, but that little prick Logan did. Anyway, he was bitten by his own snakes which is a giveaway so that case is closed."

"OK, but there's still the bit where Price did a header into Govanhill Baths. Was that Steadman's first attempt to kill him?"

"I don't think so. The Baths were locked. He was many things but I'm guessing professional burglar wasn't in his CV. Also, it seems likely the motion detectors and infrared were disabled, so someone could creep up on Price and push him in. No, this was an inside job by one of the parapsychs. Most of the people there might have had some professional jealousy as a motive but my guess it was all to do with sex."

"You think it was Sally?"

"No, she was the one who ended their relationship, as several others have attested. Love 'em and leave 'em is more her style. Besides she was right next to me so I'd have known if she'd moved."

"We'll get back to Sally in a minute but first, who *did* push Price?"

I shrugged. "Again, we'll never know for sure but my guess is Telly."

"The second murder victim. I thought you said he was a nice guy?"

"I think he was but Price had stolen away a rather amazing woman. Plus, of course, Price was an out-and-out prick. In Telly's shoes I'd have pushed him into the pool myself."

"That's a given, but you're not what anyone would call nice."

"Thanks. Anyway, pushing someone into an empty swimming pool isn't necessarily a murder attempt."

Mo did a double-take. "Head first onto concrete? You reckon?"

"Price survived, didn't he? In any event Telly's dead too so we'll never know for sure what he intended."

I hesitated for a moment. "Of course, there is another possibility. I'd never have mentioned it before but after all the demonic things Bill resorted to, the horrors he perpetrated, my mind has opened to other possibilities."

Mo blinked, he could tell this was going to be a doozy.

"Price had been robbing tombs, one of which was the subject of a demonic curse…"

"Oh, come on! You've let those parapsychs get to you."

Yes, this was getting too weird so I didn't demur. However, even with the 'conventional' explanation I had given, to my mind Price had been assaulted by one demon and killed by another. Telly had been a nice, rational guy, yet some demonic upwelling had sent him pushing Price down onto the concrete flooring of a swimming baths. Then later, it certainly hadn't been Bill's rationality that had made him cleave Price's skull with an axe.

My alternative explanation needed only one demon rather than two: something spiteful out of old Nubia.

Occam's Razor: the simpler explanation is likely to be the correct one.

That I was even considering this meant Mo was right: the parapsychs had got to me. I was also still trying, and failing, to explain away Bill appearing in my dreams.

Like me, Mo clearly wanted to change the subject. "OK, so we've gone through the crimes and the dead. What about the living? What has your bestest chum Rettner got to say for herself? One of her staff has been running riot and murdering all over the place. One of her students has been getting up to no good with snakes. Plus, her life is saved by the guy she was trying to sack. The old girl must be on the back foot..." He stopped as a look of calculation crossed his face.

I smiled and touched his glass with my finger. "This one's on me!"

"Why do I have such a hollow feeling?"

"That bit I told you about—how Rettner bit off Bill's nose. Keep shtum!"

"And why should I do that?"

"Wouldn't look good for Rettner, would it? Dean bites off lecturer's nose. That's not the sort of thing Rettner wants advertised. Not if she's going to be a Dame one day."

Mo frowned. "But wouldn't it come out at the tr..." He stopped.

"No trial, seeing how the murderer is dead."

"Inquest then?"

"I guess there will be one but not for a while. I suppose Rettner's hoping all the media interest will die and be buried with Bill."

Mo was nodding his head. "Yeah, the papers definitely left out that little detail about the nose. Hmmm, I'm beginning to see how this is stacking up. For a start Rettner must be very grateful to you..."

I'd held up a hand to stop him. "That's presupposing some humanity on her part. That's way too strong."

"OK, but that detail about biting his nose off, blood dripping off her teeth etc. You have quite a story to tell and I imagine she'd give a lot to stop you."

I smiled and lifted my glass. "Full Professor Dai Younge from now on. But you can call me Prof."

Mo did another double-take. "Full? More like—full of..." But it didn't seem like he could be bothered to finish that. Instead, he lifted his glass. "Well played!"

In fact, I hadn't really had to do anything. As Bill lay expiring at our feet and before the cops arrived, Rettner had gone into oleaginous mode. Nothing, it seemed, was too good for me.

And Philban and McKendrick had been just as amenable, eventually. During the whole time they'd been barely more than bystanders. They might have tried to get me for manslaughter but that would have involved a trial and their ineffectuality would have been revealed for all to see. They were keen for the whole business to go away. After the blowhard interrogation, when they'd got the full picture of what had happened, talk of further charges had disappeared like morning mist.

Mo was nodding. "So, as far as you're concerned it's all come up roses."

"Really? Still can't go back to my lovely flat!"

"I'm reliably informed there are other places to stay in Glasgow. Bigger and better ones to suit your bigger and better salary."

"I liked that flat. Expansive, like my personality."

"Like your ego, you mean."

An amiable silence descended as we savoured our drinks.

"But what about you?" said Mo finally. "How do you feel in yourself? Killing a man like that, in fact killing a man at all. I mean, do you think you'll suffer from PTSD?"

I looked around, making sure nobody was eavesdropping. Mo was my closest friend; if I was going to say this to anyone it would only be to him.

"You know what I feel? Nothing."

He looked surprised. "Nothing at all?"

"Nary a thing. Some stuff does bother me, like how Bill looked afterward. Bashed in skull, no nose and a lot of blood —not a pretty sight. But, when it comes to guilt or regret or whatever... well, my conscience is as dead as the proverbial witch's tit."

I knew this appalled him but he was trying not to show it. "Maybe it'll hit you later."

"Maybe," I said but I wasn't convinced. More likely I had inherited some of my parents' psychopathy after all. It wasn't a comforting thought. Demons were everywhere.

"And Sally," said Mo, changing the subject. "How's she doing?"

"Very supportive, very kind, at least when she's not suing the arse off the university. Maybe even loving."

"So, your worries, you know, about her only being attracted to you because she thought you were a killer."

I looked unblinkingly into his eyes. "But Mo," I said, "you're forgetting. I *am* a killer."

THE END

Better leave the last words to Carl Jung:

The gigantic catastrophes that threaten us today are not elemental happenings of a physical or biological order, but psychic events. To a quite terrifying degree we are threatened by wars and revolutions which are nothing other than psychic epidemics. At any moment several million human beings may be smitten with a new madness, and then we shall have another world war or devastating revolution. Instead of being at the mercy of wild beasts, earthquakes, landslides, and inundations, modern man is battered by the elemental forces of his own psyche.

Other books by Barrie Condon

Fiction

The Tethered God

The Bamboo Cocoon

Non-Fiction

Science for Heretics

Changing Trains in Ulaanbataar